THE FORGOTTEN SPARE

Endless Love
Book 3

JR Salisbury

ARE YOU SIGNED UP FOR DRAGONBLADE'S BLOG?

You'll get the latest news and information on exclusive giveaways, exclusive excerpts, coming releases, sales, free books, cover reveals and more.

Check out our complete list of authors, too!

No spam, no junk. That's a promise!

Sign Up Here

www.dragonbladepublishing.com

Dearest Reader;

Thank you for your support of a small press. At Dragonblade Publishing, we strive to bring you the highest quality Historical Romance from some of the best authors in the business. Without your support, there is no 'us', so we sincerely hope you adore these stories and find some new favorite authors along the way.

Happy Reading!

CEO, Dragonblade Publishing

Additional Dragonblade books by Author JR Salisbury

Endless Love Series
Beauty and the Rake (Book 1)
A Duke's Love (Book 2)
The Forgotten Spare (Book 3)
Love At Last (Book 4)

CHAPTER ONE

ARTHUR JAMESON, DUKE of Hightower stared in disbelief at his solicitor, Jeremy Smith. The man had always been upfront with him about everything, but this, this was different. He couldn't believe what Smith had just told him. Even more disturbing was that his parents had kept this from him. But given his parents had been murdered, he couldn't place blame on them for never telling him. The solicitor, however, was a different story. He should have told him as soon as Arthur had become duke.

That was a moot point now. He needed to process what he'd just been told.

"So you're telling me one of my father's oldest friends had been caring for my brother for all these years. Why would he and my mother even consider doing that? He was their son too," Arthur said.

"Yes, until he died unexpectedly last month. Your brother, Charles, has some unique abilities, and to be quite honest, it sometimes scares people who don't know him."

"Where is my brother now?"

"Charles is living in a cottage on Lord Denton's estate. Denton's son has been kind enough to allow Charles to continue to stay on until other arrangements can be made."

Arthur shifted his weight in the leather chair he occupied.

"You mentioned he had unique abilities. What are we talking about?"

"He can recall the most minute details of a conversation from years ago. He's extremely brilliant, but no one has been able to figure out how this came to be."

"You mentioned he's been in institutions?"

"Yes. Nothing serious, just trying to understand how his mind works. His mind is like a steel trap."

"I suppose it's time for us to meet, and I need to make a decision as far as where he should live," Arthur replied.

"Would you like me to make arrangements?"

"If you wish to make contact with the son and let him know what's going on, I would appreciate it."

"Not a problem, Your Grace."

"Can he travel by himself to London, or should I go to him and bring him back?"

"It might be best if you went to him. I understand crowds sometimes overwhelm him," Smith replied.

"Where is he?"

"The Isle of Wight."

Arthur arched a brow. "Not too far. Make all the arrangements and let Lord Denton know of my arrival."

"I shall, Your Grace. It might be advisable for you to stay for more than the day. Probably a good idea if you meet Charles and the pair of you get to know each other first. He might not like leaving with someone he considers a stranger."

"I guess we'll find out," Arthur replied. "Does he know he has a brother and sister?"

"Yes."

Arthur thought of his sister, Roxanne. She was in Italy with her husband on a delayed honeymoon. He would need to write her so she wouldn't be too surprised when she and Graham returned. Daphne, his own bride, might be able to help him with planning for his brother's arrival.

He rose to his full height and began to pace the floor. "If

that's all, I'll leave you to it. Just let me know what transpires and when I should make plans to leave."

"I shall, Your Grace."

He turned and walked out of the office and headed for his carriage. Deciding to walk back to his office in Parliament, he dismissed his carriage. There was certainly a lot to think about. He had a brother, and not just a brother, but a twin. He wondered what Charles looked like since he forgot to ask. Was he identical? That certainly would be interesting.

The afternoon was one of the rare gems. The sky was a magnificent shade of blue and this time there wasn't a cloud to be found. The kind of day that brought people outside.

He couldn't wait to tell Daphne what his meeting had been about. Of course, she would be supportive, and knowing her, she would probably have some suggestions on making Charles feel at home. She seemed to have a sixth sense about people.

Reaching his office, he soon realized he wasn't concentrating on anything but his newly found brother. He found himself writing notes about things he needed to know, things like why his brother was kept from virtually everyone for the majority of their lives. Did he have a temper he couldn't control which was part of the reason he was separated from the family?

No mention had been made as to whether Charles had a disfigurement, which would be a logical reason to hide him away. That didn't make any sense though. He could have been sent to York and not a friend of his father's. Too many mysteries and not enough answers. Arthur knew he needed to see all documentation regarding Charles. He needed to understand the reasoning behind it all.

He wrote a letter to the solicitor, asking for whatever correspondence he might have. There had to be quite a file on Charles, dating back to when he was first sent away. Arthur wanted to read anything and everything to decide what might come next. There were a couple of unused cottages that might suffice for his brother, since from what he understood, Charles stayed in a cottage on Wight. The solicitor mentioned he seemed to prefer the solitude a cottage had to offer. There were a thousand questions, and until he received information there was little to do.

Arthur decided he was at a dead end, so he stuffed the paper he'd been scribbling on into his pocket along with the letter to the solicitor. The sooner he received documents, the better. His other hurdle was going to be writing Roxanne and giving her the news. Knowing his sister, she would drop everything and be on her way home to help.

His carriage was waiting outside for him. He climbed in and gave the driver instructions. As the carriage lurched forward into the London traffic, he hoped Daphne would be there waiting at Jameson House for him. He needed to tell her and listen to her input.

As fate would have it though, the afternoon traffic in London was not for the faint of heart. After having to stop for a wagon having lost its load of fruits and vegetables in the middle of one of the most used streets, Arthur made the decision that he could walk home quicker than sitting still on a London street in the afternoon. He opened the coach door and jumped down, announcing to his driver his intentions.

He began walking, and soon Jameson House came into view. The brick facade was something he thought he'd never tire of. The structure demanded the attention of anyone who passed.

Taking the stairs two at a time, he entered the house, surprising the footman posted at the door as he divested himself of his hat, gloves, and greatcoat. Moving on, he quickly found Daphne in the drawing room feeding Sam, the macaw, pieces of fruit. She startled, not expecting him.

"You're finished for the day?" she asked.

"Partially. More like I couldn't concentrate after meeting with the solicitor."

"What could he possibly have said to you?"

"That I have a brother. A twin brother."

Her eyes widened as she took in what he'd just told her. "A

twin brother you knew nothing about until today? How is that even possible? And why would your family hide him away?"

"I'm still finding out, but evidently, he was born after me, and he's eccentric…"

"Eccentric? How?" Daphne inquired.

"He's smart, has a mind like a steel trap."

She nodded, giving Sam a piece of apple. "There's nothing wrong with that."

"No, but he is evidently prone to temper tantrums."

"And?"

"He's living on Wight for the time being," Arthur replied as he sat down in a chair across from his wife.

"Your mind must be going a hundred miles a minute with questions."

He nodded. "It is. I'll be making a trip to Wight to meet him and try and get to know him."

"Does he know about you?"

"Yes, and Roxanne too. And speaking of Roxanne, I need to go write her a letter and let her know of Charles and what has transpired."

"That would be a good idea. She would not be happy with you if she came home and found all this out," Daphne replied.

"Precisely." Arthur sat back in his chair, closing his eyes. "To think all these years Roxanne and I have had a sibling we knew nothing about. It boggles one's mind."

"I can only imagine."

He turned his head in the direction of her soft voice. "Don't we have dinner with the Smythes this evening?"

"Yes, they're hosting a small dinner party. I can send our regrets if you don't feel up to attending."

"Please."

"Consider it done. Now why don't you go to your study and write that letter to your sister?"

"You don't mind?"

"Of course I don't. I need to send our apologies to the countess about this evening."

"Thank you," he replied, standing, then planting a kiss on her cheek. "I shouldn't be long."

"Take all the time you need."

He quit the room, despite Sam's repeating his name, an indication the parrot wanted him to stay. The house was quiet as he walked to his study. A fire greeted him, the room warm as he entered. Walking across the room, he poured himself a whiskey before sitting down at his desk. Usually, he had no problem writing to his sister, but the subject matter of this letter would prove most difficult. Since she was older, he was curious to know if she might have any small memory of Charles. If she didn't, this letter might jolt any lingering memory she might have but didn't know she had.

Taking a sip of whiskey, he placed the glass to the side and pulled open the center drawer for a fresh sheet of paper. He picked up his pen and stared down, trying to wish the words onto the page. They didn't come, so Arthur began to let the words flow.

My Dearest Sister,

What I'm about to tell you will come as a shock. It certainly did to me.

Did you know we have a brother? Charles. He's my twin brother, born minutes after me. For reasons I'm still not completely clear about, he was sent to live elsewhere. I'm going to review everything the solicitor has on file going all the way back to the beginning.

What I do know is that one of Papa's friends had been looking after him on Wight. The friend has since died, which is how I learned of our brother's existence. From what I do know, Charles has some extraordinary skills, but at the same time has a sometimes-brutal temper.

I plan to go to Wight to meet Charles and try and get to know him before bringing him to London to stay with Daphne and me. Everything is very much up in the air and will be until

I meet him. I do know he is aware of our existence.

I wanted you to know about this so it wouldn't be too big a shock when you and Graham return. I hope this finds you both well and enjoying your trip to the fullest.

Arthur

He was surprised at how easy writing to her had been. Picking up his glass, Arthur took another swallow of the golden liquid before re-reading what he'd just written. Satisfied, he prepared the missive to be sent to Italy. Then he rang for a footman to make sure the letter went out in the post this afternoon.

Daphne followed the footman in holding a plate of cake and tea sandwiches left over from her tea. "How did it go?"

"Surprisingly easier than I thought it would. I hope it reaches her before they leave."

"I'm sure it will. Now you're going to come sit in front of the fire and eat something. I'm quite sure you didn't take time out for lunch after your meeting with your solicitor."

She knew him so well. One of the many things he loved about her. She liked being bossy without it sounding like that. Marriage had not changed her, or her views, and he hoped it never would. He liked her being opinionated.

WITH HIS SOLICITOR as efficient as ever, Arthur found himself faced with ledgers and files holding copies of correspondence regarding his newly found brother, Charles, the following day. He had the morning to start reading them and decided he would make good use of his time, since his afternoon would be occupied at Parliament.

Everything in the ledger was neatly noted with what the payment was for. His father gave his friend money every year for Charles's everyday expenses. If there was something involving more, Denton contacted the solicitors. It was all as it should be.

He shut the book and turned his attention to the files and found those in perfect order. The most recent correspondence sat on top. The papers were arranged chronologically. It wasn't that he was looking for something wrong, he merely wished to see where the money went and for what it was used.

It was obvious to him that Denton had done an excellent job in the care of his brother, overseeing Charles's education in every way a child of an aristocrat would be taught. Arthur noted his brother was quite proficient with swords, spoke four languages fluently, and had an eidetic memory. That piqued Arthur's curiosity, since most all of what he'd learned about Charles indicated his sibling to be far superior intellectually.

He wrote in a notebook he'd placed to one side. He would be interested in knowing if Charles was aware what he had was unique. What bothered Arthur was if his brother had emotions like loving someone. Being raised the way he had been where people thought he was unique, did people have the perception he was incapable of such emotions, or had he been raised as though he did?

Some of this he wouldn't be able to get answers to until he met his long-lost brother. Did his parents ever visit him, or had he been swept to the back of their minds? Better not seen nor heard. He couldn't fathom to have been given that choice.

A knock on the door caused him to look away from the notebook and papers. "Enter."

The door opened and in walked Daphne along with a footman wheeling a brass cart. "I assumed you were caught up in your work, so I took the liberty of bringing breakfast to you."

"You're right. I had forgotten, and thank you."

She smiled. "Finish what you're doing, and I'll fix you a cup of tea. You can choose from several things to eat."

He grunted and shut his notebook before closing the file. Standing, he made his way to a chair in front of the hearth where Daphne had placed a cup of tea. He sat and picked up the cup and took a taste while Daphne placed a plate on the table for him consisting of toast with marmalade, some apple slices, and a piece of sausage. He hadn't thought he was hungry until he saw the plate of food.

"Did you finish going over your brother's files and ledger?"

"No, but I've got a better understanding on the situation."

"Good," Daphne replied.

"I know there are other families who have endured or are going through something similar. We aren't unique. I never in a thousand years would have thought our family would be one. The fact that my father never gave me the slightest hint about Charles is worrisome right now."

"You have to take into consideration what happened to your parents. It might just be that he was going to tell you since he knew you would someday be duke, but his life was cut short."

Arthur picked up an apple slice and bit into it thoughtfully. "You're right, of course."

The room fell into a peaceful quiet as they both ate. One of the things he admired about Daphne was that they could be in the same room for hours and never feel the need to speak. Just knowing she was near soothed him.

"What are your plans? Is Charles going to live here or in Kent?"

"My intention is for him to stay in the blue suite here. It's the largest guest suite. In Kent he could stay in a separate wing. He'd have privacy when he needs it but could still eat with us. I imagine it's going to be an adjustment for him to learn to live around others."

"There's always the option of one of the cottages that isn't being used at the moment."

"That's true. It'll be easier to make a decision once I've met with Denton. The move alone from the only place he's called home is going to be traumatic enough," he replied.

"Hopefully Denton will send a reply quickly. Would you like me to accompany you?"

Arthur shook his head. "Not the first time. I don't wish to

overwhelm him. I'm not even sure he'll know there's about to be some major changes to his life."

"Very well. Would you like for me to have the suite readied for him?"

"That would be very helpful."

"Let me know what you need from me, and I'll be sure to get it done," Daphne said.

He grinned. "You can start by going over and locking the door."

"Arthur, are you wanting to be naughty? So early in the day?"

"Perhaps."

"Are you free this afternoon?"

This time he shook his head. "I'm afraid not. There are several matters I need to be a part of in Parliament."

"You're a busy man, Arthur. I know your constituents already look up to you, and you seem to savor every bit of it."

"I will admit I'm enjoying it. I never thought I would," he replied.

She kissed him on the cheek. "I will let you get back to what you were doing. I'll have the suite cleaned and aired out."

"Thank you. I'll see you before I leave."

She nodded with a grin as she walked through the door. By the time the door clicked closed, Arthur was deep in thought.

CHAPTER TWO

TEN DAYS LATER, Arthur found himself on his way to the Isle of Wight. He was going to meet his brother for the very first time. Though he was excited, he was also apprehensive. He wasn't sure what to expect. Charles knew about Roxanne and him, but how would he be received? According to what he'd been able to learn about his brother, Arthur knew Charles was extremely intelligent, especially good with numbers. There were others who thought Charles was mad and should be kept away from others, which was why he'd lived most of his life with little human contact, especially when it came to crowds. Crowds made him nervous.

Arthur had left London early in the morning in hopes of getting ahead of the morning traffic on the streets of the capital. Once the city was behind him, he sat back and opened the ledger his attorney had given him about Charles's expenses. There was one name that kept coming up in the ledger. The transactions were only deposits, and they were from a publishing house of all things. It piqued his curiosity as to what the deposits were for. He pulled a notebook sitting at his side and made some notes and questions.

Soon he put the ledger and notebook to one side and stretched his legs in front of him. Looking out the window of the carriage, he noted the sky had turned gray with no sign of it changing. The closer they got to the coast, the darker the horizon, meaning storms were on their way.

He hoped they would arrive at the waterfront before the weather changed and any boats heading to Wight canceled. It was a short journey and only happened if the water was too rough.

When they did arrive, the black skies were still on the horizon moving quite slowly. Arthur was pleased he would be able to settle in before letting Lord Denton know of his arrival. He'd made arrangements to stay in one of the finer hotels with a spectacular view of the water.

The journey across the water to Wight was not as bad as Arthur imagined it might have been. Once the carriage pulled up in front of the hotel, he informed the driver he wouldn't be needing the coach for the rest of the day, and if he did, he'd find an alternative. He wanted the horses to have enough time to rest from today's journey.

He settled in his room quickly, noting it did face the water. Having not eaten since early in the morning, he decided to order tea and make sure the missive he'd written to Denton was delivered. Hopefully, they would meet in the morning and he might meet Charles then as well.

A knock on the door brought afternoon tea. Just as he was getting settled in after choosing sandwiches and sweets and a steaming pot of tea, a bolt of thunder clapped overhead. Looking out the windows, Arthur saw the sky was changing, turning into the darkest shade of gray possible. It was met with a deluge of rain, coming down so hard it made visibility impossible. He was thankful he'd made it when he did; otherwise, he would have found himself stuck on the other side.

Taking a break from tea, Arthur walked to a table to write a missive to Denton, letting him know he'd arrive on Wight and asking when a good time would be to meet him. He hoped he could meet Charles so they might begin to get to know each other. It would make the journey to London easier. He questioned everything, realizing it would do him no good. Rereading the paper, he readied it to go out. Moments later, he handed it over to a young man who'd come to the door.

He poured himself another cup of tea and sat. Shutting his eyes, Arthur listened to the rain as it plummeted against the windows. The occasional jolt of thunder could be heard in the distance or sometimes closer. It was hard to judge the distance of the storm.

Arthur awoke to the storm still raging on, having fallen asleep. His tea was cold, as was the room. He stretched as he stood and walked to the hearth to stoke the fire, which had now become embers. He tossed some coal onto the fire and with the poker stoked the embers. It wouldn't be long until the room was a lot warmer.

Checking the time, Arthur changed clothes after deciding to go downstairs for dinner. He hadn't traveled with his valet this time, thinking too many strangers might overwhelm his brother. So, instead, he changed clothes and headed downstairs.

There were a few guests enjoying dinner, but not a lot. People tended not to eat for a few more hours. He was shown to a table near the fire. Arthur ordered the lamb. It wasn't something he had but a few times a year, and normally when he did have it was out at a restaurant such as this. The slightest whiff of lamb sent Daphne running from the source the few times they'd attempted to serve it at home.

While waiting for his meal, Arthur sat back and watched the people in the restaurant. He tried to imagine where they were from and what brought them to Wight. Was it pleasure or did they have business here? Everyone had a story. His train of thought changed as he wondered what Daphne was doing at home. She had grown into her position as duchess gracefully and liked to pass on some of her good fortune to others who were not as fortunate.

She was probably letting Sam, her parrot, follow behind her, walking through the house, cursing all the way. It was humorous how her avian friend easily made friends with the staff and anyone visiting. Sam was quick to let either Daphne or him know if he didn't like someone. He was quite the conversation piece of those who visited. Never did Arthur think he'd befriend a bird.

ARTHUR FOUND HIMSELF headed to Denton's estate the following morning. He wasn't sure what to expect as Denton seemed to be a man of few words, at least the written word. The rain was long gone, though the sky was still overcast and gray. The Denton estate was a good way off from the village he'd stayed in. The roads were still muddy from the deluge of the night before, but passable.

He pulled out his notebook and reread the questions he had for Denton. Some included the deposits from a publishing company. His only explanation was his father had some sort of financial interest in the firm and had money diverted for Charles's upkeep. He saw no other reason for the funds other than that unless Denton had answers.

The one big hope he had was that Charles would trust him and return with him to London without incident. Denton had little contact with Charles until his own father died. Initially, Denton had been agreeable to letting Charles stay for an additional month to give Arthur time to know his newfound brother. Arthur could only hope Denton wouldn't walk anything back. He would need the extra time if Charles proved to be difficult. Not knowing much about his brother made things more complicated.

The carriage continued down the road leading to the other side of the island. Before long it turned right, down a long shell-covered drive. The tree-lined drive reminded him of Kent, the only difference being the drive began to rise, going uphill. The road finally leveled out, and looking out the carriage window, Arthur noticed a large Italian renaissance-style house to one side.

It was larger than he first expected. In front was a large fountain and the landscaping complemented the house. Everything gently sloped downward from the house.

A man about his age walked out of the house and waited for the carriage to stop. Arthur exited the coach and walked nearer to the man he presumed to be Denton.

"I hope you were comfortable last night in spite of the rain," Denton said.

"Thank you. I stayed at one of the hotels and stayed dry."

"Good," Denton replied.

His host turned without word and began walking to the front door. Arthur followed, unsure what to say. A footman took his greatcoat, gloves, and hat as they entered the great hall. It was a large space with black and white marble on the floor and a fresco on the ceiling. Impressive.

Denton led him to a dark-green and gold drawing room. He walked over to a sideboard and poured two whiskeys. It wasn't even afternoon, but Arthur knew he would insult his host if he didn't accept the glass and drink. His host sat down on a dark-green damask wingback chair and motioned for Arthur to sit as well. Arthur sat in the matching chair and waited for his host to say something.

Arthur broke the silence. "Does Charles know I'm coming?"

"Yes, though I'm never sure how much or what he comprehends. My father said your brother is the smartest man he's ever met, but I hardly know him, so I have no way to judge."

"I've heard much the same thing," Arthur said. He gazed around the room. In spite of large windows and a French door, the room was incredibly dark.

"Did you know he is a writer? Writes crime novels along with other types of stories."

Arthur sat back in his chair and took a sip of whiskey. "That's why there are deposits from a publisher in the ledger. He must be good."

"Yes," Denton replied.

"When do I meet him?"

"I asked him to come to the house at about this time. We'll see what he does. If he doesn't show soon, we'll go to his cottage. I informed him he'd be going to London with long-lost family. I'm not sure how he's going to respond when he sees you."

"What do you mean?"

"You look just like him. That could confuse him. I tried to explain he was a twin, but I'm not sure he grasped what I meant," Denton replied.

"He understands he's leaving here and will be living with me?"

"Yes, I believe he does, and once he meets you it should make more sense to him. I told him to pack what he has to have, and the rest will be shipped to him."

"He's okay with this?"

Denton shrugged his shoulders. "He seemed to be, though as I mentioned, it's hard to tell what he understands much less comprehends."

"Right," Arthur replied. He was beginning to wonder just how much contact Denton actually had with Charles. Perhaps there was a man, a footman or someone, who communicated with Charles.

"I'll be sure to have my man send you an accounting and bill for anything owed."

Now came the actual truth. For young Denton this was nothing more than a financial transaction. "From my understanding, money was added to his account once a year. Nothing further is due. The money from the publisher is put into a separate account and everything else comes out of the account our fathers set up."

"Our fathers are no longer here. The deal ended with my father's death. I am not under any obligation for your brother's care."

Arthur was not going to get into a financial discussion with Denton. The man saw this as a way to make money. He didn't seem to be a man of integrity. Instead, he simply nodded his head.

He'd take care of this after he had Charles away from here.

"No, you're not under obligation to see to my brother's care. That's why I am here. To take my brother home."

Denton turned his attention to a clock on the mantel. He was obviously very precise and took his schedules seriously. "He's late. Probably forgot all about this meeting. He has a habit of forgetting time."

"If you send me in the direction of his cottage, I could introduce myself and see if he needs help packing," Arthur replied.

"No need," Denton said, shaking his head. "The estate manager seems to have taken Charles under his wing years ago. He told me earlier that your brother was packed and ready to go. There's a good chance he's taken a walk. That's something he enjoys immensely."

"Good to know. He'll enjoy walking on my estate in Kent."

Denton nodded. He was obviously not liking his day being changed. "Did you bring a wagon?"

"One was supposed to be here this morning. We could check and see if it arrived. If they're not here today, they'll come tomorrow."

That wasn't the answer he was looking for. "Let me see if it's arrived. If it has, we can see it's loaded and sent on its way to London."

Arthur was amenable to that, but he wanted to see where his brother had been living. "Please do. I'll ride with them. Perhaps Charles might have returned by now."

"As you wish."

His host stood and walked toward the door. A footman opened it, and Denton disappeared. Shaking his head, Arthur stood and walked to the French doors and looked out. His host was rather rude. While Charles had been Denton's father's responsibility, the man was rude and acted as though his brother was a burden and couldn't wait to have him gone.

The door opened and Arthur turned to see Denton standing there. "Wagon has gone on to the cottage. It's not too far a walk or I can have a horse brought."

"No need. I'll walk. Just show me which way to go and I'll head out. I don't want to take up any more of your time."

Denton chose to ignore Arthur's comments. "Come then; I'll show you the way. Not hard to find."

Following his host through the house to the front door, Arthur wondered how much Charles may have been in the house. He'd been a young boy when he left his parents' care. He had so many questions and few answers to them. With his parents gone, Arthur had only what other people knew of Charles and his personality. Even then there weren't that many people who knew of his existence. It made him wonder about a lot of things. Things he would soon have the answers to.

Once outside, Denton pointed to a path. "Just stay on this path. It'll take you right to his cottage. His cottage is just inside the tree line."

Arthur thanked him and was on his way. The path seemed to be well worn, and he could make out the wheels of a wagon which had recently driven by. It was odd that Denton seemed to want nothing to do with the situation. Arthur shook his head. Perhaps he and his father didn't have a good relationship and even though the family was in mourning, it seemed Denton was ready to move ahead.

It wasn't long before he found himself at the cottage. The structure was a good size, and there were outbuildings to the back of the cottage.

As he stood absentmindedly watching as men loaded boxes and trunks into the wagon, a red-headed gentleman approached. The closer he came, the bigger the grin on his face.

"Your Grace," the man said with a slight bow. "I'm Frazier, Lord Charles's valet."

"Frazier. It's nice to meet someone who's actually been around Charles. You've served him long?"

"I've served him since he turned ten. His father thought he needed someone to help him out," Frazier replied.

"Then you'll be accompanying us to London?"

"Aye, unless you have other plans, Your Grace."

Arthur shook his head. "You've been with my brother far too long to replace you. He trusts you or else you wouldn't still be around."

"That is true."

"Tell me about my brother."

"Not much to tell. He's the smartest man I've ever met. His memory is like nothing I've ever encountered. He walks when he's uncomfortable or needs to think something out. Crowds do make him uncomfortable. That's why he isn't here. He's either walking or he's watching what's going on."

"Interesting. I understand from Lord Denton that Charles is aware he's moving. Does that upset him?"

"At first it upset him, but he and I have discussed it many times and he seems more comfortable knowing he's finally going to be among family."

"He'll have his own suite of rooms when we return to London. Do you think he'll be okay with that arrangement? When we return to my estate in Kent, we can re-evaluate things and see what he might want."

"I think he'll be fine. Just a word of advice… don't rush him. Let him adjust to changes in his own time. This is a huge one for him."

Arthur nodded. "You're absolutely right. I might need you to remind me of that at first."

"Not a problem."

"Did you set aside a case to go with us on the carriage?"

Frazier nodded. "I did."

"I suppose we ought to find my brother and see if we can't be on our way."

"I know exactly where he is. I'll get him. That's probably easiest and then the two of you can meet."

"Thank you, Frazier. Whatever you think best. You're making this a lot easier than I imagined."

Frazier grunted, turned, and went in the general direction he'd indicated moments ago.

Arthur knew he still had hurdles to overcome, but just the fact that someone who knew Charles was going to stay on made him feel more at ease. He would find out what the man was making in this position. Surely not enough. A raise would probably be needed for everything he did.

He walked in the direction Frazier had gone. How would this go? Would Charles accept him, or would he need help to overcome his fears? He was about to find out.

CHAPTER THREE

Aʀᴛʜᴜʀ sᴛᴏᴘᴘᴇᴅ ɪɴ his tracks and stared at what he saw. In front of him stood a young man. Charles. He was talking lowly to Frasier, but then his eyes locked with Arthur's and the two stared at each other. He was amazed. It was like looking at himself in a mirror. There were some slight differences, but only he and probably Frazier would notice them. Charles wore his hair longer; it went to his shoulders and was slightly lighter due to all the sunlight he got. He was muscular from all the labor he did to occupy his time. The men stood in silence, each taking the other in.

Finally, Arthur decided to try and break the silence. "Hello, Charles, I'm your brother Arthur."

It took a minute or so for Charles to process what was going on. He kept standing, not a muscle flinching.

"Yes, I know. You look amazingly a lot like me."

"Indeed, you do. Are you ready to head out to London?"

Charles hesitated with his answer. Frazier was right there with him. "We've talked about this. We're going to London. Arthur is an MP. Then we'll go to Kent."

"Can I go to Parliament to watch?" Charles asked.

"Of course you can. But first we need to get to London," Arthur replied.

"Yes, I am ready."

"Excellent," Arthur said.

"We go by boat to the mainland, and afterwards we'll head to London," Charles said.

"That is correct," Frazier said, trying to reassure any doubts or fears Charles might have.

The threesome started to walk to the cottage Charles had been living in. The wagon was being loaded when they walked by. Charles slowed down to observe how the men were progressing but quickly caught up to Frazier and Arthur.

Finally, they came upon the carriage.

"Do you wish to say goodbye to Denton?" Arthur asked.

"No, he probably wouldn't see me. He doesn't seem to like me, so we can leave immediately."

Arthur hated the fact that Charles had lived his life in a bubble, always being protected from the possibility of someone taking advantage of him. With time and his brother's acute awareness, Arthur was determined to see he overcame his anxieties. He could make inquiries about Charles seeing a new doctor and see if that might help. That was not something he would push. Right now, they needed to build trust between the two of them.

It came to him that he hadn't inquired about the money Charles seemed to be earning from a publisher. He had to have written a book to receive that kind of money.

They left Denton's estate in Arthur's carriage. Speaking further with Denton proved to be impossible. Arthur was turned away. He shook his head and climbed into his carriage. Charles sat across from him. He was looking around the interior of the coach. Arthur wasn't sure if he was considering bolting or just taking everything in.

"Are we going directly to London?" Charles asked.

"No, I thought we'd find a place after we've crossed."

Charles looked notably nervous. "We mustn't stop, except to rest the team. We must reach London today."

"Is there a reason?"

"I do not like being idle. Staying at an inn would make us idle."

Arthur nodded as though he understood. He knew his brother had idiosyncrasies and he would have to learn them, or at least be patient with him. "Very well. I'll tell the driver as soon as we're crossing."

"Thank you," Charles replied.

"You must tell me if you're not comfortable with anything. At least until I know your ways."

The conversation completely took a turn. Arthur understood this was a way Charles managed some conversations. "Tell me about Roxanne. What is she like?"

"You will like Roxanne. She and her husband live close by in Kent. She's very kindhearted and will do anything for you. She's older than us by a couple of years."

"So that makes me the youngest."

"Yes, it does," Arthur replied.

They were waiting for the coach to be loaded onto the barge that took people and items to Wight. He would give his man the new orders. The last thing he wanted was for Charles to get out of sorts.

Once he returned to the carriage, he found his brother with notebook in hand, furiously scribbling away. He wondered if it were some sort of journal he kept.

"Are you planning to write another book?"

"Yes. Soon."

"What was your previous book about?" Arthur asked. He didn't know and wasn't sure how many there were.

Charles arched a brow and stopped writing. "I've written three books. Each book is about a period of English history and how they influence today's world."

"That sounds like it takes a lot of research. How do you choose which period to write about?"

"I don't. The subject matter chooses me."

"Interesting," Arthur replied. "Do you do speaking engagements?"

"Rarely. If my publisher receives an invitation, we discuss the matter. They go through them for me. Oxford is wanting me to come speak."

"Will you accept the Oxford invitation?"

Charles ran his hand through his hair and then scrubbed his beard with his hand. "At some time. They ask every time I come out with a new book."

"I suppose you should. It speaks volumes on how well received your books are."

"Yes. It's just one subject matter that I'm passionate about. Perhaps I'll be able to expand into something else at some time."

Arthur could tell his brother had been well schooled and that he had a passion for things most men wouldn't. He wondered what he wanted to expand into but decided that was enough for one day. "Are you hungry, Charles?"

"Yes. Why do you ask?"

"I'm going to stop and purchase a hamper so we can have something to eat while we're heading back to London."

Charles grunted, his attention on something else. He stayed silent. Arthur knew he stayed on one subject for only so long. But in a matter of minutes, he recalled his conversation and answered. "Excellent idea."

Any further conversation was halted. At least on Charles's end. Arthur engaged the coachman when they pulled up in front of an establishment. He sat back until the man returned carrying a basket. The coachman handed it in to Arthur and in moments, the carriage groaned as it pulled out onto the street.

Once they were on the way to London, Arthur opened the basket which was sitting beside him. "We've got some Cornish pasties, two varieties of cheeses, apples and pears, a loaf of crusty bread, and a bottle of wine."

Arthur began to take items out of the basket and lay them on the seat next to him. He found two plates and handed one to his brother. That was still a strange word to come out of his mouth.

He sliced cheese and an apple and pear. Charles didn't seem to have any trouble in helping himself to what he wanted. Arthur followed suit, though he took less, making sure there would be plenty. He noticed that his brother ate like there was no tomorrow. He wondered why.

Once everything was put away, Arthur placed the basket on the far side of the seat he occupied. He looked across and found Charles settled back, his eyes closed, taking a well-deserved nap. He imagined the recent days had been tiring for him. He'd been through quite a few changes. Denton's father had died, leaving Charles precariously in an odd position. If Arthur hadn't found out his brother existed, he may well have been taken advantage of. He'd thought that when he first set eyes on Charles, but the more he was around him, the more he understood it was a partial act. Charles knew he could learn much more if he played ignorant. People thought him odd anyway, so playing into that thought, he could pretend one thing while he was learning; he would take things in stride.

Arthur picked up a book he'd brought along with him but found he couldn't concentrate on the words in front of him. After several tries, he set the book down and closed his eyes. It was the last thing he remembered.

The next thing he recalled was Charles trying to wake him up. His first thought was they'd reached London. "Arthur, we're getting closer to London."

"How can you tell?"

"Traffic has become heavier. More people too."

"You would be correct," Arthur replied. "We're still about an hour outside London."

"How do you know?" Charles had a puzzled look on his face as he looked out the window.

"I recognize that field," he replied, pointing to the window on the opposite side of the coach.

Charles nodded and peered out that side of the coach. He didn't say a word. It was as though he were trying to remember every detail of that field for future encounters. Finally, he sat back and closed his eyes. Arthur knew Charles's mind had to be going full speed. He was certain he would in the same situation. Charles was basically a stranger. Neither knew the other, and Arthur was sure this was going to be more delicate than what was going on now.

He and Daphne had discussed where Charles should live when they headed back to the country. There was a separate wing that was barely used. Sometimes it was occupied by guests, so the rooms got used. Other times it sat empty. It also had a full kitchen if Charles liked it and wanted to use it. If he felt uncomfortable, Charles could also live in one of the spare cottages, like he did at Denton's. There was one cottage that came to mind to Arthur. It sat on the edge of the meadow, hidden by trees and brush. It had a small stable and outbuilding and was close enough to the main house that Charles could walk the distance.

The cottage might be the best option At least for a while, until Charles acclimated to the huge changes in his life. Arthur would still let his brother make his choice, but he would also talk to Charles's valet and get his input. He would make a point to do so while they were still in London.

Arthur tried to close his eyes, but sleep wouldn't come this time. Instead, he pulled a notebook out of a pocket of his greatcoat and began to make some notes about Charles, his attitude, where he might be more comfortable living. Turning a page, he began recalling things from Parliament he was working on and what he needed in order to comment on anything. He thoroughly enjoyed being an MP. It gave him a chance to help people and the country. Though he kept his personal life private for the most part, this new chapter with Charles was certainly going to wag some tongues. No one would doubt his claim that Charles was his brother. They looked exactly alike. Still, he didn't want to expose his brother to unneeded publicity.

When he finished his thoughts, he replaced the notebook into his pocket. For some reason, he glanced up and saw Charles studying him with keen interest.

"I was writing notes on some bills I'm working on. It makes it easier for me when I get to my office to work if I have something to go by."

"I understand. Can you take me through Parliament?"

"Yes, of course I can."

Glancing out the window to his right, Arthur spotted some houses mixed with smaller offices. Officially, they were in London.

Right then, there was a change in Charles's mood. He was somber, watching with keen interest at what they passed. Never saying another word, his jaw seemed to set as though he was full of questions but refusing to ask Arthur anything further. As they neared the house, he only got more tense.

Arthur kept an eye on him as they traveled through London. When the carriage pulled up in front of the house, Charles jumped out and onto the street before Arthur even knew what was happening. Frazier was there to guide him to the front door.

"Your Grace," the butler greeted him.

"This is my brother, Charles."

The butler nodded. "His rooms are ready whenever he'd like to settle in."

Suddenly, Daphne appeared. Sam could be heard in the distance calling to her. "Charles, it is so nice to meet you."

"Do you have children?" Charles asked.

"No, not yet. That's Sam, my parrot. Would you like to meet him?"

Charles gave her a look of horror at the thought of such a creature living in the house among humans. "No, I do not wish to meet him."

"Very well. Just let me know when you want an introduction." She locked eyes with Arthur, as if not knowing if she'd done something wrong.

Charles grunted. "I should like to see my rooms."

His valet, Frazier, came out of nowhere. "Come. I'll show

you. I think you're going to love them."

Charles said nothing, nothing to Daphne or Arthur. He didn't even try to make eye contact. Instead, Arthur nodded and watched as the pair walked across the hall.

"I guess this is a huge change for him," Daphne said. She stood next to Arthur watching his new-found brother disappear up the stairs.

"Yes. I can't even imagine. He's lived in one place and now he's been uprooted and moved."

"Would Denton not let him stay on for a while? Just until Charles got used to the idea of moving."

Arthur shook his head. "He couldn't get rid of Charles fast enough. If he had stayed, it would have come at a price."

"Greedy man?"

"From what I could see, yes."

"Is there anything I should know?" Daphne asked.

"He's moody. We were having a nice conversation and then he shut down."

"Oh, my. But like I said, he's been through a lot. Everything is new."

"Just beware. I'm not sure how he's going to act."

Daphne nodded. "I will. Let's just give him some time to acclimate."

"I think that's a good idea," he replied. "Now if you'll excuse me, I need to go through correspondence."

"There were some packets brought from Parliament for you to review. I put them on your desk."

"Thank you," he said, bending down and kissing her. "It's nice to be in familiar surroundings."

"Would you like some tea or something to eat?"

"No. I'm fine," he replied. "I promise I won't be long."

She let a giggle slip and put her hand over her mouth.

"What's so funny?"

"I promise I won't be long. Really, Arthur?"

CHARLES STOOD IN the doorway of his suites, unsure whether to enter. Frazier pushed him aside and stepped into the small sitting room.

"Come on. I think you'll like these rooms. I checked them out myself for you." Frazier knew his charge better than anyone. The late duke had chosen him to act as a valet and friend to his second son. They'd been through thick and thin together and Frazier knew Charles was highly intelligent, but he had trouble interacting with others, and it was made worse if he didn't know the person.

Walking into the sitting room, Charles immediately walked across the room to the window. It overlooked a large garden on the backside of the house. He would have to go outside for a walk and check out what was where. Knowing where everything was, was important to him. Made things seem a little less disorderly.

"Excellent." He turned and began walking to the bed chamber. After that was the bathing chamber and storage closet. Everything had recently been cleaned, and he concluded the duchess, his sister-in-law, had something to do with it. It seemed Her Grace was a hands-on sort of lady.

"Would you like to clean up and change clothes?" Frazier asked from behind him.

"Yes, it was a dusty ride even in that fancy carriage my brother has."

Frazier led the way to the bathing chamber where he'd already laid things out by the tub. "What are your feelings about Arthur?"

"I can't say. I don't know him."

"Come on, Charles. You spent a long time with him. All the way from Wight. Surely you must have an opinion?"

He shook his head as he headed over to the copper tub. "It's too soon to do so. I can tell you he's articulate, intelligent, and seems to genuinely care." Charles paused. "But you already knew all that."

"I'll let you have this one, but mind you, I will ask again."

"I'm sure he had to be in shock when he learned about me. Anyone would, don't you think?" Charles said.

"I know I would be, especially because you two are identical twins," Frazier replied.

Climbing into the tub, Charles lowered himself in, leaving just his head showing above the water. "I suppose that plays into the grand scheme of things. I'm sure his colleagues and friends are going to be doing double-takes." He laughed.

"You have a sister as well. Roxanne, she's a couple years older."

"Yes, so I've been told. I suppose we'll meet her in the up-coming days."

The fact was that Charles felt some hesitation in meeting his sister. He didn't know what to expect from her, just as he wasn't sure about the duchess either. Women were strange creatures. He hadn't spent a lot of time around them but found them hard to understand. Some preferred to be docile and others were the opposite. Independent. Arthur's wife seemed to be like that. Independent.

"Yes, if she and her husband are in London. You might want to get to know your brother's wife, Lady Daphne," Frazier said from across the room. Frazier was never the sort of man who stood sedentary. He was always doing something.

"I will," Charles replied with a cheeky grin as he grabbed a bar of soap.

"Not in that way, milord. You won't be able to fool her; at least not for long." Frazier was referring to a scar Charles had along his shoulder on his back. It happened years ago and had faded, but it was still there. A long-ago training accident while learning to fence. Lord Denton had hired Charles tutors through the years, and this particular one did not believe in coddling his students. A hard lesson learned for Charles.

"You spoil everything, you know that?"

Frazier shook his head. "That's what I'm supposed to do. Keep you from doing something stupid."

"I don't do stupid things. I think things through before I act on them."

"Yes, you do. Now when you're finished with your bath, I've laid out clothes. I thought you might like to take a walk in the gardens."

"Why would I want to do that when there's a perfectly gorgeous park just blocks from here?" Charles replied.

"Because you can do that alone. You don't need me to look after you."

Grinning, Charles stood up, water dripping from his lean, muscular body. "I will this once. I need to see if Arthur would like me to go over the books in regard to my upkeep while living on Lord Denton's estate."

After changing, Charles was drawn to a knock on the door. He was about to answer it when Frazier appeared out of nowhere and took care of matters. Opening the door, the butler stood.

"I hate to disturb you, milord, but the duchess wanted to invite you to tea."

"Tell Her Grace I'd love tea and I'll be there momentarily."

"My lord." With that, the butler disappeared with the shutting of a door.

"Now you don't need to take a walk in the gardens," Frazier quipped.

"At least not now. I need my jacket, Frazier. Then I'll see what tea is all about."

The valet shook his head. He knew Charles always questioned being included in anything. People, he thought, wanted something. It made Charles leery of everyone. Frazier helped him with his jacket and watched as Charles fussed with minute details.

"Do you need me to help you find your way?"

"No, I'll figure it out on my own," he replied as he opened the door and looked back, as though he thought he might have forgotten something. Satisfied, he walked through the door. He had an eidetic memory and finding his way to the drawing room was easy. He never got lost, no matter where he was. The gift, as Frazier referred to it, had saved them on more than one occasion. A good thing, too, because some of the areas they went to were not all that savory.

Portraits of previous dukes and their families lined the walls along with hunting scenes and garden paintings. Nothing seemed to have a purpose as to why it was placed where it was. It was an eclectic mishmash of art. Some of it not very good either. The older portraits needed to be taken down and cleaned by an artist specializing in such things. A lot of people didn't know of such matters, therefore, their portraits seemed to fade with age when actually it was a buildup of smoke, air, and age. Something to mention to his brother and his Lady Daphne.

Finding the drawing room wasn't hard. A nearby table with cut flowers sitting in a crystal vase with a footman next to the door gave it away. There again was no reason for the table to be that close to the door. He nodded to the young man who then opened the door to the drawing room.

"Ah, Charles. I take it you had no problem finding me," Lady Daphne said as she came across the room to greet him. A rather large iron cage stood not too far from the fireplace. Atop the cage sat a huge brightly colored parrot. This must be the one she had been speaking of earlier.

"No, no problems at all." He eyed the bird, then Daphne. "How did you come to have a parrot?"

"My father. His name is Sam, and he talks a lot for a parrot. I will warn you not all his language is nice. He knows how to curse like a sailor when he wants to."

"He's being quiet. Why is that?"

"Perhaps because you are a mirror image to Arthur and he hasn't figured that out yet."

"In other words, he may think I'm Arthur?"

Daphne arched a brow and thought for a moment. "That's

entirely possible."

"Fascinating," Charles replied.

"Come, tea arrived just before you, and I've set it up in front of the hearth. It's still a little too cool for tea on the terrace."

Charles nodded. "That sounds delightful." He diverted his gaze to Sam for a second. The bird was still watching him with great interest.

"If you're not comfortable with Sam being here, I can have one of the footmen remove him."

"No, that isn't necessary," he said, shaking his head slightly. "I'd actually like to hear him talk."

"Very well." She led the way to where the tea service and treats had been placed on a low table next to the chairs they were about to sit in.

Charles looked in amazement at the tiny sandwiches, cake, and sweets set before them. Tea usually consisted of a cup of tea and a large piece of cake or pie. Those were usually left over from Denton's tea and given to him. Over the years, he'd taught himself to bake pies and cakes.

He accepted the cup of tea from his sister-in-law and placed it on a table next to him. Picking up a plate, he filled it with cake and sandwiches, without realizing how hungry he was.

"I'm sure this all came as a huge shock," Daphne said, picking up her teacup and observing Charles closely.

He shook his head. "Not at all. I've always known I had siblings. I just assumed my parents were punishing me for being different. I'm very smart, you see."

"Yes, so I've heard," she replied. "But wasn't meeting Arthur a shock to your system? Seeing someone who looks just like you?"

He picked up his plate holding a piece of marmalade cake. Taking a bite, he put his fork back on the plate. "Yes. Not as shocked as I thought I'd be, but then they say everyone has at least one person in the world who looks like them."

"That's scary," Daphne said. Out of the corner of her eye, she saw Sam climb down from his cage and begin to walk towards them. Charles had seen Sam's actions but seemed to be content watching the parrot.

"Your bird is walking across the floor," he finally said uncomfortably.

"He does that often. He likes to follow me around the house when he can. Sam also does it for attention."

Glancing at Daphne and then the bird, Charles didn't appear too happy with the idea. "You allow him near food we eat?"

"It's not like he gets on the table and begins eating."

"That may be, but he still has an opportunity should he decide that's what he wants," Charles insisted.

Daphne smiled and put down her teacup. "I can assure you that won't happen, but if it'll make you more comfortable, I can put him in his cage."

"If you don't mind," he replied.

"Of course not."

He watched as his sister-in-law stood and walked a couple of steps before bending and putting her arm out to the parrot. The bird jumped on without a word. That all changed the minute Daphne put him at the door of his cage and closed the door behind him. Sam began screeching and trying to flap his wings from the cramped interior of the cage.

"I didn't know he'd be so upset," Charles said, watching the bird continue his tantrum.

"He associates his cage as a place to go if we're not here or it's time to go to bed. Putting him in during the middle of the day can cause him some confusion."

"I don't wish to cause him discomfort," Charles said.

"He'll settle down. I promise. He thinks the attention will get sympathy from someone and he'll get out."

"Smart."

"They are that."

"Has anyone studied them as far as their abilities? It would be fascinating to know where and how he learned to talk."

"The only thing I know for sure is he learned a lot of naughty words on the ship that brought him to us."

"Don't you wonder if he understands his actions?"

"Not particularly," Daphne replied.

Charles rose from his chair and walked across the room where he stood to observe Sam. "I wonder if the fact he's upset might have something to do with the fact I look like Arthur, but do not act like him."

Daphne's hand flew to her mouth for a moment, clearly shocked by his statement. "You're right. I hadn't thought about that. It's entirely possible he's confused."

"The theory can be tested once Arthur arrives."

"You mean the two of you approach Sam to see his reaction?"

Charles nodded. He was still standing in the same position near the cage, watching Sam watch him. "Precisely."

"Arthur should be here shortly so we can test your theory."

He said nothing but turned away from the cage and walked back to his chair where Daphne was refreshing his tea. He picked up his empty plate and chose two sandwiches and a raspberry tart.

"Are you anxious about your move from Wight and what lies ahead?" Daphne asked.

"I haven't given it much thought because I don't understand why I was abandoned and put there by my father. No good answer has ever been given to me."

"But you have been informed."

"If you want to call it that. I've learned more from Arthur than anyone else."

"How do you spend your days?" Daphne asked quietly.

Charles seemed to be deep in thought on how to answer her. He scrubbed his beard with his hands before picking up his teacup once again. "I take a lot of walks. I find it keeps my mind clear."

"Arthur does that as well. He also rides his horse for the same reason," she replied.

"Arthur likes to do what?" a familiar voice said from the

doorway.

"Lady Daphne was inquiring into how I spend my time."

Arthur came across the room in three steps and sat down next to his wife. "Was she? Well, you and I have an appointment with the solicitor tomorrow."

"No one's ever included me on such meetings," Charles said.

"Now you have," Arthur said, accepting a cup of tea from Daphne. "I thought we might stop by Parliament afterwards and see if anything is going on."

"How long will we be in London?"

"I'm not sure. I'll know better when I see what Parliament is doing. We're to have a break for a fortnight but it still depends on bills, and the like."

"We have an experiment to do. Sam seems to be confused. He knows I look like you, but he knows I'm not you. I thought it might be a good idea to show him there are two of us."

Whenever Charles didn't feel comfortable with a subject of conversation or he didn't want to be bothered with details, he changed the subject. It had always worked for him before. But then he'd never kept much company except Frazier. This was something new he was going to have to get used to.

"Yes, that seems like the logical thing to do. I keep telling her the bird is too smart."

"He is," Charles replied.

Shortly, Daphne crossed the room to Sam's cage, opened the door and let the bird hop onto her forearm. She walked back to where the men were and stopped. Sam looked at both Charles and Arthur before letting his voice be heard.

"Bloody hell!"

"That's not nice, Sam. Charles will be living with us, so you better be on your best behavior," Daphne scolded him.

"Sam good."

"Yes, you are for the most part," she replied.

Sam continued to sit on Daphne's arm. She fed him a piece of apple she had brought from his cage top. He greedily took it from her hand and ate it as he continued to look from one man to the other. Another apple slice appeared in Charles's hand. Charles extended his hand, palm up, to see what the parrot might do. Once again, greed for his treat overtook any suspicions Sam might have about Charles. Treats won out every time.

"More!" Sam demanded.

Charles pulled his hand away as soon as the macaw seemed as though he was going to jump on his arm. "I have no more," he replied.

He heard his brother snicker beside him. "Do you find yourself questioning why you're talking to a bird?"

"No, why would I? It is obvious Sam has some intelligence, though how much he really understands is questionable."

"Would you care to take Sam back to his perch?" Daphne asked, holding her parrot-ridden arm in his direction.

"No, another time perhaps?" he said, adding, "Would you mind if I got a book from the library? I thought I might read before dinner."

"Yes, of course. Don't feel as though you have to ask," Arthur said.

"He's right, and dinner is at seven-thirty. We gather in the drawing room around seven," Daphne said as she walked back to the parrot's perch and cage.

Charles nodded and rose from his chair. "I shall see you then." He turned and walked toward the closed door. It had been the only excuse he could come up with to get away. Even conversation with his newly found family found him withdrawing to his safe spot. He would have to overcome this. But not now. He'd bought himself some time to relax on his terms. He would try it again at dinner.

Inside the library, he found two walls lined with books. A grand piano sat in the center of the room with the furniture placed so everyone could enjoy music. Perhaps another time. Playing would just invite people to come and listen, and he didn't care for the idea. His music had always been something very personal to him. He quickly found a book on the War of the Roses he hadn't read. Shutting the door behind him, he once again walked back to his rooms. He found himself alone, Frazier probably downstairs taking care of something on his behalf.

CHAPTER FOUR

CHARLES AND ARTHUR sat in front of the desk of Jeremy Smith, the family solicitor. Smith had wanted to not only meet Charles in person, he had news to share with him.

"You've written three rather successful books. Have you ever considered where the royalties were going?" Smith inquired.

"Royalties? No. I signed a contract which is good for three more years, I believe. I've never seen any royalties from any of them."

"Your father set up a bank account in your name and that's where they've been sent. Your father's name was on it of course, but when he died, Arthur's name replaced your father's."

"If you want, I can have my name taken off the account, Charles," Arthur said.

"No. No changes need to be made," Charles replied.

Smith picked up a black ledger book from his desk and handed it to Charles. "This is a full accounting of your royalties. It is up to date as of the end of last month."

Charles began to leaf through the book, holding it where Arthur could also see it. He tried not to reveal his emotions as this was far more than he ever imagined. "This is for the first three books?"

"Yes, it is. Nothing has been taken out."

Looking at Arthur and then Smith, he tried to find the words.

Finally, simple words left his mouth. "This is a tidy sum."

"It is," Smith replied.

"Thank you for showing me this. Can I expect a copy each month?"

"If that's what you wish."

Charles shook his head. "Only if money goes out, and any deposits which are made."

Charles sat back and listened as Smith and his brother went over other matters. He couldn't get his mind to focus on anything else. He'd never had his own money. Denton had always taken care of his needs through money his father regularly sent. He even made sure Charles had pocket money for the times he did go to the village. If something was more than he had, Charles simply had it billed to Denton.

"Charles?"

He glanced over at Arthur. "Yes?"

"Are you ready to go?"

Charles nodded. "Yes, whenever you're ready."

"If you have any questions, please don't hesitate to let me know," Smith said, extending a hand to both brothers.

"I'm sure I will once the shock has worn off," Charles said. "Thank you."

The pair walked out into the sunshine and headed to their waiting carriage. Charles would have preferred to walk to Parliament, but his brother insisted they'd get there just as quickly by taking the carriage. He climbed in after Arthur and sat. "Are we going to your office?"

"Yes. I thought first we might have lunch in the Parliament dining room. The food is superb, and after that we'll go to my office and check on what I might have missed."

"Do you miss it when you're away?"

"This is my first session, but I do enjoy it. Ask me that question in a year or two when I'm more seasoned," Arthur replied with a grin.

"I won't forget." He wouldn't either. Charles had a memory

like a steel trap which had so far proven to be quite useful in his life.

The carriage pulled up in front of the buildings which housed Parliament. This was a first. He climbed out ahead of Arthur and waited on him. He glanced up at the imposing sky. When they had left the house, the sky was a beautiful shade of blue. Now a storm seemed to be approaching. He hadn't paid attention to it when they left Smith's, probably because he was in a daze as they walked out.

Walking beside Arthur, Charles took his surroundings in. There were people walking in and out and when they did enter, it became more apparent that there was so much more to where laws were passed than he ever imagined.

"Let's go to the dining room first and get something to eat," Arthur said.

Charles nodded as they made their way through the crowd. He was hungry but hoped it would be quieter in the dining room. He disliked crowds, always had.

He was not prepared for the large number of people inside the dining room, though it was quiet considering the multitude of men having lunch and discussing whatever it was men in Parliament talked about outside the chamber. The tables were closer together than he liked, but if he had to guess, they were trying to accommodate a larger number of guests. MPs with their wives, or businessmen. Charles knew he had to be careful and ignore what might be going on around him or he'd find himself fleeing.

They were seated at a table in the middle of the room, one of the few empty tables available. Arthur gave the young man their drink and food orders and he quickly disappeared.

"I hope you're okay with what I chose. Their steaks are memorable. Most popular item, I believe," Arthur said.

"Yes, that is fine. I haven't had a steak in a long time and that was when my first book had been published," Charles replied.

Arthur absentmindedly ran his hand through his hair before

he spoke. "That is quite a long time. I'll ask Daphne to put steak on the menu so you can have it at least a couple of times a month."

"Please don't trouble her with something so unimportant."

"Trust me, it's no bother. Daphne is still finding her way as duchess, and this is one area she seems to enjoy."

"What would that be?" Charles asked.

"Making sure the household is at its best, the meals the best. In fact, you're in for a treat. When we're in Kent, she makes a point of serving new dishes she might want to serve at some soiree we might be having."

"The two of you have a unique relationship. You complement each other very well."

"Thank you, Charles. That means a lot. You're very observant."

"I'm told it's one of my redeeming qualities," Charles replied with a lop-sided grin.

"An excellent quality to have."

Trying to keep the noise in the room from overwhelming him, Charles realized he was going to have to work hard to accomplish that. He hadn't told anyone about it since he left Wight. He didn't want people making a big fuss over him. It was something Frazier had tried and tried to help him with. Every time he felt he couldn't take it, people in general, he slipped away. He sometimes took long walks, other times he went to one of his hiding places on the estate. If he was going to stay with Arthur, he would need to find places he could retreat to in times like this.

"Have you ever been to Tattersall's?" Charles asked his brother.

"Yes, quite a few times. Have you been?"

"Once."

"We could go if you want to pick out a horse. If not, I have several for you to choose from in Kent."

An older man arrived at the table with their lunch while

another poured each of them a glass of wine. Charles held his breath until they left. It was getting harder and harder to sit with all the noise, but he was determined to.

"I think I'd like to see what you have first."

Arthur picked up his glass of wine and took a swallow before cutting into his steak. Rare to perfection. "Roxanne's husband Graham has some exceptional animals, though I'm not sure what he has available. It might be a good idea to see what he has."

Staring down at his food, Charles nodded. He cut a small piece of steak and pushed it around on the plate. "That sounds like a good idea as well."

Watching his brother push his fork around on the plate, Arthur couldn't help but wonder if he wasn't particularly fond of rare meat. "If the steak isn't cooked the way you like, we can have it sent back."

"No, that isn't necessary."

"It's no problem. They won't mind."

"It's perfect," Charles replied. He speared the piece he'd cut and popped it into his mouth. Arthur was right. It was tender and quite delicious. He nodded his head after swallowing.

Just then a fellow MP happened upon their table. He was an older man and quite boisterous. Charles wasn't sure if that was his personality or if he'd had a bit too much wine.

"You never said you were a twin," the man said loudly.

"Yes, I am. This is my brother, Lord Jameson. Charles, this is Perry Young, Earl of Blackshire."

"A pleasure, Lord Jameson. I expect we'll be seeing a lot more of you. Do you live in Kent as well?"

Arthur interrupted. "He does."

The man turned and loudly spoke to an adjacent table about Arthur and Charles being twins. It was more than Charles could bear. Without a word to Arthur, he stood and walked out of the dining room as fast as he could. He didn't stop until he was back outside in front of the Parliament building. The sky was still a foreboding shade of gray, but the skies had not opened up. He stood there trying to catch his breath and decide what to do next.

His instinct told him to walk. Walk he did. He crossed the street and disappeared down one of the side streets. The longer he walked, the better he felt. He knew he had to get his aversion to crowds or small gatherings under control. Arthur was left having to explain why his brother left.

Before today's incident, he and Frazier had been working on just that. He would put himself in situations such as looking in a shop. The results weren't always what they'd hoped for, but he had made some progress. Today's incident had been caused in part due to the boisterous man who visited their table. Charles knew there were lots of men in the world like that one, and that he was going to have to get used to being around them, especially when in town.

He continued walking until he came upon a park. He knew it was near Grosvenor. Finding a bench, he sat down. The skies were still gray, but it hadn't stopped people from coming out for a walk. There were more than he figured would have been outside. They would go scurrying home the moment the rain began. He didn't want to go home because that would be the first place Arthur would look for him. His conscience wouldn't allow him to worry that his brother, newfound or otherwise, was out looking for him. Sitting for a time, caught up in people watching, Charles finally rose and began walking toward the house, estimating it was at least eight blocks from the park. He needed Frazier to help him put this right. He didn't need his brother being ashamed of him, but Arthur needed to understand him better.

He felt peace within himself as he saw the house come into view. He hoped it was quiet and not a lot going on. He'd rather not run into anyone. All he wanted was to go to his rooms without having to answer a lot of questions from well-meaning people.

A footman opened the front door and Charles walked past, leaving his hat and coat on a chair. He was walking toward the steps that led to the family's quarters when Daphne came toward him out of nowhere.

"Arthur stopped by and mentioned what happened," she said.

"I didn't mean to worry him."

"He understood why you left and said if he had been in a position to, he would have fled too," she replied with a smile. She grabbed hold of his hand and began pulling him toward the drawing room. "Come have a cup of tea with me. I'm sure you must be chilled."

Charles understood he was caught and shouldn't be rude and decline. "That sounds nice."

He entered the drawing room and a blonde-headed young woman caught his eye as she sat on a settee near the fire. She was a slip of a thing, wearing a lavender and gray day dress. He couldn't take his eyes off her. Never had he encountered such a beauty. She smiled demurely at him.

"Cathryn, may I introduce my brother-in-law, Lord Charles." She turned to Charles. "Charles, this is a very old friend of mine, Lady Cathryn Beckman."

Charles nodded as she extended her hand. "Lady Beckman, a pleasure, I'm sure."

"Very nice to meet you as well. I wasn't aware until today that Lord Arthur had a brother. Daphne explained it all. Amazing likeness."

"We're identical twins," he replied.

"Would you care for a cup of tea, Charles?" Daphne asked him with a bemused smile on her face.

"I don't wish to interrupt. I need to find my valet and go over some matters with him. Another time."

"Frazier isn't here. He went to pick up some shirts I believe you'd ordered," Daphne said.

"He could have had them sent to the house." He sighed and sat down on a gold damask high back chair.

"Will you take a cup of tea now?" Lady Cathryn asked. She was smiling, and looking at her made his insides act strange.

"Yes, thank you. No milk or sugar, please."

He noted Daphne had a smile on her face. Women tended to do that a lot. Why, he wasn't sure. His knowledge of women was limited. Mostly older women. People thought him an oddity and kept their daughters away from him. He rarely went to social events. His life was changing, and intermingling with the fairer sex was something he'd have to get used to.

Accepting the tea from Lady Cathryn, Charles stared down at it for a moment. "Is your father an MP?"

"No," she replied, sitting back down. "He had some business here and my mother wanted to shop so he brought us both along."

"That seems to be a favorite thing among the ladies."

"It is," Daphne replied. "Lady Cathryn is an accomplished musician. I've never heard anyone play as well as she does."

He arched a brow. "I play as well."

"When did you start? I believe I was about seven when I began," Lady Cathryn inquired.

"I really don't remember a time when I didn't play."

"Lady Cathryn's playing at a musicale we've been invited to. Perhaps you'd like to join us, Charles," Daphne asked with a twinkle in her eye.

Recalling today's events, he wasn't sure if that wouldn't be a disaster as well. He took a sip of tea before answering his sister-in-law.

"Let's see what Arthur has to say since I wasn't included in the invitation."

Lady Cathryn placed her teacup on a table beside her. "I'm sure they wouldn't mind, and I'd love for you to come hear me play."

There was something about Lady Cathryn that had his body reacting in ways that it normally wouldn't. She intrigued him. Not only was she beautiful but she had the most amazing lavender eyes he'd ever seen, and her voice was soft and soothing. She wasn't pushy, vying for his complete attention, but rather let him speak when he wanted and took an interest in what he had to say. On top of all that, his cock was hard and caused him to try and sit without anyone noticing.

"If you want to come along with us, I can inquire with our hostess and see if she would mind one more guest. I don't think she will since you're Arthur's brother," Daphne said.

"Daphne's right. I'm sure they'll be delighted to have you."

He scrubbed his beard with a hand and looked at each of the two women. "If you don't think it's rude to ask to bring an extra person, go ahead and ask."

"Wonderful!" Lady Cathryn said.

Daphne looked at him for a moment. "I'll double check with Arthur first, but I'm sure he'll agree."

"Thank you." He looked about the room. "Where is Sam?" He'd learned quickly that the parrot was always nearby.

"I had him removed because he was saying too many naughty words," Daphne replied with a grin.

Charles grinned as well. "They must have been really bad if you banished him."

"Trust me, he was."

Picking up a plate, Lady Cathryn addressed him. "Would you like some cake or sandwiches, Lord Charles?"

He needed to get out of here and go to his rooms. She was a distraction he didn't know how to deal with. Looking at Daphne out of the corner of his eye, he knew he had better accept her offer.

"Yes, a piece of seed cake would be nice," he replied.

As Daphne poured him another cup of tea, Lady Cathryn added a slice of seed cake to his plate, along with two sandwiches.

"Here you go, Lord Charles. Your sister-in-law has an excellent baker. The seed cake is delicious."

He took a bite. She was right; it was delicious. There was so much out there calling his name. His entire life had been one of being alone, eating whatever he cooked or made. He'd never been exposed to delectable treats like this seed cake. The cake was just the tip of the iceberg, and he wanted to try it all. He then picked up a cucumber sandwich which was quite dainty and only took him one bite. The second one was made with eggs, and after eating it, he couldn't decide which was better. The egg or the cucumber.

Hearing the clock on the mantel chime, he knew he'd overstayed his intended time. He needed to go to his rooms and look for his notebook. He had a lot to write about today. Maybe writing his encounter and feelings about Lady Cathryn would help him understand better, though he doubted it. No one had taught him about the fairer sex. This was uncharted territory to him.

Finishing his tea quickly, he stood to his full height. "Ladies, this has been enjoyable. It was a pleasure to meet you, Lady Cathryn," he said, adding, "If you'll excuse me, I need to find my valet to see if a package has arrived."

"It was nice meeting you as well," Lady Cathryn replied with a smile.

He walked across the room as quickly as he thought acceptable. The moment he was out of range of the closed doors, he quickly went up the stairs and to his suite of rooms. Shutting the doors behind him, he went to look for Frazier who was putting away freshly cleaned clothes.

"Did my package come?" he asked anxiously, referring to a supply of notebooks, pens, and pencils.

"Yes, it's on the desk," Frazier replied with a nod.

"Excellent."

Frazier turned toward him with a smirk on his face. "Rumor through downstairs has Lady Daphne inviting you to tea with her and her friend, Lady Cathryn."

"Yes, I thought it would be rude to decline," Charles replied. He turned to walk to the desk.

"You would have been correct."

"I need to make sure this order is correct so I can get back to work on my book."

Frazier grunted as Charles walked out of the dressing room.

Charles quickly cut the string holding the paper around his order. Gently, he lifted the stack of paper out. The pens and notebooks had been on top of the paper. He put them aside to make sure the paper was the correct type he wanted. Seeing it was, he opened the right-hand desk drawer and placed it on top of the remaining few sheets he had left.

The notebooks were nothing fancy. Two were of the size that they could fit in his pocket and the other two were larger. He preferred these for making notes or writing his daily activities if there were something worth writing about. His introduction to Lady Cathryn and his odd feelings made it perfect to put this to paper.

Frazier walked in the room. "I understand you had a hard time at lunch."

"Who told you?"

"One of the footmen who travels with the duke."

"Then you know I walked out of the dining room and kept going."

"Yes, though why you did it, they did not convey."

"A rather loud and obnoxious gentleman stopped by the table and began going on about Arthur and me being twins. I couldn't take it."

"You're going to have to learn to accept and live with the fact that there are all sorts of people. Some are nice, some are not. His Grace doesn't know you that well yet. I'm sure it made him frantic until he realized that leaving was a coping mechanism for you."

"I'll make my apologies to Arthur when he arrives home."

"I know he'll appreciate that. You are trying, I will say that much. You're taking walks and putting yourself in uncomfortable situations. I call that trying, and you certainly have done a lot of that."

"Your encouragement has helped me."

Frazier ignored the compliment for a moment. "Dinner is at

seven-thirty with drinks in the drawing room at seven."

"That leaves me with some time to relax. Make sure I have plenty of time to change."

CHAPTER FIVE

TWO EVENINGS LATER, Arthur, Daphne, and Charles were quietly sitting inside the carriage, waiting for it to move away from the front of the house and into the London evening traffic, people going to the theater, soirees, and musicales like the one they were on their way to. This evening's event was being held at the house of the popular MP, the Marquess of Bath and his wife.

Charles had tried for two days to prepare himself for what would come. Strangers, but a lot of them friends or acquaintances from Parliament. He and Arthur had had a few discussions on how to act, which meant not to react. They were there to listen to the music, not socialize like one would at a ball.

He had to keep his focus on that, especially on Lady Cathryn. She had been almost all he thought of for the past two days. He hadn't been able to stop thinking about her.

His sister-in-law seemed to be aware of this and tried to gently reassure him. "You'll be fine, Charles. Everyone is there to listen to the music. We don't have to stay afterwards, do we, Arthur?"

Arthur shook his head. "Of course not. If you wish, we can stay for a short time. If not, we can immediately leave after the performance."

"Since Lady Cathryn was kind enough to secure me an invitation, I will need to thank her and commend her on an extraordinary performance."

"She would enjoy that," Daphne replied. She smiled knowingly at Charles.

The coach stayed quiet for what seemed like an eternity before anyone spoke again.

"Since Parliament has a break now, I thought we'd return to Kent," Arthur said.

A thousand emotions flowed through Charles. He did want to go to the country. He could ride or take long walks. He just wouldn't be able to call on Lady Cathryn like he wanted, though he wasn't sure exactly how to go about it.

"Does everyone go to their country homes?" Charles inquired.

"For the most part, yes," Arthur replied. "I'll show you around the estate once we arrive."

"That would be nice."

Finally, the carriage came to a stop as they waited to exit. Looking outside, Charles could see a throng of people talking and walking into the grand manor. A footman opened the carriage door, and Charles stepped down and waited for his brother to assist his wife. He had to admit Daphne looked very much a duchess in her deep-purple gown. He knew very little about women or their fashions, but comparing her to other ladies around her, she certainly stood apart from them.

"Remember what I said," Arthur whispered near his ear. "Deep breaths. You'll be fine."

Charles nodded and followed Arthur and Daphne into the marquess's home. The musicale was being held in the ballroom in order to seat all the people invited. It seemed the marquess knew a lot of people. Daphne had told him the marquess's wife had died three years prior and he was just now looking for a wife to bear him an heir. Surely, he wouldn't have any problems finding a woman, just gauging on how women seemed to react to him. Why shouldn't they? He was wealthy, handsome, and had a way with women.

The trio took their seats and waited for the music to begin. First, though, their host introduced each young lady. He was far too familiar with Lady Cathryn and personally made sure she was comfortable as she waited her turn. From the paper they'd been given, she was to be the last one to play. Charles noted that rather than the usual composers pianists went to, Lady Cathryn had chosen Handel, a German-British Baroque composer. The man had left behind a large catalog of music, and Charles found himself curious which pieces Lady Cathryn would play.

The first pianist began to play Bach. Charles sat back in his chair, closed his eyes and listened to the music. She was good, but she didn't seem to bring much emotion to her playing. Still, with a good tutor she would easily overcome her shortcomings. The next two young women were similar. One played Mozart and the other Beethoven. Both unique composers and each of the pianists played them well, but again with little emotion.

He sucked in a breath as the marquess reintroduced Lady Cathryn. She made herself comfortable before launching into her music. Her fingers flew over the keyboard, leaving everyone in the room speechless. If they'd been whispering before, Lady Cathryn had them eating out of her hand as she magnificently played. By the time she ended, she had applause from the audience that lasted well over two minutes.

The marquess invited everyone to stay for refreshments and to meet the young ladies. From the looks of the room, it appeared that's what most were doing.

"Why don't we congratulate Lady Cathryn? She was by far the best performer," Daphne said to both him and Arthur.

"That's an excellent idea," Arthur said. "What do you think, Charles?"

"I concur."

The trio neared Lady Cathryn. She looked away from the couple she was talking with to smile and nod to Charles. He smiled at her, noting an older couple nearby. He took them to be her parents as they never let her out of their sight.

Arthur and Daphne spoke to all three, then introduced Charles to her parents. He didn't panic but began to carry out a short conversation with Lady Daphne.

"You said you played, but I was surprised at how well you play."

"Thank you, Lord Charles. As I mentioned, it's a passion of mine."

He nodded. "It's obvious in your playing." He was about to say something more when the marquess interrupted.

"Lady Cathryn, let me find you somewhere comfortable to sit." He stared at Charles as though he expected Charles to make his leave, but Charles stood his ground.

Remembering not to make a scene, he relented—sort of. "I look forward to continuing our conversation, Lady Cathryn." He watched as the marquess took her arm and began leading her away. She glanced back at him and smiled at him.

Charles turned back to Lady Cathryn's parents and Arthur and Daphne. They were talking among themselves, but Charles had a distinct feeling they'd all been observing what had just played out and it made him uneasy. Another couple approached and Charles backed away a few feet.

Everyone said their acknowledgments and then Arthur took the lead, seeing Charles's uncomfortable look. "This has been a most enjoyable evening. I'm afraid we need to take our leave."

Charles walked behind Arthur and Daphne all the way to the carriage. The evening was pleasant, cool, with a quarter moon lighting the sky. He climbed into the carriage last and sat across from the pair. He wasn't good at small talk and hesitated to even try. But the only way he would get comfortable in society would be to try it.

"Thank you for including me. It was quite enjoyable, though I didn't care much for the marquess."

Arthur gave him a lopsided smile. "He's one of those people who takes some time to get to know. He's an odd duck."

"He's more than that. From the gossip I heard this evening, he's looking for a wife and what he wants he will get," Charles said solemnly.

"A young lady who has a sizeable dowry," Daphne added.

"Why would a man do that unless he's broke?"

Arthur smiled again. "You answered your own question."

"I see."

"Does Lady Cathryn interest you, Charles?"

"I don't know. I do know she is smart, well-educated, and played better than any of the other young ladies."

"I'm sure something else can be arranged if you'd like to see her again."

"I don't think her parents would approve of me courting their daughter."

Arthur cleared his throat. "You don't have to start out courting, even if that's what you want. There's no reason you couldn't be friends."

"I plan on marrying her," he replied.

Daphne and Arthur smiled at each other. "Is that so?" Arthur teased.

"Yes."

"I understand she and her family are leaving for the country in a day or two," Daphne said.

"Where in the country?"

"Their estate is in Kent so she wouldn't be too far," Daphne replied.

"I see. Perhaps I can call on her at some time. I need to work on my book first and don't need to be distracted."

"When you feel the time is right, just let us know," Arthur said.

Charles nodded. "I shall. Tell me how it is you think I have an interest other than friendship with Lady Cathryn?"

He first needed to figure out what these feelings were that he was having. It was odd, and he wasn't sure he liked it. His life had always been predictable and structured. He wasn't sure he wanted to change that.

"We don't," Arthur replied.

"You seem to like to talk with her," Daphne added.

"Yes. She is quite intelligent and easy to talk with."

He shut his eyes to the outside world. They weren't far from the house and, when they did arrive, his first move would be to go to his suite. His head was beginning to throb because of all the new stimuli he'd experienced today alone. He would be glad to get out of town and to the country. He wanted to see the cottage Arthur mentioned. It might be perfect, though Daphne explained he would have his own wing in the manor house. That would give him the privacy he preferred. A lot of decisions to be made, and on a scale he'd never had to deal with.

The carriage was approaching its destination. It slowed and a moment later came to a stop. He cracked an eye to see what was going on around him.

"We're home, Charles," Arthur said.

Gathering his hat, he waited for the pair to leave the carriage. Once they did, he followed a short distance behind. Once in the grand hall, he bid them both good night and bounded up the stairs two at a time to his chamber. He found a fire burning low in the hearth, and in the bedroom he found the bed turned back and his night clothes laid out on the bed. As usual, Frazier saw to his needs, knowing he liked structure in his life.

Walking back out into the sitting room, he poured himself a brandy. He carried it back and after taking a healthy swallow, Charles began to change out of his clothes, after which he climbed up on the bed and picked up a book from the bedside table and began to read.

He found his eyes heavy and unable to stay focused on the words before him. It took every effort to read the book on the Roman Empire. He should know it. The book was similar to others; this one simply had a spin on where they landed and when. The author was doing the Romans no favor by how he wrote. Others had written about this before, but were easier to read. It was almost as though the author wanted the reader to find fault in his work. Charles was surprised a publishing house would print this in its current form. It obviously hadn't been well edited, and the author wandered off the track all the time.

Finally, he set the book aside and picked up the brandy snifter. He swirled the dark amber liquid and raised the glass to his lips and swallowed. The brandy was smooth going down, so he drank until the glass was empty. He lay back against the pillows and closed his eyes.

TWO DAYS LATER while they were on their way to the country, Charles thought he'd been here before. Had he really been here or did he see it in a dream? Things really looked familiar as they drove down the drive to the house. A lot of memories came back to him. Why didn't Arthur recall them? They were twins after all. Perhaps Arthur didn't remember because he lived here all his life. The memories Charles recalled were that of a young boy. One who was shunned by his classmates because he was different than the rest of them. Arthur even joined in the taunting, but had told him later when Charles asked him about it that if he hadn't, they would have turned on him as well. Charles saw no point in reminding his brother of those times.

Walking into the entrance hall, Charles felt a rush of memories. He and Arthur were running around here, being chased out by the housekeeper. He passed his hat and coat to a waiting footman.

"Do you want Frazier to come and show you to your wing?" Arthur inquired.

"Thank you, no. I can find my way. I remember the house very well."

Arthur ran a hand through his hair and briefly looked at his wife. "Just ask any of the staff should you have a problem."

"I shall, but I doubt I'll need anyone's help."

He ascended the stairs to the family space and finally found the hallway leading to his wing. It was sealed off by two heavy oak doors. He walked through them and found his way to the staircase leading to the bedchambers. His was in a corner and was larger than any of the others. He walked through the door and found Frazier putting away some of his shirts in the dressing room.

"You really did find your way."

"It wasn't hard," Charles replied.

Frazier nodded as he shut the drawer. "You remember then."

"Yes, but I don't understand how that's possible. I was a mere babe myself."

"The mind is a strange thing," Frazier replied.

"Yes, it is."

"Are you hungry, my lord? Should I have a tray and tea brought up for you?"

"Yes. That would be nice. While you're doing that, I'll go explore. Have the trays taken to the small drawing room. I can't imagine being too long. I know where everything is."

"Very well, my lord," he said and quickly left the room.

While he was waiting, Charles began by walking through the rooms. There were two dining rooms, one that was quite large and the other was one for having tea or breakfast. As he walked, he made his way to a music room. A baby grand piano sat just off to the side with a small table next to it with sheets and sheets of music. He would have to take advantage of this. It was calling his name. Did he dare? One short piece would be enough to satisfy and by the time he finished, the food ought to have arrived.

He sat down at the keyboard and gently lifted the cover from the keys. Warming up with some scales, Charles then went directly with a tune he had heard some time ago while still living on Wight. Someone living in the village had been playing it with their windows open to enjoy the nice day. He remembered standing and listening to the person behind the curtains.

That had been ages ago, one of the few times he went to the village as his needs were usually taken care of. People talked, just like they did in London and probably would here as well. He tried to ignore the fact that people thought him an oddity of some sort.

His brother hadn't thought him an oddity. He'd taken him along while they had been in London. Arthur wasn't embarrassed by him. He was learning what his brother Charles was all about and trying to accommodate him. Arthur was a quick learner and after the encounter at the MPs' dining room, knew what made his brother uncomfortable. Having someone else besides Frazier who understood him helped.

Finishing the tune, Charles closed the cover over the keyboard and rose to his full height. He wished his mind would slow. There were always more than one or two thoughts going on in his mind. It had been that way all his life. Walking and sometimes playing piano calmed his mind, but other times nothing seemed to help. Writing had a calming effect on him as well.

He wanted to pay a call on his sister but needed some advice on how to do it. Since she was his sister, did he just show up at her door, or did he send her a note telling her of his intentions? He could ask Frazier which he should do. Sending her a request sounded like the best way to handle the situation. If he just showed up, he might be sent away by staff. Arthur would be a better person to ask. He knew their sister quite well. She lived close by but Charles wasn't sure where.

Hearing sounds coming from near the front, Charles walked in the direction of the sound and voices. As he approached, he noted a pair of footmen leaving. He made it to the smaller drawing room. Yes, there was food placed on platters and plates alike. He looked around, but found no one, not even Frazier. Walking over to the table, he picked up a plate and began making his selections. There were so many delicacies to choose from. Cold smoked salmon, cheese, warm bread. He also found a plate with roast chicken. He was so hungry it was too hard to choose, so he took at least one of everything in order to see what he liked best. The salmon was mouthwatering. He was sure it'd been caught in Scotland because every time he had salmon this good, it had come from Scotland.

The cheese was sharp and pungent like Stilton should be. He immediately wondered if it was made locally or if Arthur made cheese on the estate. He vaguely recalled someone talking about the cheddar made there, but that was years ago, and he couldn't be sure.

He heard someone behind him and turned to look and find Frazier, his valet, walking in. "His Grace would like to know if you will be joining them for dinner this evening."

"I suppose it would be best if I ate with them. It would save Cook from having to prepare separate meals."

"She's used to doing large dinners and with little notice," Frazier said.

"That may be, but even to eat the same as my brother and wife, it would be seen as a slight. I will, for now, join them."

"Very well, my lord. I'll go tell Cook to expect three."

Charles nodded, but his attention was not on dinner; it was on the food in front of him. He tried everything and then spied a piece of marmalade cake on a plate to one side. It was his favorite. Frazier always made sure people knew that when dining out. He wasn't too fond of trying different sweet desserts.

Once finished, he placed his napkin to one side and rose from the table. As he had plenty of time until he needed to get ready for dinner, he decided to go outside for a walk. Frazier still hadn't unpacked all his things, and he didn't want to begin digging through things, making the valet irritated.

Going down the stairs to the main entrance, Charles walked out the front door. The sky was overcast, but he didn't think it was too serious looking. He walked down a path which led to the formal gardens. There was a maze, which he knew he'd have to try. Flowers were everywhere. From roses, peonies, lavender, the scents were unmistakable. He was amazed by how precise some of the shrubs had been trimmed. It took a master gardener to create some of the spectacular shapes and keep them up.

Charles had always preferred the Japanese miniature trees and had spent a lot of time learning from a man on Wight. He nurtured several of his own but had given them to the master when he knew he was leaving, afraid they might get damaged in the long journey.

For his part, the Japanese master had given Charles four starter trees for him to start once he made it to his destination. It was one of the things he waited for Frazier to unpack.

He looked up at the sky, as he thought he felt drops of rain on his shoulder. Indeed, it had turned dark enough for rain to change the afternoon. He rushed back to the house, instinctively finding the fenced kitchen garden and door. As he surprised the staff with his presence, he quickly walked through the kitchen and down a hall to a set of steps leading upstairs to the main floor.

As he arrived on the main floor, he heard the distinct sound of Sam, the parrot, as he walked toward his wing. The animal seemed agitated, so Charles decided it was best to look in on the bird. He peered into the drawing room and saw Sam on the floor peering up at his cage. A wooden ladder which allowed him to walk up and down was lying on the floor. Since the macaw couldn't fly, he had no way to get up to his cage.

Charles walked over to the bird and bent down to pick up the ladder. As he did, he stroked the bird's feathers. "How did you manage to do that, Sam?"

"Bloody hell! Sam no do!" the bird squawked in reply.

"Right." He made sure the ladder was firmly in place and as he began to leave, he watched the parrot walk up the ladder making odd noises.

"Sam happy."

Charles shook his head as he exited the drawing room. An odd choice for a pet, but he remembered the bird was a gift from Daphne's father and she was rather attached to the macaw.

As he walked down the hall, he was met by Arthur. "Are you finding everything okay?" Arthur inquired.

"Yes, I went for a walk until the weather had other ideas. Sam's ladder was on the floor, and he was having no part of it. I fixed it for him."

Arthur chuckled. "A word of advice about Sam. He's smarter than he lets on, and the ladder on the ground is a favorite trick of his to get attention."

"You mean I was outwitted by a parrot?"

"I'm afraid so," Arthur replied.

"Glad to know."

"Are you finding your way around okay?"

Charles nodded. "Yes, it's strange but a lot looks familiar, like I've been there."

"A displaced memory being released, I suppose."

"That's what it has to be. I don't like it though."

Arthur arched a brow. "Why?"

"It's like a portion of my life is missing and now bits and pieces are coming back."

"Does it scare you?"

"No, it's just an odd sensation because I have no control."

"Let me know if I can help solve anything," Arthur said. "Are you going to join us for dinner?"

"Yes. Right now, I need to see if Frazier has unpacked all my things."

Nodding, Arthur smiled. "Of course. I'll leave you to it and see you for dinner."

Charles heard not a sound when he entered his bed chamber. Frazier must have finished his duties as he was nowhere to be found. He knew there was a study in this wing and that would be where his valet would have put all his books and papers. He turned and left the room in search of the study. True to form, Frazier had organized his desk with two black notebooks sitting to the right of the desk. One he would keep on him to jot down things that interested him, book ideas. The other notebook would be a journal starting from today, his first day at the family ancestral home.

Another thing he wanted to know was about the history of the family, from the very beginning to now. It might not be great reading for some, but he might find something that would be suitable for writing into one of his books. As he sat down in the chair behind the desk, he noticed there were two pens sitting on the desktop just waiting to be used.

He opened the top left drawer. This is where he always kept the manuscript of what he was writing. It didn't matter what desk or where, the left drawer was always used exclusively for his current manuscript. He took it out of the drawer and placed it before him. Since he hadn't written in recent days, he decided to refresh himself by reading it before he continued. Taking one of the pens, he began to read the words. His words. He made notes in the margins. Questions, ideas, did a certain part need to be rewritten? Thus, when he finished, he would send it to his publisher a little more refined than what he stared at right now.

Reading the manuscript took longer than he anticipated. It didn't help that he fell asleep when he was close to the end. It had been a long, eventful day. So many new things, so many forgotten memories resurfacing after decades of hiding in his mind.

He'd written notes not only in the margins, but on a piece of paper. This would be what he'd go by if he needed a reminder of what he'd written, even though he never used them. He had perfect recall. It was more for other people who had something to do with his books.

Once he put everything back in the drawer, Charles took out fresh paper and began writing the next chapter. He'd outlined what came next in his head since he finished the last chapter. He was invigorated to have time to put his thoughts on paper. When words flowed like this, he couldn't put his pen down. He had to finish. The outside world didn't exist when he wrote. He heard nothing but the pen and the sound of his breathing. Not even his valet could bring him out of his trance-like state when he was writing. Frazier knew not to disturb him. He would not hear him, or he would pretend not to hear the valet. Frazier would try in spite of this. Sometimes it worked, but only on a rare occasion.

"My lord," Frazier began. "You must stop now and change for dinner."

Charles didn't hear him, didn't even move a muscle to indicate he was going to finish. He continued on furiously writing his story out.

Frazier knew there was no stopping him. He'd let His Grace know Charles wouldn't be joining them and why. He was sure they'd understand.

Hearing someone behind him, Frazier turned and saw the duke standing there. The valet motioned for His Grace to retreat from the study and shut the door behind them. He explained the situation to the duke, who remarkably seemed to understand. His Grace told the valet to have a tray fixed for Charles. He didn't want his brother to stray from what made him comfortable. The duke understood his brother better than Frazier thought he would after this short time. Then again, it could be something to do with them being twins. Frazier had noticed similarities between the two men despite them not being around each other the majority of their lives.

CHAPTER SIX

CHARLES MADE HIS way down to the breakfast room the following morning. He was tired, having spent most of the night writing. He found his brother reading a newspaper from a pile to his left. He sat down and let the footman know he preferred coffee this morning.

"Good morning, Charles. I take it you had a productive evening?"

"Yes, I did, and I apologize for being absent for dinner."

"Did you get a tray?"

Charles nodded. "Yes. It was nice to have a break. I usually don't take any, but the food smelled too good."

"I'm glad you liked it," Arthur replied. "Have you plans for today? I thought we could ride the estate. I have a horse I think that will be perfect for you."

"That would be nice. Can we look at that cottage you mentioned?"

Arthur nodded and smiled. "You don't like your wing?"

"I do. I'm just not used to so much room with such magnificent furnishings. I've lived a fairly simple life."

"Then we'll ride to the cottage. There's lots to see."

A footman brought a plate filled with sausage, eggs, bacon, and buttered toast. A cup of coffee was set down as well. "This looks good," Charles said. "And I'm sure there's plenty to see."

"More than we'll be able to see today," Arthur replied.

"I'm sure," Charles said between mouthfuls. "Didn't you say Roxanne and her husband live nearby?"

"Yes, they do. Neighbors."

"Hmmm, that's nice for her to be close by."

"Yes, it is."

Charles put down his fork and picked up a piece of toast. He slathered strawberry jam on it and took a bite. "How much is made here on the estate? I know the Stilton and cheddar are. What else?"

"There is much. It depends on the time of year. Jam like this, cheese, smoked meats. Mother would always give tenants a basket at Christmas filled with goods. She made sure they got a wheel of their favorite cheese and a goose for the holiday."

"Do you carry on the tradition?"

"Yes, Daphne is looking forward to continuing what our grandmother actually started."

"The tenants are going to love her."

Arthur smiled. "They already do. She had me take her to meet them all after we married."

Just then, a huge red setter came bounding into the room. Obviously, Arthur's dog, as the beast sat down right next to his brother's chair, his tail thumping the floor.

"This is Roddy. He'll be joining us on our ride," Arthur said. He petted the top of the dog's head.

"He's beautiful. He hunts?"

"No, he couldn't get the hang of it. He tries, but he's too interested in everything else around him. Thus, he's my dog," Arthur replied with a smile.

"He thinks a lot of you."

"Actually, he's hoping for a morsel."

"Spoiled," Charles replied, adding, "I will go put boots on. I'll meet you in the main entry hall?"

"Yes, say twenty minutes?"

"I will see you then."

Fifteen minutes later, Charles was waiting on his brother in the grand hall. He noted there were vases of fresh flowers on the tables that were different from yesterday when they arrived. He assumed they came out of one of the gardens. He walked around the room as he waited on Arthur, which wasn't long because the Irish setter came bounding into the hall, his hind legs coming out from under him because of the speed at which he was running. Recovering quickly, he ran circles around Charles and bounded over to Arthur when he saw him.

"Shall we?" Arthur commented as a footman opened the front door.

At the bottom of the stairs, Arthur began leading them to the path that went to the stables. Charles realized where he would have ended up yesterday if he'd chosen this path. Moments later, as they walked, fencing began to appear. Pastures and paddocks for the horses, depending on their needs. As they neared the building, Charles noticed a groom with two horses tethered. The boy was checking the saddles and other equipment one last time before he turned the horses over to them.

"The chestnut is the horse I was telling you about. He is solid, dependable, and well mannered."

"He's well-muscled and tall. How old is he? He looks like a youngster," Charles replied.

"He's five, I believe."

"Good age."

"Yes. Now like I told you, don't feel obligated to him. If you still want to go to Tattersalls the next time we're in London, we'll go. There's also a bay mare you might like if the chestnut doesn't work for you."

"I'll keep that in mind," Charles replied as he stroked the chestnut's neck before putting his foot in the stirrup and swinging his leg over the animal's back. The groom came around and helped him adjust the stirrups and made double sure the saddle was well placed.

Arthur had already mounted and was walking the black stallion around waiting for Charles to finish. Charles nodded he was ready, and the two began to walk next to each other down another path leading away from the stables. Charles was amazed at how well maintained the stables were. The ones on Wight he was familiar with needed repairs.

"Where to?" Charles asked.

"I thought we would ride through the meadow and then to the small lake nearby. After that, I'll show you the orchards, and after we can ride to the cottage I was telling you about. It's not too far from the orchards."

"Lead the way."

Charles followed his brother toward the meadow. Roddy, the setter, would circle them before going off to some scent he'd picked up. He watched as the dog took off from sight. The horse he was riding didn't seem to like the dog circling them. Getting the animal to accept Roddy was a matter of the horse getting used to the dog being around. It would take time.

They made it to the edge of the meadow. His horse wanted to do something beyond walking or trotting. Arthur picked up on that.

"Would you care to canter across the meadow or at least part of it? I think the horses would like to stretch their legs."

"Absolutely."

Arthur urged his stallion into a canter with Charles and the chestnut following not too far behind. Roddy, in the meantime, was running at breakneck speeds.

When they slowed to a walk to give the horses a rest, Charles glanced up at the blue sky. It was clear with only a couple of puffy white clouds floating by. It was the perfect day to be riding. He wasn't sure about what to expect from a ride with his brother. It was obvious that Arthur spent a great amount of time in the saddle. He sat a horse quite well. Almost like the two were one.

Charles hadn't had a lot of opportunity to ride on Wight. Not that he hadn't wanted to, it was simply the way things were, especially when he was younger. Perhaps now he would have time to learn a lot of new things.

"What are you thinking so hard about?" Arthur asked.

"Learning new things. Improving my riding skills. I would also like to learn to drive a curricle or something similar. I was never given the opportunity."

Shaking his head, Arthur spoke. "There's no reason you can't, if that's what you wish. My stable master is the man who taught me. He has quite a way with horses. If you're interested, we can talk to him later."

"Yes, I would love that."

"Come, the lake I was telling you about is just over that ridge, through the tree line."

"Is there a path?"

"Oh, yes. Mother used to love coming here during the summer. Father would sometimes join her. Roxanne and I learned at an early age that that was their time together and we weren't to bother them."

"I understand," Charles replied as he blew out a breath.

"What is it?"

"I missed out on so much being sent away. I never had a normal childhood because people didn't understand me or didn't want to."

"I can't say I understand what you had to accept as normal, but it seems unfortunate things couldn't have been handled a bit differently."

"My temper was a large part of the problem. If I got in a rage, there was no telling what I might do. Frazier's the only one who was able to help me keep it under control."

That was all true. Though Frazier had shown him ways to calm his temper, there were times when he had to go off by himself so he didn't go off in a rage. He never knew when it would happen or what would set him off. Writing was just one of the things he learned to do during these times. He could closet himself somewhere where he'd be alone, calm himself before returning to something he was in the middle of writing or making notes for an upcoming book. He was never disturbed. Sometimes he would go to a particular tree in the woods, sit on the ground, and make notes in a notebook or just sit with his back against the tree trunk and close his eyes. Listen to nature.

His thoughts were interrupted by Arthur. "Are you all right?"

Charles brushed it off. "Yes, of course I am. Just trying to remember things."

"Come, we're almost there. After we're done here, I'll show you the cottage."

Charles nodded. "Has the cottage ever been lived in?"

Arthur began walking his stallion toward the tree line. "The estate manager's parents lived in it until they both died. It's been sitting empty for about two years."

"Two years?"

"The estate manager keeps it up. Sends men to clean up the outside and inside when necessary."

Charles followed his brother, nodding in response to his questions. The walk through the trees was short. On the other side, the sun was reflecting off a small body of water. To one side, partially hidden by shrubs and trees, sat a small house made with a lot of glass, reminding him of a conservatory. Lots of windows meant lots of sunlight.

Dismounting the chestnut, Charles secured the horse to a small tree. He noted from the side Arthur doing the same exact thing while coming off his stallion quickly. He tethered the animal by himself. The only one who leapt around with not a problem was Roddy.

Arthur motioned for him to follow. They neared the glass house. It wasn't huge, but large enough for one or two people. The front of the house, the parlor, had a spectacular view of the lake in one corner of the room. The rest was hidden from view. The portion with the view was still partially hidden to the untrained eye. One would have to know what they were looking for.

Farther back there was a bed and a small kitchen with a

hearth. The furniture was more than he anticipated. It appeared someone had lived there not too terribly long ago.

"This is nice and quiet. I can see why Mother loved to come here."

"Yes," Arthur replied. "On occasion during the summer, she would bring Roxanne and me here."

"She was afraid of me. I remember that."

Running his hand through his hair, Charles looked out at the small lake. It was a painful memory to have, knowing your own mother was afraid to be around you because you were different from your other children. What he did know was that he couldn't stay in this cottage.

"I want to see the orchards and this other cottage."

"You don't want to spend more time here, explore the lake side?"

Charles shook his head. "No, I've seen enough."

Once they'd remounted, Arthur told Charles to follow him. Charles watched as his brother and dog galloped off. He tried to keep up as best he could but was no match for his brother's stallion. He hoped he hadn't upset Arthur by not wanting to spend more time. The truth was it had long been something he tried to erase from his mind. He never knew his mother because of her fear, and though his father came to visit him perhaps once a year, the two never knew each other in the way some father-son relationships developed.

He caught up with his brother a minute or so later. Arthur was standing on a ridge as the black stallion held his ears back and teeth bared when Roddy came running up next to him, circling him. Charles brought his horse to a halt as he surveyed the trees.

"That's a lot of trees," Charles murmured as he approached.

"It isn't. There are the usual apple trees. Pear, peach, and a few cherry trees. The fruit from these trees are used for jam, pies, cakes, to name a few. What isn't put back for the family is given to tenants and the church in the fall."

"Along with the wheels of cheese?"

"Yes."

"So the estate is self-sufficient," Charles said.

"Yes."

"I'm impressed," he replied. "Shall we move on?"

Arthur nodded and began walking his horse along the edge of the orchard. Soon, he took a turn into a wooded area. A white-washed cottage sat in the middle of a clearing. There was a small barn and two other outbuildings. Dismounting, Charles followed his brother to the front door of the cottage. It wasn't locked, leaving them to walk right in. The cottage was more spacious than it looked on the outside. It boasted a large hearth to heat the house and to use for cooking. There was an area designated as a kitchen and another as a living area. Through a doorway which had been partitioned off was a main bedroom. A ladder was positioned. Above the ladder was a large room which must have been used for children. There were only a few pieces of furniture that had been left behind.

"What do you think?"

"Well maintained. I'd like to see the stables and outbuild-ings."

Arthur nodded. "Let's go."

Looking around one more time, Charles followed his brother out and walked to the nearby stables. There was a nearby paddock and what appeared to be a small pasture beyond that. The stable was small with enough space to house three horses. The outbuilding held extra hay and grain. It was a perfect fit for the cottage.

"Your estate manager's parents had a nice place here. Is there any reason it hasn't been inhabited by another?"

"Repairs were made, the roof is new, and so is the paint. I decided I wanted to think about it before anyone was assigned the cottage. When I met you, I decided you might be interested in it. Even to use as somewhere you can get away to write. Same goes for the lake house."

"It seems a waste to just use it as a place for me to come part of the time."

"I wasn't sure how you were going to accept being in the main house. I wanted you to have an option."

Charles arched a brow. "You're very observant."

"You've lived a very different life from me. I'm sure mine can be overwhelming."

"Yes, at times. I realize being brother to a duke, I don't have the same privileges as you. Second son and all."

"You're still entitled to more than you're used to. If you want it," Arthur replied.

"Very well. Let me think on it, but if there's someone more in need for a place to live, please see they get it."

"Very good," Arthur said. "Why don't we head back, unless there's somewhere else you'd like to see?"

Shaking his head, Charles mounted the chestnut. "I can't think of anywhere else right now."

He followed Arthur as they headed back to the stables. There was a lot to think about. He had his choice of a place to live. There had been many changes in his life in a matter of weeks. He had his own wing in the house. He could hire his own staff and live independently from everyone else. If he chose this cottage, he certainly would be alone as he had been on the island. It was time for a change, but first he would weigh the pros and cons of each building, and he'd speak to Frazier about everything. He was always good to listen to him when he was trying to make decisions like this one.

When they finally walked into the house, Daphne greeted them. Charles had liked her immediately and was glad his brother had found her.

"Did you enjoy yourself, Charles?" she asked with a smile.

"Very much."

"Well, I have some news. Graham and Roxanne have returned from their wedding trip and are having a hunt next week and we're all invited. Knowing Roxanne, it'll be wonderful."

Charles looked at his brother who was standing next to his

wife. "Will the chestnut be suitable for a hunt?"

"He's never been on one, but the bay I told you about has been on several. He would probably be your best mount."

"I'll have him saddled and ride him, perhaps tomorrow."

"Feel free to ride whenever you wish, Charles," Arthur said.

"Thank you."

"No need to thank me. This is your home too."

CHARLES DECIDED TO enjoy the sun later that day and had lemonade and fresh baked seed cake brought to him on the terrace. He sat with a book he thought he might read and his notebook he wrote down random thoughts in. After taking a long, refreshing swallow of the lemonade, he sat back in his chair, closed his eyes, and let the sun do the rest. He was close to falling asleep when a voice jolted him back into reality.

"I didn't mean to startle you," Daphne's soothing feminine voice said from behind him.

"I'm fine. I thought it would be nice to enjoy the fine weather rather than be cooped up in the house."

She sat down in a chair. It was hard to see her with the sun behind her. "I have to agree."

"Would you like a glass of lemonade?" he inquired, noting the second glass and plate on the tray.

"Lemonade would be nice, but I can serve myself." She smiled as she reached over to the tray. He watched her pour a glass.

"Are you looking forward to the hunt?" he inquired.

"Yes. Roxanne and Graham put on a great one. I believe this is their second and I see it becoming an annual event."

Charles nodded. While he wanted to participate, he was unsure what was expected of him. His social skills were lacking when it came to his peers. He'd been taught, probably by his parents. Before he was sent away. Then it was just part of normal routine.

"Are you nervous about going?"

He shook his head. "No, not at all." It wasn't the entire truth but the last thing he wanted was pity from others.

"Besides the hunt, I believe there'll be trap shooting afterwards," Daphne said. She took a sip of lemonade and reached for a slice of cake.

"I don't know how to do that either."

"Arthur can show you before we go."

"I'm sure my brother has more important things to do than teach his brother to shoot trap," he replied.

"We'll ask him at dinner." She took a bite of seed cake and closed her eyes. "Cook certainly outdid herself on this batch."

"It is good, isn't it?" Charles took the remaining bite of his slice and eyed a second.

"Feel free to ask Cook if there is something you want. Even if it is something she doesn't normally make. It doesn't mean she doesn't know how."

"I'll have to remember that," Charles said, adding, "Do you know who's attending this hunt?"

"I'm not sure. I haven't had a chance to ask Roxanne. I imagine neighbors and perhaps some friends from nearby counties."

He nodded. Not good with crowds or even small groups, the last thing he wanted to do was embarrass anyone in the family because he was inept in social skills. There had been too many changes in his life. Things needed to slow down so he could take in what was going on around him.

"Do you and Arthur host many affairs?"

"No. We're still considered newlyweds and there's been so much going on with Arthur taking his seat in Parliament there honestly hasn't been a lot of time for hosting events. I'm thinking of hosting one in late summer."

"You should," he replied. "This is all terribly new to me."

Daphne smiled at him. "I know, and you're doing splendidly.

What did you do when you were on Wight?"

"I wasn't included in any social events, if that's what you're asking. It was a rare time if I went to the village. Frazier and I usually would go, but it was mostly for purchasing needed items. We would go walk along the beach from time to time, but that was all."

"That's a pity."

"That's the way my life was. I was considered an oddity, and it got worse once the lord's son inherited."

"That's in the past. Look forward, take your time, and you'll settle in nicely."

Charles finished his glass of lemonade and poured another. "I thought I might go for a walk."

"That sounds like a wonderful idea. Enjoy yourself. I need to get back inside and go over menus with the housekeeper." She rose and, as she began to leave, she placed her hand on his shoulder and patted it.

"You'll be back for tea?"

"I don't know. I'll make sure to take my pocket watch so I don't lose track of time."

"Enjoy yourself."

Charles finished his drink and sat back in his chair for a moment. From the position of the sun, he figured it to be mid-afternoon. Still plenty of time for a walk, but where to? There was so much to explore, he didn't know where to start. First off, he would take his books back to his rooms and retrieve his pocket watch. Then he'd take a leisurely walk. He remembered a path that appeared to go up to the top of a hill. He used to go there to hide but had no idea how he knew that bit of information.

Frazier was nowhere to be found when he entered his bed chamber. Going to the dressing room, he still didn't find the valet, but instead found his pocket watch and stuck it in his pocket and walked out of the rooms and out on to the terrace.

He found the stairs leading down into the gardens. Walking through, he gave himself time to see the various types of flowers and plants. A lot of the plants were older and had been in their places for years. Others may have been newer but from the older ones. That was what he learned from the gardener on Wight.

Leaving the formal gardens, he found beds of wildflowers and wondered who had thought to plant them. It certainly would keep the garden refreshed as this was an extension of the formal garden.

Continuing, Charles found the path which led to the top of a hill. For some reason, he was sure it was one of the tallest, if not the tallest, spot on the estate. From what he could see, the path had been kept neat and tidy, which made him wonder if Arthur came here. At the top he found a felled tree which had also been cleaned up and one could use as a spot to sit and gaze out on the view of the estate.

He sat there on the tree, looking about the land below him. The house was not in view and the stables were off to his left and were just barely in view. Charles wondered how many years it had taken to get the entire estate looking as good as it did.

He'd never had time to put much thought into his sudden departure from Wight, the only home he'd really known. Really, it hadn't been a home since he'd been placed in a cottage on another part of the estate where he lived with Frazier. Apart from the occasional visits from a doctor or priest, he'd been isolated. His caretaker came to check on him at least weekly and to see if there were any needs he might have. Other than that, he was alone. People were afraid of him, plain and simple. Thought he was mad, they did.

Now he was back on his family's ancestral land, and he was trying to make sense of it all. Here he was, a duke's brother, a second son. He was an adult but had no job. His schooling had been by tutors. He knew how to speak French, Italian, Spanish, and German. He could play piano like any maestro, and he could write better than most. Charles chuckled. He was a genius when it came to math. Calculating sums in his head was a strong point of his.

Sighing, he rose and walked around for a moment before sitting back down on the fallen tree. Though he had wanted to move into the cottage, he chose to stay in his own wing of the house. He was forcing himself to live among his family and household staff. Learning to socialize was an important part of life now. If he had chosen the cottage, he would have isolated himself, and that wouldn't be good.

He pulled his watch out of his pocket and looked at the time. He'd been on his walk for over an hour, and he should start back. There would be time for him to take his walks and learn the estate's secrets. To cover that, he remembered he had found a book in the library about the family and estate. He would have to pull it out and read it. It should give him a timeline of when things were built or happened over the years. See how far the book came forward. Something he would be very good at doing. Details, statistics.

He retraced his steps and went back on to the path where he kept walking until he saw the house come into view.

CHAPTER SEVEN

GRAHAM AND ROXANNE'S hunt party came quickly. He'd ridden the bay several times and felt quite comfortable with the beast. Arthur had sent their mounts over to his brother-in-law the day before so they could acclimate to their new surroundings.

The trio of Arthur, Daphne, and himself rode over to the nearby estate in one of the duke's carriages. Arthur had insisted the horses be fresh and ready to go for the hunt. It was a perfect day for outdoor activities.

He watched as the countryside changed ever so slightly. The ride wasn't that far and upon turning down the long driveway, Charles noted a couple extra carriages, their occupants having long left and were most likely inside.

As the carriage stopped, Arthur jumped down and offered his hand to his wife. Charles followed. The heavy oak door opened and there was the butler and his sister, Roxanne. Seeing him, she rushed over.

"I'm so glad you came. I think you're going to enjoy the hunt."

"It sounds like a lot of fun."

She turned and looked back. Her brother and sister-in-law were walking behind them. "Lunch is a buffet on the terrace."

"We should share a table," Daphne said.

"I already have set one aside," Roxanne replied.

"We'll see you outside," Arthur added.

Charles was aware his brother had already seen some associates amongst the small crowd. Charles continued to the drawing room with his sister. Immediately he could see where his sister had recently had new wall silk hung. A few pieces of furniture had also been reupholstered to match.

"Lunch is a buffet. If you'd like, I can get you a plate, or if you prefer to wait in line, I believe you'll need to go right to the bottom of the stairs."

Roxanne led him on to the terrace and walked down the stairs with him. As they descended, Charles noted Lady Cathryn standing in line talking with two other women. Sisters? Aunts?

He nodded to her and her companions. "Lady Cathryn, lovely to see you."

Glancing at her, he noted the dark-blue riding ensemble she was wearing. It was striking with the black piping.

"Milord. May I introduce my sisters, Lady Agnes and Lady Violet. They are serving as my chaperones since our parents are on the Continent along with my brother."

"Nice to meet you. Are you riding the hunt?" he inquired.

"I am," Lady Cathryn replied.

"I look forward to it."

He turned and saw Roxanne had moved to the bottom of the stairs. She was watching him, a small smile on her lips. He continued until he was at the bottom and said nothing.

"Lady Cathryn is an accomplished rider, so expect her to be in the mix today."

"I'm surprised her parents would allow it."

"They're trying to see her married."

"I gathered as much last time I met her," he replied.

He heard her sigh softly. "If you'd rather not wait, I can have one of the footmen bring us each a plate."

"I don't mind waiting. The queue is moving much quicker than I thought it would."

"I need to see to my guests. The table is over there." She

pointed to an area with tables set up.

"Go visit with your guests. I'll be fine."

"Thank you. I'll see you shortly," she replied.

Charles grunted and moved ahead. Watching his sister walk away, he was suddenly curious about her. She was older so she might remember things he hadn't, and she had the patience to sit and explain to him.

Finally, he made it to the food. Picking up a plate, he began making his selections. There was quite a bit to choose from. Nothing too fancy but some hearty selections. He chose sliced beef with roasted potatoes, a fruit mixture and cheese selection, and hearty bread.

When he arrived at the table, Arthur and Daphne were already enjoying their lunch and had obviously had their food brought to them. Another man he recognized as his brother-in-law, Graham, was leaning back in his chair with a piece of cheese in one hand.

"You didn't go through the queue, did you?" Graham asked.

"Yes, I did. Roxanne stayed with me for a while. I saw no point in having someone else choose my meal. The queue moved fairly quickly."

Graham waved at someone. "Speaking of Roxanne, I see my lovely wife is beckoning me."

"Yes, go," Arthur teased him.

Charles continued eating while that was going on. It was one of those situations he didn't understand how to react or should he react. He picked up a piece of Stilton and bit into the creamy blue-veined cheese and listened to Daphne and Arthur banter among themselves.

"Whenever you're finished, we can go find our horses and prepare for the hunt," Arthur said.

"Let me finish this delightful cheese first," Charles replied.

"That's the same Stilton we have," Daphne said. "Roxanne got a couple of wheels a couple of months ago."

He nodded and finished the pungent cheese before drinking

the last of the wine. He hadn't seen Lady Cathryn since he saw her standing in the queue with her sisters. She'd once again caused his body to react in ways he wasn't sure of. It wasn't a bad feeling, just one he couldn't control his body about. He turned and saw Arthur and Daphne watching him in a curious fashion. He pushed his chair back and rose to his full height.

"Shall we go find our horses and get ready?"

The pair of them nodded with smiles on their faces, never saying a word. The trio began to walk across the gardens to a space on the outside where everyone was headed. He kept his stride, trying not to think too much. He had to learn how to deal with situations like this.

Upon seeing Frazier holding the bay, accompanied by two stableboys, they walked up to them. Out of habit, Charles checked the girth to make sure it was tight and made sure the bridle was in top shape before nodding to Frazier that he was ready to mount. He didn't do this to double check his valet's work because that wasn't it at all. Once on Wight, he was going for a ride and one of the grooms had cut the girth and reins just enough so when Charles tried to turn or stop, they would finish breaking and he most likely would have been hurt. A bad prank with a possible devastating ending. Since then, he always checked his equipment if he hadn't done it himself.

Throwing his leg over the saddle, he put his feet in the iron stirrups to check they were the right length. He refused a whip since this was only one of the handful of times he'd ridden the horse and he didn't like to use one unless the animal was lazy.

Across the way, he noted Lady Cathryn. She was mounted and attempting to talk with one of her sisters. At about the precise time, brandy was served to the riders. Another tradition Graham had told him about earlier.

As the hunt got underway, Charles chose to stay back in the pack of riders. He'd never been on a hunt, and he wanted to be sure he understood and was comfortable with the crowd. Making sure his horse was comfortable with the hunt was important too.

He didn't need the bay going sideways and acting scared of the close proximity of the others.

He'd lost track of Lady Cathryn in the madness of the start. In fact, he'd lost track of everyone. He kept riding, which was the easiest thing to do since he wasn't familiar. Charles was enjoying the pace even if he'd slowed down.

Cantering his horse around a sharp turn, he noted a small fence to jump. No one was around so he thought he would give the bay a chance at it. After clearing the jump, he slowed the bay down when he noticed a horse without a rider. He immediately rode over to the stray, looking around for its owner. It was then he saw Lady Cathryn. It was obvious by her appearance that she'd fallen. Her hair was askew, her hat lost, and her dress caked in mud and dry dirt. Quickly, he dismounted.

"Are you hurt?" he asked as he rushed up to her.

"Only my pride," she replied.

"What happened?"

"I pulled back because the mare wasn't liking some of the horses around us. We came upon this jump, and she refused to try to get over it. She stopped suddenly and I went sailing over her and the hedge."

"You were lucky you didn't get hurt worse."

She nodded. "Yes, I know. To add to it, the mare has lost a shoe." She held up the missing shoe.

He noted she'd ridden in a proper saddle and not a side saddle. He wondered if her sisters knew of her preference. It was a brilliant move on her part. Side saddles could be dangerous and weren't made for everything.

Lady Cathryn needed to be looked after. He could leave her here and go find help or he could put her on his horse, and he could lead her mount back. It might work, even though the bay was not as docile as her horse.

"This is what we're going to do," he said. "You're going to ride in front of me on my horse. I'll sit behind you, and we'll lead yours back. I don't want to leave you here alone."

"Are you afraid I might be kidnapped or something?"

He was puzzled by her remark. It was an odd thing to say. "Certainly not. Now, are you going to let me help you up, or are we going to talk?"

Moments later, he assisted her onto the bay. He gave her the reins of the horse she'd been riding as he swung up behind her. He hadn't even gotten comfortable when he felt his body betraying him. His cock was hard and throbbing as he tried not to think of the reasons why. He was attracted to Lady Cathryn, but wasn't aware attraction led to something like this. It had happened far more than he'd remembered it happening before he came here.

Charles clucked the bay into a walk. He could tell by the animal's ears the extra weight wasn't boding well with him at all. They continued in silence, which suited Charles just fine. Women tended to want to engage in small talk, but she said nothing.

Finally, he felt he should at least ask her how she was doing. Make sure the ride wasn't too much for her bruised body. "You okay?"

"Sore, but I'll make it. We should almost be there."

"You've ridden here before?"

"No, but I did get up and walked the course this morning."

"Really? That was quite smart of you."

"Thank you. Knowing approximately how many people would be coming today, I felt I needed to know the best route."

"Do your sisters disapprove?

"Neither of them wanted me to ride today. Said hunts are a dangerous sport."

He readjusted his seat and tried to imagine she wasn't there. Her nearness hadn't waned his body's reaction. "So you mentioned."

"Look," she said suddenly, "we're at the finish. Everyone is here."

True, and they were the last ones, which everyone seemed to know because both her sisters came rushing over to them. Out of the corner of his eye, he noticed Graham and Arthur on their way as well.

"Where have you been?" her sister Agnes inquired, eyeing Charles up and down. "And what are you doing riding astride?"

"I always ride astride," she replied. "Lord Charles came to my rescue after he realized my horse had thrown me."

A stable boy had come and taken the horse while another held the bay's reins. Charles swung himself off the back of the saddle and on to the ground. Carefully he assisted her down. Her sister grabbed her by the arm as her feet hit the soft grass.

"Thank you for your assistance, Lord Charles, but I've got her," her sister Agnes said. She had a look on her face Charles was familiar with. In her eyes, he was a madman, someone who shouldn't be out of an institution.

"Thank you again, Lord Charles," Lady Cathryn said softly.

Instead of saying another word, he turned and walked away. He noticed Daphne with a brandy in one hand standing off to one side.

"It's a good thing you happened upon Lady Cathryn."

"I'm not so sure of that," he replied. "Her sister thinks I'm some sort of monster."

Daphne laid her hand on his forearm for a moment. "You are overreacting. I'm sure Lady Agnes is just concerned for her sister."

"I'm sure you're right," he replied. Glancing back over to where Lady Cathryn and her sisters were, he noted Arthur and Graham talking with the trio and the two sisters being quite adamant and vocal with displeasure.

People who were nearby were starting to glance over at him. He knew when that happened it was time to leave. If he didn't, he'd be the gossip for the day. He knew how this all worked; he'd been through it before.

Not wanting to draw attention to himself, Charles spoke to his sister-in-law. "If you'll excuse me. I need to walk. I'll see you back home."

"Don't you dare. Don't let those two win."

"I have no intention of that. I simply don't wish to cause a problem for Roxanne and Graham."

"You aren't."

"It's best for me to go." He turned and began walking a path away from the crowd.

He passed almost no one as he stopped in front of the house. He knew Graham's estate backed up to his family's so he began to walk to a path that would lead him in the general direction. He'd then pick up the pace and would soon be somewhere near the house.

A few light-gray clouds dotted the afternoon sky but he was undeterred by the sight of them. He instead continued his walk. Keeping up a swift pace, he finally reached a large meadow. Before he could cross it, he had to get over an old rock fence. Charles glanced about the fence, looking for any break in it. Not finding any opening, he walked the fence line for a moment or two when he found a gate. It opened easily and Charles walked through it before finding his way back to the path.

It was about at that time that Frazier found him. From the look on his face, something was seriously not good. His face was like the gray clouds above them.

"His Grace sent me to find you. He wants you to go to the house and wait for him in your rooms."

"What have I supposedly done?"

"Lady Agnes is accusing you of making inappropriate advances to Lady Cathryn. She is demanding satisfaction."

"I never did any such thing! What does she want?"

"I don't know. His Grace finally got Lady Agnes to agree to speak about it privately rather than airing things in public."

Charles kicked his boot along the ground. "I can't bring shame to my family."

"Let His Grace handle the situation."

Charles nodded. "That's all I can do for the moment."

"That's right."

"Very well. Tell him I'll be waiting on him."

"I'm coming with you," Frazier replied.

Charles began walking. "Come on. We need to hurry. Those clouds look as though they're going to part at any time."

The valet peered up at the darkening sky. "We do indeed."

Without further word, the pair walked as fast as they could. By the time they made it to the house, a rumble of thunder sounded followed by a flash of lightning. The rain came down hard.

He followed Frazier into the kitchen and requested a pot of tea. It always brought a smile to his face to see the look on the kitchen staff's faces when he came into the busy room. Charles saw no reason not to. After all, he had very little memory of living here and had always had access to anywhere he wanted to explore.

Once in his sitting room, he sat close to the hearth to warm the chill as he waited for tea. Finally, he walked over to the windows where the wind was blowing the rain sideways and the lightning frequently lit up the sky.

Frazier walked in with a footman carrying a tray filled with not only a pot of tea but sweets and sandwiches to hold him over until dinner. He followed them to a large table and waited. Pouring a cup of tea, he took a plate of egg sandwiches and a slice of cake covered with cream and strawberries. He found a comfortable chair and set everything on a table in front of him. The cake was rich and the tea strong.

"I'll leave you, milord."

"Very good. Tell me something, Frazier. How does Lady Agnes think she can accuse me of anything, or demanding right be made? She's not a man and women have no authority in matters like this, do they?"

"She is the oldest and perhaps her father left her in charge of her two sisters. There may not be a male relative. Or at least one close by. I'm sure His Grace will know the answer."

"I'm sure he will. It just struck me as odd that Lady Anges

would be so bold. But you're right, there may not be a male relative."

Another crack of thunder caused even Charles to jump, and when he turned in Frazier's direction, the valet had disappeared into thin air. Just like he always did. He took a sip of tea. Deciding it was still too hot, he set it down on the table.

⤞⫷⫸⤝

"CHARLES. CHARLES. WAKE up." A hand on his shoulder shook him lightly.

It was a familiar voice. Slowly he opened his eyes to find Arthur standing next to him. Charles sat up straighter and gazed at his brother.

"What is it?"

"We need to talk," Arthur replied. He sat down in the chair next to his.

"We do? What about?" Charles picked up his tea, but it had cooled so he returned it to the table.

Arching a brow, Arthur sat back. "I'm sure your valet has informed you something of Lady Agnes's accusation."

"He shared what he knew at the time. I find it odd that she would go so far as to accuse me of something I didn't do when earlier in the day she wanted nothing to do with me. I was a monster in her eyes."

"I thought the same thing," Arthur replied.

"Tell me exactly what I'm being accused of and what she wants."

"She's claiming you ruined Lady Cathryn."

"Ruined her? All I did was help her mount my horse."

Arthur tapped the arm of the chair with one hand. "I believe you, but Lady Agnes is making the accusations on behalf of her sister."

"Is that so? I wonder."

"Wonder what?"

"What does Lady Cathryn have to say about the matter?" Charles asked. He ran a hand through his hair and waited for the answer.

"She hasn't said a word. She's just let her sister speak for her."

"I thought a male member of the family was in charge for such a claim. What does she want?"

"Her father, brother, and mother are on the Continent and there are no other male relatives nearby to take charge."

Charles responded quickly. "Can that be done?"

"It's rare, but in cases like this, yes, it can."

"What does she want besides money?"

"Marriage to Lady Cathryn."

Charles felt his heart skip a beat. "I don't understand."

"It's simple. You took advantage of Lady Cathryn. You've ruined her. The best-case scenario is marriage."

"No. I will not marry based on a lie."

"Lady Agnes and Lady Cathryn will be here late tomorrow morning to go over the details. You will, of course, be present and can ask any questions."

"No!" Charles shouted. "I will not. I did nothing wrong."

Arthur slammed his hand down on the table in front of him. He understood and he would use Charles's "ailments" as a way to put an end to this. "You are not going to ruin our family's reputation and good name. If all else fails, you will marry the chit."

"You know what I think? I think the entire incident has been planned."

"What are you saying, Charles?"

"That Lady Agnes and her sisters planned this all out. Don't you think it odd that Lady Cathryn's incident happened when I was the only one around?"

"It's a moot point."

"No, it isn't. I thought her parents had their sights set on someone else. A duke's son or something."

"You're right. I remember that from the concert."

"That must not have panned out the way her parents intended. But why choose me? I'm a second son and one some call mad." He snorted at the description.

"Why don't we do this. We'll meet with them tomorrow. In the meantime, I'll see if I can find out anything about this gentleman Lady Cathryn's parents wanted for her. I'll also send word to my solicitor in London and see if someone can find out about the family makeup. See if there are or are not any male relatives who should be making these decisions."

"That sounds fair enough. Perhaps we'll be able to put them off long enough for you to hear back from your people."

"That's what I'm counting on," Arthur replied. "I suggest we go downstairs. Daphne was going to have something light for dinner."

"She doesn't have to take care of me."

"What are you going to do? Hire your own staff?"

"I haven't decided."

"Well, don't. I think you'd hurt her feelings if you did."

"Very well," he replied.

The two brothers made their way through the halls and stairs and found Daphne had dinner ready in the breakfast room. Fruit, cheeses, a roasted chicken, and bread made up the light meal.

Daphne had been sitting waiting on them. She smiled when she saw the two brothers. It would be easy for a stranger to mistake one brother for the other at first glance. Charles, however, sported a beard and longer hair than Arthur. If he was clean shaven like his brother, it would take a minute to try and determine who's who.

"Are you nervous about the meeting?" Daphne asked.

"No, more curious than nervous," Charles said.

"We'll get through it tomorrow. Nothing will be resolved, and I'm sure that's going to make Lady Agnes unhappy."

"I have a wicked idea if everything goes their way. I will move to the cottage and Lady Cathryn will not get to live in the main house like I'm sure she wants to. Make her live humbly and maybe I'll be able to get the truth out of her."

Both Arthur and Daphne smiled at his words. "That's mean, Charles, but I like it," Daphne said.

"I'm surprised at you, Daphne. I would have thought you would want her living here," Arthur said.

"Tricking a man into marriage. She deserves it. Perhaps a month or so in the cottage might humble her."

Charles broke off a hunk of bread. "I was thinking more like a year, maybe two."

"Charles!" Daphne exclaimed with a laugh.

"Hopefully it won't come to that," Arthur said.

"Maybe Lady Cathryn will have a change of heart and reject her sister's idea," Daphne said.

All he could do was hope something like that might happen. The idea of being with a woman for the rest of his life that he was forced into marrying made his stomach churn. It was trickery plain and simple. He even thought of finding somewhere to stay on the estate unseen from all. Let them think he'd gone off on one of his days or weeks-long walks.

"That would be nice, but somehow I don't see it happening," Charles said.

"I guess we'll find out tomorrow," Arthur said. He cut a piece of cheddar and bit into it.

Everything was going to come down to tomorrow. Charles knew his life would come down to what this meeting brought.

CHAPTER EIGHT

CHARLES ROSE EARLY the next morning. During a sleepless night, he decided to ride early enough that Arthur and Daphne wouldn't be up. Walking straight to the stables, he waited as a groom saddled the bay.

He headed to the lake. While there on his and Arthur's ride a couple of days earlier, he noticed there was a wide stream that fed into the lake, surrounded by woods. For some reason, he had been drawn to it and imagined perhaps he played there.

Once he arrived at the lake, he began to walk his horse on the bank. He was looking for something but had no idea what. The farther he went, the more his surroundings changed. He urged the bay on. Finally, they came upon the opening to a cave. It wasn't a deep cave, if you could even call it that. The entrance was hidden by vines and overgrowth.

He dismounted and took a look inside. It was dark inside even with pushing aside some of the vines. It wasn't huge and didn't seem to go anywhere but he could make do. What he needed to do was gather supplies and some food. Always be prepared, and if things didn't go well later, he would have a safe place to go. Luckily, it was warm out during the day and the nights were not bad to sleep outdoors.

When he walked into the house again, he noticed a carriage sitting out front. Their guests had arrived. Early, but they'd arrived nonetheless. Rather than go and change, he walked into Arthur's study where four pairs of eyes regarded him. Daphne was the only one not present.

"Did I have the time mixed up?" he asked, looking at his brother. Arthur was standing by the fire, and his look was not a happy one.

"No, you don't have the time wrong."

"Yes, come and join us, Lord Charles," Lady Agnes trilled. "May I present our solicitor, Mr. Brown."

Charles glanced at his brother for an explanation. Not getting one, he spoke on his own. "Why would you need a solicitor?"

"To represent Lady Cathryn and our family."

"The only male relative lives in America, and her father and brother are on the Continent," Mr. Brown said.

"So their parents left them with no one to act as their protector?" Arthur inquired.

"That is correct."

"I find that odd," Charles said.

"That's not important," Lady Agnes said. "We need to finalize this while we're here."

Mr. Brown, their solicitor, cleared his throat. "Lady Cathryn has accused Lord Charles of inappropriate behavior and as such has ruined her for any other man. Is this correct, milord?"

Charles sat there in disbelief. He still couldn't believe he was being used like this. He would never ruin a woman's reputation. Looking Mr. Brown in the face, he shook his head. "No, that is not correct. She took a fall while jumping and her horse threw a shoe. The rest is a fabrication."

"My lord, I do not understand why you won't own up to what you did to my sister. She has sworn you touched her in inappropriate places on her body," Lady Anges seethed.

"I did no such thing."

"So how are we going to fix this?" Arthur asked, clearly frustrated by the accusations being thrown at his brother.

"Really, Your Grace. There is only one solution to this dilemma. Your brother will marry my sister."

"Lady Cathryn. Please. Tell them the truth; that I didn't do any of the things I'm being accused of."

She said nothing but instead stared at her folded hands.

"All right. I think this has been decided," Mr. Brown said, looking at Charles and then Arthur. "I trust you will get a special license and this marriage can be finalized in the next few days."

"There is the matter of where they will live," Lady Agnes said. "I assume they'll live here?"

Before anyone could answer, Charles stood up. He'd had enough. He was going to have to disappear, at least for a while. Perhaps some of these people would grow tired of their charade. He quickly looked at everyone in the room. Lady Cathryn looked as though she would cry and everyone else appeared angry. He walked to the door and opened it.

"Charles, where are you going?" Arthur asked.

"I need some air."

As he bolted across the room to the door, he heard Arthur tell them he'd be back in a few minutes. Not a chance. If he were going to have to go through with this, he would do it when he was ready to give in. By the look on Lady Cathryn's face, he was sure she didn't like the position she was in.

He made it to his wing of the house and went directly to the master suite. Heading over to the sitting room, he moved a panel, opening it with a hidden lock. In the past it had been used for servants to come and go, mainly to check or light the fires. It had also been used as a place for family members to hide. There was a hidden door giving access to the servants' hallway to other parts of the house and a set of stairs which led up to a private room in the attic.

Once in the attic room, he looked around to determine what he would need to stay. He couldn't very well go to the stream hideaway until there was a moon. He would have to work at night to make it inhabitable. For now, this would work.

He retraced his footsteps. He needed to inform Frazier what

he was up to so his valet could be on alert when it came to his brother and Lady Cathryn and her family. As he neared the hidden panel, he overheard Arthur and Frazier's voices. His valet assured his brother he'd not seen him and Arthur sounded frustrated.

"Lady Agnes has left her sister here. Said she was Charles's problem and that she was not going to have the family name sullied."

"I don't think I've ever met someone so set on getting what she wants."

"That's all I wanted to tell you in case you hear from him. I know he goes for long walks that can last hours or longer, so he might be sighted."

"That's always possible. I'll do my best to convince him to come back if I run across him," Frazier replied. "How is Lady Cathryn getting along?"

"Heartbroken that her sister cast her aside. Her Grace has been doing her best to try to cheer her up, with little results."

"Do you think Lady Agnes made all this up?"

"Absolutely, I do," Arthur replied.

Upon hearing all this, Charles backed away from the exit. He went and sat down at a table just off to the left of the entrance. The idea that one's sibling could do something to another was so heartless and went beyond comprehension.

"If I see him, you'll be the first to know, Your Grace."

"Thank you, Frazier."

Charles heard the sound of a door closing and his valet mumbling to himself. A few minutes later, Charles heard the servant's door open and close and suddenly it was completely quiet. He paced up and down the hall for a few minutes. He wanted to make sure Frazier was indeed gone.

When he did emerge, Charles quickly penned a note for his valet, grabbed his notebooks, pens, and some apples from a nearby table. He knew Frazier would know what to do. He'd see to it that he got food, some blankets, and other necessities to keep him sustained.

What bothered him now was Lady Cathryn being left by her sister. Would she stay here to wait on him? Or would she find somewhere else to go? From the few times he'd met her, she seemed docile. When he found her during the hunt, his first impression was that she was capable of more than most young ladies. Today really surprised him. He'd expected her to stand up for herself. He wanted to believe it was all her sister's doing, but something told him to keep his distance.

He headed back through the opening and closed the panel. He would go up to the attic because the window was going to be the only source of light. Once it got dark, he would have to rely on a candle, which he would have to use cautiously in case someone happened to look up at the house and saw light coming from the attics.

Entering the attic room again, he set the notebooks, pens, ink, and everything else he'd been able to carry onto a table under the window. It was then he realized he had forgotten matches and a holder for the candle. This was a conundrum. The only reason one could see in the hidden hallways and stairs was because there were lanterns near doorways for the servants to use. They weren't all lit but they were there waiting for use.

Realizing he'd be taking a risk, Charles thought he'd go down and try to find a lantern already lit and bring it back up with him.

The task was easier than he anticipated, and he even found some matches sitting nearby. At least he wouldn't be in the dark all the time. So, before going back upstairs, he walked to the hidden door to see if Frazier had left him what he'd asked for just outside the door.

A couple of heavy blankets and other necessities along with a hamper were waiting on him, just inside the door. Frazier had figured out where he was. Not what he wanted, but it was probably better he did. He knew his valet would keep his secret.

The room had been where his father would lock him away whenever he had a major tantrum, as his father called them. Back then he had a mattress and a couple of crates, nothing else. His father was afraid he might try and climb up to the window and try getting out on the roof to escape. When locking him away from the household, his father sent him first to a home which dealt in infirmities such as he had. After that didn't help, he sent him to live on Wight.

Opening the hamper, he found a note from Frazier, along with some fruit, a loaf of bread, cheese, and roast chicken. Two bottles of wine were to one end of the hamper.

Frazier mentioned he would leave him food once a day and would try to do more if he didn't raise any eyebrows with the kitchen staff.

After eating and putting everything up, Charles noted it had gotten dark. He'd written a list of things he'd need for the place by the creek. Perhaps, if the moon was out, he'd try and sneak out and return early in the morning. He lay down on the blankets and fell fast asleep, until he woke sometime in the middle of the night to the sound of thunder and the flash of lightning. Hopefully the storm would move on before morning. If not, it meant everyone would be in the house for the day. He wondered about Lady Cathryn. It couldn't be easy for her, her sister casting her aside.

He wouldn't mind talking to her since he was very attracted to her. Or so said his body. She seemed to be easy to talk to. That would need to wait. He needed to let everything settle to see if her sister changed her mind. He doubted that would ever happen.

WAKING UP SLOWLY, his senses were hit by the smell of coffee and sausages. He sat up from the pallet he had made the night before and found a covered plate on the small table. Frazier had brought him a tray. There was also toast, butter, and marmalade to one side. When he opened the lid keeping the rest warm, he found two types of sausages and a spoonful of scrambled egg. Replacing the cover, Charles looked around the room and found a change of clothes, a basin with water, and soap and a towel. Pulling the chair up, he took a sip of coffee, then began eating the hearty breakfast Frazier had brought. Everything tasted amazing.

What he was going to do for the day was limited. He couldn't afford to be seen by any of the staff. A sighting would make its way back to Arthur, and he wasn't ready for that discussion. He needed time to himself to think. How would he respond to Lady Cathryn's sister's accusations? Or would he? He had denied the accusations though his declaration had fallen on deaf ears. He felt as though he was going in circles.

Remembering Lady Cathryn liked to take long walks, he thought perhaps he could use that to his advantage. He could have Frazier perhaps find out where she went. Did she have a preferred time to go on her walks? If he were careful, he could leave earlier and be there waiting. She would probably startle, but he needed to see what she was about. From his observation, he was fairly sure she had not agreed to what her sister had proposed.

He had nothing to offer her except the books he had published. The income they generated was unpredictable. No one had really seen he was properly prepared for life in the world. He was the second son of a duke. Traditionally he should have become a priest or gone into the navy or army. But everyone had been sure Charles would never become either. That he would remain in seclusion forever. No one, not even his siblings, would ever know of his existence until he passed.

He'd been through this numerous times. For years he questioned his own existence. Very few questions had ever received answers. Now and then he heard words thrown around like crazy, idiot, mad, all used to describe him. Charles had proven them all wrong.

It was raining. He could hear it beating down on the roof above him. The day was going to be long and dismal. Writing on his new book would be how he spent this day. He also had observations he needed to put to paper because perhaps they might become a part of a story. In reality, he had plenty to keep him occupied.

Waking up to sunshine beaming through the dormer window in his hideaway, Charles smiled at the sight. Even though he couldn't step outside for fear of being discovered, his day would be much more content.

There should be a moon tonight and he decided that after the house was asleep, he would sneak outside and take a walk through the gardens. He'd also decided his decision to move to near the creek wasn't feasible. He couldn't saddle a horse for fear of being discovered, and walking to and from the location would take longer than the time he would have to work. So in the middle of the night, he decided until he was sure his point was made, he would stay right where he was.

Frazier came with breakfast which consisted of fruit, bread, a hunk of cheese, and coffee. The two men talked for a while with the valet telling him what was going on in the house. Lady Cathryn was still in residence, her sister completely ignoring her and Arthur's letters. Daphne and Arthur were trying to make her feel welcome and decided she should stay for the summer if her sister didn't have a change of heart.

His valet scoffed at the idea of Lady Agnes changing her mind about anything. The woman, he found out, had never been married, not even a prospect. That would explain part of the reason for her bitterness toward Cathryn.

She had a dowry, Charles knew that much. A substantial one if he remembered what Arthur and Agnes discussed. It wasn't like she would profit from the marriage. He, Arthur, and the solicitor would be the ones controlling the money.

"Do you know how long Lady Cathryn's parents will be away?"

"I heard Her Grace mention late summer, early autumn."

"I wonder if her father knows anything about this?"

Frazier shook his head. "I doubt it. If he knew, he'd be headed back to England."

"Point taken," Charles replied.

Not wanting to get caught coming out of the passageway, Frazier left, saying he'd keep his ears open for any more information.

Charles spent his day working on his next book and making notes of things that came to mind. He didn't take a break until he looked up and noticed the sun was setting. The room was darkening so he got up and lit the lantern. He put everything in a neat pile at the side of the desk. Frazier had brought him a decanter of brandy earlier. Charles poured himself a glass and sat down on the pallet he'd made. Leaning against the wall, he sipped brandy and tried to close his mind down. That task was easier said than done. From where he sat, he could see moonlight shining down. He couldn't wait to smell the outside.

Polishing off the brandy, he sat back against the wall and listened to the sounds of the house. It seemed to hum much of the day. When everyone slept, the house was quiet.

Much later in the evening, once the house seemed to be asleep, Charles snuck out and into the gardens behind the house. The moon was at three quarters full, making it quite bright on an otherwise dark night. Walking around on the crushed shell paths, he breathed in deeply. He caught the scent of some of the night flowers. This was just what he needed.

He came upon the opening of the maze. There should be a bench in the middle of the puzzle. They were easier than most people thought them to be. One could never truly get lost in one. He entered, taking his time as he slowly walked between the tall hedges. The light from the moon was almost like daylight. No clouds covered the skies.

As he was about to turn the final bend into the center, he thought he heard someone, a female, sneeze. He shook his head. That was impossible and he determined he hadn't heard a thing. Charles slowly walked into the center of the maze. A bench sat at the far end and a young woman sat there. Not just anyone. Lady Cathryn.

He walked closer to the bench, and her head quickly snapped up to see who it was. She appeared to be as startled to see him as he was to see her.

"Lord Charles, where have you been? Why did you leave so abruptly?"

He cleared his throat. "I sort of panicked. I couldn't sit there and listen to your sister dictate my future with her accusing me of things I did not do."

"I understand. She finally got fed up and left, leaving me here."

"She's giving up her nonsense?" Charles inquired.

"Heavens, no! I imagine she is plotting her next move," Lady Cathryn replied.

"I had the feeling she hadn't told you what she was up to."

"Not a clue. I was so embarrassed I couldn't speak. I didn't know what her next move might be."

"I find it interesting that she left you here."

Cathryn smiled ever so slightly. "She doesn't want the family name to be dragged through the mud. Her reputation is on the line as well."

"What do you think she'll do next?"

"I think she'll not only see the solicitor, she'll contact our father and ask for his guidance. Father will return home."

"That'll take several weeks, if not longer," Charles replied.

"The duke and duchess have been so kind."

"Yes, they are."

She looked at him square in the face. "Are the rumors true that you're mad?"

Charles snorted. "It depends on your definition of mad. My mind just works differently than most men's."

"I don't think you're mad. Eccentric perhaps, but not mad. You're highly intelligent, way above most men."

"I'll take that as a compliment," he replied.

"It was meant as one. Are we still going to have to marry?"

"It appears we will, I'm afraid. Once your sister gets word to your father, he's going to insist."

"But we can tell my father the truth. That'll help change his mind."

He shook his head. "By the time he returns, I'm afraid your sister will have done enough damage."

"Then we must come up with a way to thwart her plans."

"I agree. Two heads are better than one," he replied.

They sat there in a comfortable silence for a moment. Charles wondered what she was thinking. She was, after all, a smart, talented young woman. He'd never heard anyone play piano as perfectly as Lady Cathryn. She was an angel in his eyes. No woman had ever made him feel as she did. Certainly, he hadn't spent a lot of time around women growing up. His social life had been limited for fear he might have one of his "fits" and scare everyone around him. Now he'd met her, and it seemed everything had turned upside down and he wasn't sure what he was supposed to do about it.

"May I say something personal?" she asked.

"Of course."

"Why aren't you angry with your parents or your siblings about the way you grew up?"

"Honestly, I can't be upset with my siblings. They were too young to know what was going on. As for my parents, they thought they were doing the right thing after listening to the so-called experts. It could have been worse. My father could have left me in an asylum and forgotten about me."

"I understand. What you say makes sense."

"One doctor did convince my father to put me in an asylum. That didn't last but a few days. He came to see how I was getting along and to speak with the doctors about their plan to help me recover. He didn't like what he saw."

"So that's how you ended up on Wight?"

"Yes."

Looking up at the moon, Charles figured it was getting very late. They'd been here talking for hours, and daybreak wouldn't be too many hours away. He hated the idea of leaving, but he couldn't afford to get caught just yet.

"I hate to bring this to a close, but we've been here talking for ages, which I must tell you I've thoroughly enjoyed."

"As have I. Would you like to continue again tonight?" she asked.

"I would," he replied.

He assisted her to her feet where they both stood in silence, neither sure what to say.

"I will think about our conversation and see if I come up with anything regarding my father's upcoming visit," she said.

"You're sure he's going to come?"

"Yes."

Tucking his finger under her chin, Charles tilted her head and, before he knew what he was doing, kissed her gently on the lips. He'd never kissed a woman like this before and deduced he'd done it right because she didn't pull away in horror. She seemed to like it because he felt her respond.

"Come, I'll escort you back to the house," he finally said.

"I'll be fine."

"I insist. You'll enter first. I'll wait a few minutes before going in."

She nodded. "I enjoyed our talk, Lord Charles, and look forward to our next."

"Charles," he said. "Please call me Charles. Lord knows you of all people should call me by my Christian name."

"Only if you'll call me Cathryn, Charles."

He smiled and opened the kitchen door for her. "Until later," he said. Before she could respond, he was gone.

When he returned to his secret room, he paced the floor for a moment. He was surprised with the feelings that had come about just being in Cathryn's presence. He didn't want to wait until after dark before seeing her again. There was a need, and he couldn't explain it. Being in her company and just talking with her brought him happiness he'd never known. His cock had been hard the entire time, and he was grateful the light wasn't any brighter or she might have seen.

To top it off, he kissed her, and she didn't pull away. It had only lasted a few moments, but he would never forget how she tasted and how she responded to his actions.

Sitting down in the chair, he pulled off his boots, jacket, and trousers until he was in his smalls. He lay down, drawing the blankets up over him. His eyes were heavy, and it was only a matter of minutes before he fell asleep.

Waking up hours later, he sat up for a moment to get his bearings. He dressed and found a light breakfast sitting on the table along with a couple of newspapers. The coffee was lukewarm, indicating to him that Frazier had been here earlier than normal. A change of clothes was neatly placed at one end of the table. What he wanted was a bath. Perhaps one could be arranged. Something he'd speak to his valet about.

He read the newspaper after eating his fill. Charles didn't see anything earth shaking going on, so he stood and began to get dressed. As he finished, he turned to see the door opening and his valet coming through.

"You were sleeping rather soundly when I was in a few hours ago."

"First good night's sleep I've had in a while," Charles replied.

"I thought you'd like to know what's going on."

Charles cocked his head. What could possibly be going on that involved him? "What is it?"

"Thought you'd like to know that Lady Cathryn's parents will be here in three days. Her father wants her reputation intact by having her marry you. Her mother, on the other hand, wants to send her to a convent."

"That's a little extreme."

"It is, but if something can't be arranged for the two of you to marry, they will do whatever needs to be done, and that includes sending her away to a convent."

"What is wrong with these people? Lady Cathryn isn't a race-horse who hasn't lived up to their breeding. She's a smart, beautiful, and talented young woman."

"Spoken like a man in love," Frazier replied with a lopsided grin.

"Love doesn't happen that quickly. It's something that develops over time."

"There are many ways Cupid's arrow will pierce your heart."

Charles sighed. "Any advice?"

"You could elope. Take her to Gretna Green and jump the broom. Leave early in the morning before the house is awake. Go to London, catch the train to Edinburgh. From there you two can take a coach to Gretna Green. You'll be husband and wife before her parents arrive."

"So in their eyes I'd be admitting I ruined her."

"Won't matter by then, will it?" Frazier said.

"No, it won't."

"You don't have to come right back. You could spend some time at the family estate in York. I don't think anyone would think to look there."

Charles nodded. "You're right. I need to get word to Lady Cathryn and see what she thinks about the entire thing. The sooner we're on the road, the better."

"If you write something to her, I'll make sure she gets it and bring word back to you."

"Very well. Give me a half hour to write to her. I want to make sure I get it right."

He sat down at the table, lost in thought, not hearing his valet leave. Was this truly the thing to do? Marry Cathryn? He was certain her parents would do something awful like send her away to a convent. He wanted to save her from such a fate. If they married, her father wouldn't be in a position to make monetary demands. Nor would they be able to have the marriage annulled, and if they did try, it would be unlikely they'd succeed.

Providing for her wouldn't be a problem, and he was sure they could reside on the family estate. Spending time in York might be an idea while everyone adjusted to the fact they were married. If not, they could always take a wedding trip to the Continent. He'd been once. Trying to prove a point, he set out with little money and a lot of ambition. His father put a man on it and had him brought back to Wight.

His fingers were writing the words, but his mind was elsewhere. It always was. The best thing to do might be to return to Kent after they wed and confront everyone. If her parents had left, he would send word, and they would go to them. If they didn't disown their daughter. That was always a distinct possibility.

Explaining his plan to Cathryn wasn't hard. He kept it simple. The details would follow. All he wanted right now was for her to agree to his plan. They would figure the rest out later.

But what would happen if she didn't agree and didn't wish to elope? Or marry him at all. That wasn't something he was going to let his mind wander to. All he could do was hope for the best. The rest would follow. They had the rest of their lives to get to know each other.

CHAPTER NINE

CHARLES GAZED ACROSS the compartment. Cathryn was trying desperately to keep her eyes open, but the gentle rocking rhythm made it a losing battle.

"Go ahead and sleep," he said. "It's a long journey."

"You sure you don't mind?"

"Not at all. I may be right behind you." His eyes were indeed getting heavy from the motion. The train was headed forward toward Edinburgh. While the weather was decent, he hoped it would stay as it was. Dry. That could all change the farther north they went.

He had gotten them their own compartment for the long train ride, so they'd have privacy. He hadn't wanted to share with others.

Several hours later he awoke to the sound of the train stopping in a far northern village to pick up more passengers. He noted Cathryn was fast asleep, not even waking when the train made a jerking motion as it pulled out and began to pick up speed.

When they arrived in Edinburgh, he'd need to find the options available to get them to Gretna Green. Once they were married, they'd spend the night there and decide between them where they wanted to go. They could go back to Edinburgh for a day or so before moving on to the family estate in York.

"Do you know how much longer until we're in Edinburgh?" a sleepy voice asked from across the compartment.

"We have several hours still."

"Have you slept at all?"

He nodded. "Yes. I only awoke when the train pulled into a station. I forgot to check where it was."

"That's fine." She rose and walked around the small compartment. She sat back down and gazed at him.

"Are you hungry? My valet put together a small hamper. He had to do it in private so as not to raise the cook's suspicions."

"Not right now," she replied. "I think I'm going to try and sleep some more."

"Excellent idea. I think I'll go see if I can find us some tea."

She smiled at him. "That sounds heavenly."

Closing the compartment door, Charles went down one corridor of the car in hopes that finding a cup of tea wouldn't be a challenge. He finally came upon a porter who informed him it was late but that the service should be started in a few more hours.

He turned around and made it back to their compartment. As he opened the door, he tried to be extra quiet so as not to wake her. As soon as he sat down across from Cathryn, he realized he was still tired. He arranged himself in the corner and found his eyes growing heavy. This time dreams and visions crawled into his sleep. Cathryn's parents disapproving of the marriage and attempting to see about having it annulled. Another flash was that they were beaming that their daughter had done well in finding a husband. No, that would never happen. They wanted their beautiful, talented daughter to marry far better than the second son and brother of a duke. But here they were, on their way to marry, and that wasn't a dream.

The next thing Charles remembered was Cathryn gently waking him up, informing him they'd arrived in Edinburgh. He sat up straighter and scrubbed his beard.

"How will we travel to Gretna Green?"

"There's a coach. I've made arrangements. We need to walk to their offices and purchase our tickets and leave our luggage there since the coach won't leave for a couple hours," he said.

"Is their office very far?"

"No, I was told it was just outside the station."

The walk was short, and Charles was able to get everything taken care of. A porter even brought their luggage while they were getting their tickets.

"Would you like to get some breakfast while we wait?"

"Oh, yes. We never did eat last night," she said.

"No, we didn't. There's a hotel down the hill that has an excellent restaurant. Breakfast is supposed to be quite good."

She nodded as he opened the door for her. "I could surely use a cup of coffee now."

"Me too," he replied. He smiled to himself as he felt her tuck her hand into the crook of his arm. There was something soothing about such a simple act. They would be okay. It was like they were meant to be together.

Finding the restaurant proved to be easy. Inside, the dining room was nearly to capacity with people who had been traveling. They were seated against a wall, and the waiter told them what the specials were. They each picked the same one, and while they were waiting, their much-appreciated coffee was brought to their table.

"Do you suppose our absence has been discovered?" Cathryn asked with a grin.

"It's very possible since I left a letter on my brother's desk, and you left one on your bed. Arthur rises early to get his paperwork and correspondence taken care of."

"I don't think either Arthur or Daphne will be surprised, do you?"

"No."

Once they pulled into Gretna Green, Charles helped Cathryn down from the coach which was parked in front of the hotel they'd be staying at. The skies were a deep, rich shade of blue with an occasional large, fluffy white cloud floating by.

He guided Cathryn across the street to the hotel. Inside he led her to the registration desk where he and the clerk had a discussion about the rooms and how to get married. Next, he signed a ledger marked "weddings."

There would be a couple of hours wait, so he escorted Cathryn to the room he'd rented for them to spend the night after they were married. He was sure she might like to change clothes or take a bath before she did that. While they waited, he would also change and clean up. The journey by coach had been a dusty one.

Cathryn sat down at a small table and faced away from her intended. Making use of the basin and water pitcher, Charles cleaned himself before changing clothes. He chose a dark-gray suit with a crisp white shirt and a red cravat.

Once he finished, he walked over to Cathryn. "I'm going to find someone to replace the basin and get some fresh water for me. I shouldn't be but a few minutes."

"Very well. While you're doing that, I'm going to lay out my clothes."

He grunted and walked out the door. It didn't take him too long to find someone to do exactly what he needed. In a matter of minutes, everything was the way Charles wanted it. Cathryn had laid out her clothes on the bed and sat in the chair waiting on his return.

"I'll take a walk while you're changing," he said.

"No need. I'm going to need your assistance with something since I don't have a maid with me."

"What would that be?" he asked.

"My corset. I will need assistance taking it off and tightening the new one."

He arched a brow at her words. "Just don't wear a corset," he replied.

"My dress won't look right without one."

"Very well. Just tell me when you need me. I'll be over here," he said, indicating the table with his hand.

"You might as well loosen this one while you're so close."

He turned and saw she was no longer in her dress, but in her stockings and underwear. "I've never done this before."

"Really? Well, it's quite easy. Simply unlace me in the back."

He found where he needed to start, and quickly she could breathe a sigh of relief. Then he walked over to the table, avoiding any eye contact with her or her state of undress. He sat with his eyes closed for what seemed to be hours. When she did speak, she was quiet.

"I'm ready for you to help me with this new one."

"I've never done this before." Moments later, she was strapped in, though not as tightly as a maid might pull it.

"Really? You did quite well. If it'd been my maid, she would have had it so tight I would barely be able to breathe."

He sat down in the chair. "Is there anything else you need me to do? If not, I'll go downstairs and see what's going on."

"No, but don't think you have to leave. We'll soon be married."

"I just thought you might want some privacy."

"I'm fine."

He rose and found her by the basin. "I'll be back in thirty minutes. Will that be enough time for you?"

"I can make it work."

"Very well. I'll return then."

He shut the door behind himself and headed to the stairs. The lobby seemed to be bustling with people. It made him wonder how many couples were here to do the exact same thing as he and Cathryn. He sat down in a dark brown leather chair and began to watch the different people as they went about their business. Couples dressed in their finery strolled blissfully through the lobby and upstairs. The latest couple to be wed in the blacksmith's shop.

Charles looked at the large clock mounted on a wall and decided he'd been here long enough and would go check on his bride. He knew she was going to be beautiful in spite of how hurriedly they'd left Kent.

When he opened the door to their room, he found her sitting on the side of the bed waiting for him. She wore a stunning lavender dress with dark purple piping. She was beautiful beyond words. Her hair was worn down, flowing past her shoulders. Charles had never seen her with her hair down. She would have to do it more often.

"For a moment I thought I'd entered the wrong room," he said. "You are breathtaking."

She smiled. "For a second, I was afraid you had a change of mind. That you fled, leaving me behind."

"I would never do that," he replied.

Standing up, she walked toward him. "Shall we go and marry?"

His breath hitched as he simply nodded his reply. Words would not convey what he was feeling at that exact moment. Whatever it was, he hoped it never ended.

As they walked outside in the crisp air, he felt her once again tuck her hand in the crook of his arm. He didn't look down at her; instead, he patted the top of her gloved hand as they walked across the street. The smithy's shop was neat, causing him to wonder how he got any other work done aside from marrying couples.

What happened next was a blur of emotions. In one second, he found himself questioning everything. From the recent changes in his life, to standing here in front of a few select people. Instead, he repeated his vows in a clear, steady voice. It was after that he vaguely heard the man pronounce them husband and wife. He leaned down and kissed her on the lips, for perhaps too long.

As they walked back across the street, Charles once again wondered how much his bride knew of consummating the marriage. It would have been a discussion her mother would have had with her. Women were fickle creatures. Most didn't know anything but the fundamentals, or at least that's what he understood. He would be gentle and together they'd discuss this.

Upon returning to their room, he gathered her in his arms and kissed her greedily. It dawned on him that this may be something either of them had never experienced. He certainly hadn't, but it seemed the proper thing to do. When they broke the kiss, he saw she was flushed. On the table was a bottle of champagne and two glasses beckoning them. He'd made sure it would be in place for when they returned. Besides toasting their marriage, it would help take the edge off and relax them.

"Come, sit down while I pour us a glass of champagne."

"Of course."

Moments later, he passed her a flute and joined her in a simple toast. After finishing the glass of champagne, he said, "I certainly don't feel any different." He placed the empty glass on the table.

"What do you mean?" she said.

"I don't feel any different now that we're married."

She smirked. "You really didn't think getting married would change you, did you?"

"I suppose not, but it got you to smile."

"It did."

"There is something I'd like to discuss with you now."

"What's that?"

"What would you say to us holding off consummating our marriage until we arrive in York?"

She smiled shyly. "I would be forever grateful to you if we did that. I'd rather save it for somewhere we can truly be alone."

"Good, I'm glad you concur for the same reasons I have."

She bent over and removed each of her shoes and climbed up on the bed. Patting the bed, she beckoned him to join her. He obliged her by removing his shoes and jacket and joining her. Then she asked him a curious question.

"Will you allow me to continue with my music?"

"Of course. You don't even need to ask such a question. Yes, you may. Your talent is extraordinary, and I would never expect you to give anything up. Especially your music. I know how much it means to you."

"Thank you."

He would move mountains for her, and he'd never had those feelings about anyone. They seemed to be able to talk to each other about anything. Not even the fears he harbored since childhood phased her. She was quite remarkable.

"What would you think about living in London?" Charles asked.

"All the time?"

"Not in summer. Everyone escapes to the country during the summer. I was thinking of purchasing a house there. One of our own where we wouldn't have to live with family members."

"London does make sense. Isn't your publisher there?"

"Yes. I thought living there would help tremendously. I would be close by for meetings and the like."

"I think that's a splendid idea," she replied.

"I've been thinking about it for some time. I need to invest some of the money I've earned through my books."

She said nothing. It was as though she was deep in thought. Finally, she took his hand. "We could leave here and go directly to London. Once we've finished conducting business, we could go to Kent. I don't think anyone would mind since we've just married."

"You're right."

She leaned against him, placing her head on his shoulder. He held her like that until she fell asleep. She soothed him. Just to hear her speak made his body lose some of its tensions. Though they were still technically strangers, he felt more at ease with her close by. They were slowly getting used to each other, what they liked and disliked. His eyes heavy, he gave in and fell asleep next to his bride.

LOUD, DEMANDING KNOCKING on the door the following morning startled both Charles and Cathryn. Walking over to the door, he asked who was on the other side. He heard the familiar voice of his valet, Frazier, and immediately let him in.

"Frazier, why are you here? Is everything okay?" Charles asked.

"Are you ready to leave?"

"What are you about, man?"

Frazier went and gathered the luggage. "I've rented a carriage. I'll tell you all about it once we're on our way, but we must go now."

The pair followed his valet down the stairs to the carriages outside. He walked to one and as they neared, a young man opened the door. Cathryn stepped in while Charles followed. For a rental carriage, it was quite nice. The curtains were drawn, making it dark inside.

Frazier popped in and closed the door. He tapped on the roof and the carriage jerked forward. "I'm sorry to be so mysterious, but your brother sent me."

"Why would His Grace do so?" Cathryn asked. She was sitting next to Charles and their eyes met for a second as they waited for his valet to tell them more.

"Your parents are on their way to Gretna Green. They have the notion they can stop your wedding from happening."

"They're a little late for that," Cathryn replied, shaking her head.

"They want the marriage annulled in spite of His Grace telling them it wasn't going to be possible."

"Where are we going?" Charles asked.

"To York, but not to the main house. His Grace sent word to prepare the dowager summer house. It's not near the house and can't be seen unless you're looking for it."

"Do you really think they'll go to York?" Cathryn asked.

"Yes. It is my feeling they'll spend the night in Gretna Green or somewhere on the road."

"Did my brother send correspondence with you?"

Frazier nodded, pulling a hamper from underneath his seat. He opened the lid and took an envelope sealed with the duke's insignia and passed it to Charles.

He read the letter, which was short, and passed it to Cathryn who read it with great care. Shaking her head, she read through it a second time before setting it on the seat beside her.

In the meantime, the valet had the hamper closer to them before he tapped the top of the carriage to have the coach stop. "I'm going to ride up top and get some fresh air. Keep the curtains closed until we're farther down the road." Frazier was out of the carriage quickly and they began their journey to York again.

"I don't know about you, but I'm hungry." She glanced into the hamper and pulled out a loaf of bread. "There's this and butter and some marmalade. Also a couple of scones and cheese. What would you like?"

"Some of each," he replied.

She nodded and went about taking a plate and filling it with his choices and handing it to him. "There's also a bottle of wine, if you'd like some."

"I guess we'll have to make do." He leaned forward, opened the bottle of wine, and poured them each a glass.

While Charles was doing that, his bride made her own plate with the food provided. Even though it wasn't typical breakfast, her husband's valet had thought of them. They both sat there in a comfortable silence and enjoyed their food.

Once everything was put away, Charles beckoned Cathryn to sit closer to him. After she settled in, he took her hand and kissed the back. "I bet you didn't realize how exciting life would be when we married."

She giggled, which made him feel better. He'd been worried

she might regret marrying him.

"I must admit it has been far more appealing than going through what my mother would have had me endure. My decisions have been mine and mine alone. Not her nagging and convincing me on how and what should be done."

"Good, that's what I want to hear."

The next thing he knew, she was kissing him on the cheek. "I'll never regret marrying you, Charles. You're an amazing and caring man. Remember that."

He didn't want to burst her happiness, but he hoped she'd feel the same after seeing him in one of his outbursts.

Rain began to hit the roof of the carriage. The curtains had remained closed, but Charles leaned over and opened one covering the door next to him. The sky was a dark gray, and the rain was coming down at a steady pace. Then the carriage came to a halt and Frazier joined them.

"I hope you don't mind. I didn't bring rain gear. Coachie is well prepared."

"Of course, you can join us. I would hate for you to become ill because we didn't," Cathryn said.

"That's very kind, milady."

Charles, who had been peering out the window at the weather, turned toward them. "Is this weather going to hinder our travel?"

"We should be fine as long as the roads don't become untravelable."

The three continued to look out the windows at the rain pelting the carriage. After not too long, Frazier and Cathryn were fast asleep. Charles, on the other hand, still stayed wide awake. He could not remember when he had slept soundly in the middle of a storm. Having a tree come down on the roof of his cottage during a storm while on Wight had been the start of his habit. He'd been lucky. Lightning had split a tree near the cottage and sent it falling onto the roof. After that he never slept during a storm. Not intentionally.

He needed to get them settled as soon as possible. Spending time in York was still a good option, but with her parents looking for them, he wasn't sure what to anticipate. He would talk with his valet about it all as soon as they had a chance. His bride would like to have a place to call home. Once they settled for a while, he would make inquiries into properties for sale in London.

The storm pressed on but the closer they got to York, the lighter the rain. Eventually, the rain stopped, and the sun began peeking its way through the clouds. They needed to stop and change out teams. The four pulling now were exhausted, no doubt.

While the team was being changed at a coaching inn, everyone went in and had a hot meal. Stew with crusty bread and cheese seemed to do the trick. Finally, they were on the road again, heading to York. Charles knew they wouldn't make it today. They could either keep going or when they arrived at the next coaching inn to change out the team, they could spend the night and get an early start the next morning. He was anxious to make it to York.

CHAPTER TEN

THE DRIVE AND house were lit up the evening they arrived at the estate in York. Word had been sent to the staff to expect them. Never had Charles been so glad to put his feet on solid ground. The first thing Cathryn wanted was a long, hot bath before she did anything else.

The housekeeper led them through the house to the duchess's suite, showing Charles the door separating his suite and his wife's. He kissed Cathryn, telling her to come to his suite when she finished, and they would see about dinner.

Cathryn followed the older woman to the bathing chamber where a young chambermaid was preparing the bath. The maid picked up a bottle of bath salts and poured it into the water. It was vanilla and orange.

As Charles stepped into the hot, steaming water, he wondered if his wife was enjoying her bath. He certainly was. He submerged himself up to his neck and lay against the back of the tub and closed his eyes for what he thought were a few minutes.

He woke up when Frazier threw a bath cloth, hitting him on the side of the head. "How long have I been asleep?"

"Long enough for your bath water to begin cooling," the valet replied.

Grunting, he picked the cloth out of the water, found the soap, and began scrubbing the dirt off his body. His hair was next, and he submerged himself to wet it. Once that was taken care of, he stepped out of the tub and took the towel Frazier passed him and began to dry his body. He then sat through Frazier shaving his beard.

He then dressed and went to sit in the drawing room. Dinner would be served, and Cathryn would enter at any minute. He was looking forward to spending some private time with his bride. If they weren't too tired, he intended to have her stay the night with him. The marriage needed to be consummated. Thinking about that brought a hum through his body. Especially his cock which had a mind of its own whenever she was around, or when he thought of her.

When Cathryn entered the drawing room minutes later, she literally took his breath away. Dressed in an emerald-green silk gown, she showed poise and confidence like he hadn't seen in her before.

Charles immediately rose and walked across the room where he took her outstretched hands and kissed the back of them. He drew her closer to him and, taking one hand, he tipped her head up and kissed her. Gently at first but demanding as they continued.

"You look exquisite," he said when their lips parted.

"Am I overdressed?"

"Not at all. Let me see if dinner is ready."

"Wouldn't they come and announce that it's ready?"

"Yes, ordinarily they would, but if we continue what we just did, there will be no dinner."

She giggled. A sound he would never tire of. "Then you had better check because I'm quite ravenous."

"I'll be back momentarily."

Finding a footman approaching him as he closed the drawing room door, the young man informed him dinner would be ready momentarily. He took that as good. Returning to the drawing room, he found Cathryn sitting in a chair near the hearth. Their eyes locked as she looked up at him as he neared.

"Dinner is served, madam," he announced. Extending a hand, he helped her rise from her chair.

"Excellent," she replied, placing her hand in his and letting him lead the way.

Two place settings were at the end of the long, mahogany dining room. A crystal vase, filled with fresh flowers, greeted them midway down the table. Charles stood and waited for Cathryn to sit before he did. A footman poured them each a glass of red wine as the crab bisque soup was served with bread.

"This is lovely," Cathryn said, picking up her spoon. She delicately tasted the liquid, closing her eyes as the taste invaded her senses.

"I don't think I've ever had this before."

The main course of Scottish salmon followed. It was served with a dill sauce and asparagus spears. Charles had asked that a nice dinner be served for their first official night in the house, but he wasn't expecting this. This would have taken longer prep time to gather the items. This had all the makings of Daphne or Roxanne taking charge. He may not know them well yet, but he knew of their kindness and support.

Dessert was a marmalade cake followed by a cheese plate. The cake was fresh and moist. The variety of cheeses impressed him. There were four different types and two he'd never had. He tried them.

"I almost think I like the cheese more than the cake," Cathryn said. "I don't have a huge sweet tooth."

"Both were good. Do you know what these two cheeses are? I've never had them before."

Cathryn stared at the plate for a moment. "There is a Dutch gouda, and the other is an Italian, though I don't recall what it's called."

He reached and grabbed a piece of gouda and popped it into his mouth. "This is quite good."

"I thought you would like it."

Finishing the cheese, he picked up his glass and finished his wine. "Why don't we head upstairs?"

She nodded, not knowing the meaning behind his words. "I think that's a splendid idea. I'm exhausted from the past few days."

Charles leaned over in her direction. "Who said anything about sleeping? That'll come later."

Realizing what he meant by his remark, Cathryn's face turned a deep shade of red. He wanted to laugh, but knew it was best if he didn't. He didn't want to embarrass her any more than she already was.

Pushing her chair back, Cathryn rose to her feet. She stopped at her husband's chair where he remained seated.

"Come."

Standing to his full height, Charles followed her out of the dining room and up the stairs. Both were quiet, but words weren't needed at the moment. As they stood in front of the door to his suite, she squeezed his hand. He reached for the door handle and pushed in. The sitting room was warm from the fire in the hearth, the lights were dimmed, and a bottle of champagne sat in a bucket on a table along with two glasses.

He watched her as she walked around the room before choosing a dark-green couch to sit on. It was close enough to the fire to ward off any chill. "Why don't you pour us a glass?"

"I was just about to do that," he replied. He carefully opened the bottle, not wanting the cork to go shooting across the room. He poured them each a glass and walked to her. Handing her a glass, Charles sat down next to her.

He lifted his glass. "To us. May our marriage be strong and prosperous."

"To us," she replied. Taking a sip of the bubbly wine, she wrinkled her nose. "It tickles."

"It does."

"No regrets?" she asked him. She placed the empty glass on a table next to the couch.

"Absolutely none."

Charles put his glass down and drew Cathryn closer, kissing her long and slow. When he thought she was beginning to relax, he parted her lips with his tongue, and the kiss became a little more urgent. Finally, she opened to him as they explored each other. He tasted the champagne on her tongue. When the kiss broke, they were both panting. Charles began kissing her neck in slow, deliberate kisses. She moaned at his touch. His cock had never been so hard.

"Shall we move somewhere more comfortable?"

"Yes," she replied breathlessly.

They never made it to the bedroom. Instead, he got her out of her green dress and her undergarments. He disrobed inches from her and twice caught her looking at him. Had she never seen a man naked before? He took her hand and placed it on his cock. In a moment, she began to touch him, causing him to groan when she touched his balls. Knowing he wasn't going to last much longer, he picked her up and took her to the bedroom and deposited her in the center of the bed.

Charles covered her with his muscular body, lining his cock up with her wet passage, and began to enter slowly. She clung to him, anticipating what was coming next. Not saying a word, he kissed her, hoping to distract her. He pushed hard and fast until he was seated within her. Hearing her moan, he stiffened, afraid he might have hurt her.

"Are you okay? I promise after this time, things will be more enjoyable." How he knew that he had no idea. He had to have heard it some place at some time.

She said nothing, still clinging to him as he began to establish a rhythm. He wasn't going to last long, but the marriage was consummated and now they could begin to enjoy marital pleasure. At least he hoped she would enjoy it.

Close to his climax, Charles pumped harder and faster until he finally exploded, his seed filling her. He pushed one more time before remaining still, enjoying this intimate moment with her.

Waiting a few moments, he slowly withdrew from her and as

he did, he kissed her deeply. Pulling her close to him, he felt her hand on his chest.

"Thank you for waiting," she said softly.

"I didn't want the memory of our first time together to be of some place like the inn at Gretna Green."

"This was much more personal."

"It was," he replied, reaching down and pulling a blanket over them.

"I think we're going to be just fine, Charles," she said.

"Yes, I concur."

The room became quiet, and he heard her breathing. She'd fallen asleep and was snoring lightly. Smiling, he knew she was content, and yes, he would tease her about snoring. He closed his eyes and continued to listen as his eyes grew heavy.

His dreams made no sense at all at first. Cathryn appeared in them. For the first time in his life he had someone permanently etched in his life. He had someone who depended on him. Never before had he had such responsibility.

At some point during the night, Cathryn turned onto her side and he instinctively laid his arm over her body and held her close and fell back asleep for a time.

The next time he awoke, dawn was upon them. The light was faint coming through the windows. More important than that, he found his cock hard and wanting her. He brushed her hair away from her neck and kissed her, gently turning her over on her back. Spreading her legs, he ran his hand up and down her thigh. She was still wet from their earlier coupling. He inserted a couple of fingers into her passage. Yes, she was wet and warm. She called out as his thumb rubbed her magic spot and broke apart in euphoria as her climax overtook her body.

"My God, Charles! What was that?"

"You had an orgasm. Your mother never told you about such things?"

"Only the basics, and one was to just lie there and let you do the rest. I learned more from my sister than my mother, but nothing about this," she replied.

"Hmmm. Your mother was brought up in a different time."

"I know. She has no opinion when my father is around, pretending he knows all."

"I thought she might be, and I'm sure she's quite opinionated among her friends."

She arched a brow. "You can read people well."

"Just one of my many quirks, that's all."

"And you're modest too," she replied.

He reached out to her and pulled her toward him. "Why don't we see if we can get some more sleep."

"You're right, we should. Can we go on a walk if the weather holds?"

"We can do whatever you wish," he replied.

"Maybe there are some saddle horses we could use and ride instead."

"I'm sure there are. Now sleep, my dear. Sleep."

Sleep didn't elude either one. Charles heard a soft knock on the door. Grabbing a sheet, he wrapped it around himself and went to the bedchamber door. Frazier stood on the other side.

"I took the liberty of having breakfast brought to you. It just arrived and I had it put on the small table in front of one of the windows."

"Thank you. I'll wake Lady Cathryn now."

"Is there anything else you need?" the valet asked with a smug grin on his face.

"No, that'll be all for now."

"As you wish, milord."

Charles waited until his valet had shut the door behind him. Walking over to the table, he saw breakfast looked scrumptious. He snatched a piece of bacon and walked back to the bed. Cathryn was already sitting up, her legs swung over the side of the bed. She had grabbed a robe and was putting it on. "Did I hear something about breakfast?"

"Yes, indeed you did."

"Good. I'm famished," Cathryn replied.

"As am I." He walked over to a chair near the entrance to the bathing chamber and picked up a robe. Dropping the sheet, he put it on.

Sitting down, she poured them both a cup of coffee. While waiting for it to cool, Charles watched as she took off the lid keeping her plate of food warm.

"This looks fabulous," she said as she slathered strawberry jam on a piece of toast.

He grunted in agreement, picking up his fork and taking a bite of egg and then sausage. He then picked up his coffee and took a sip. Still hot, but drinkable.

"I asked Frazier to see what the availability of two horses might be. We could ride the estate. That is, if you're not too sore from our activities."

"No, I'm not. I just need to take a bath."

He wasn't sure if she was saying that for his benefit. Women were complicated creatures.

※

CHARLES WAS UNFAMILIAR with the estate grounds. There was a lot going on as this was truly a working estate. At a far end, away from the manor house, there was a mine in use for coal. From what he understood, his great-grandfather had started the venture. It had continued, bringing quite a profit to the estate. It also kept a large number of people employed. They would visit the mine site another time. Today he wished to learn the layout of the land with his bride. His valet, Frazier, had given him a quick run-down on the layout of the estate so he would know a little more about how things were set up. His thoughts were interrupted.

"Charles, we're at the orchard."

He reined in his gelding and stood to admire the multitude of fruit-bearing trees. "Ah, so we are. It's massive."

"How many trees would you guess there are?" she asked.

"I wouldn't even stand to guess. A couple hundred, if I had to guess."

"That's a lot of jam, pies, and cakes."

"It is," he replied.

She patted her horse's mane, and they sat side by side. "I wonder if some of the fruit or products from the fruit is sold or given away?"

"I'm sure some of it is. The revenue from the sales would go back into the estate."

She nodded. "Where to now?"

"Why don't we see what's at the far end of the orchard?"

"Yes, and while we're walking through, we could make note of what types of trees grow here," she replied.

"Excellent idea."

They began to walk through the orchard on a path on the perimeter of the orchard. They passed apple, pear, peach, which were most familiar. Finally, at the other end of the orchard, was a small meadow fenced off with rock walls. It didn't take but a moment to understand why the walls were there.

A small herd of Belted Galloway cows were grazing just beyond the wall. Charles had never seen this particular breed of cow before, and he sat on the back of his horse and watched. The breed originated in Scotland, and from what he could recall, they were not uncommon in northern England.

"Fascinating, aren't they?" Charles said, watching her reaction.

"They are. I don't think I've seen them before."

"Neither have I." He glanced up at the sky. The sky was changing. The beautiful cornflower blue was quickly being taken over by gray clouds which took over the landscape. "I hate to end our lovely ride, but I'm afraid we need to return to the stables before the sky opens up."

Looking up at the skies, Cathryn grinned. "Lead the way,

husband. All we can do is hope it stays away."

"Come, follow me," he said.

"Do you know a quicker way?"

"No, but we need to hurry."

"Look," she said, pointing to a portion of the sky which still had blue sky and white clouds. "That wasn't like that a couple of minutes ago."

"You're right, but we still shouldn't dawdle. I would hate it if you were to get sick from my decision."

Charles led her back the way they came through the orchard. When they reached the small meadow leading to the stables, he broke his horse into a gallop. Cathryn followed, clucking to her horse to try and keep up with him. She was a better rider than most young ladies and he wondered how since her mother was more interested in her daughter's piano playing.

The sky was still a mixture of blue and darkening gray when they arrived at the stables. They began walking to the house, still mindful of the weather.

"That was very enjoyable," she said.

"I take it you didn't get a chance to ride much."

She shook her head. "Heavens no. If it weren't for my father, I would have never ridden, even sidesaddle."

"That's a pity. You're quite a good rider."

"I love the freedom riding gives you," she said.

"It is very liberating, isn't it?"

"Hmmm."

They walked around to the front of the house and entered into the main entry hall. As Charles was about to close the door, the rain began coming down at a good steady pace.

"We made it just in time," he said.

"Do you have anything you should be doing?"

"I need to write my brother, let him know we arrived in York and see what's going on in Kent and how long he thinks we should stay here before returning."

"Excellent."

"I came up with an idea. We wait for Arthur's reply and see what he says. We could take the train to London and spend a couple of days before returning to Kent."

"That would be fun. Does your family have a box at one of the theaters?"

"I'm not sure, but I could ask Arthur."

She smiled. "Why don't you go to the study and write your letter? I'll order you some tea before I go upstairs to change clothes."

"Perhaps I should wait on my letter to Arthur and help you."

"I think you should write your letter. If you don't do it now, it won't go out until tomorrow."

Sighing, Charles nodded his head. She was right, but the moment he finished, he intended to have his cock buried deep inside her. "You're right. Why don't you join me when you've changed?"

"Very well. Let me order you some tea and head upstairs," she replied.

He watched her as she sashayed across the remainder of the hall. She would go to the kitchens for the tea unless she ran across the housekeeper and then upstairs to change.

Finding the study, he rang for someone to come start a fire. It was damp in the room and it surprised him that one hadn't been lit. Walking around the room, he decided to wait until he got the fire situation under control before he commenced with his letter to his brother. It took no time for someone to answer his call. The young maid brought a bucket with coal and proceeded to get a fire lit. Charles made sure to thank her as he could tell she was nervous, leading him to believe she had forgotten to light the fire in the study.

He sat down at the desk and began looking through the drawers for paper and pen. Quickly, he placed everything on the desktop exactly as he wanted it. As he was about to pick up the pen, a knock on the door was followed by a footman pushing a trolley filled with a teapot, small sandwiches, and cakes. He noted there was two of everything. Cathryn was joining him. That made him smile.

He rose and strode over to the cart to fix himself a cup of tea and a plate of sandwiches and a scone. This time when he sat down, he placed the tea in a specific location to his right and the plate at the top.

Picking up the pen, he held it for a moment before writing. He informed Arthur that they had married in Gretna Green and if he hadn't heard, they were in York. Charles mentioned her parents had tracked them to Scotland, but by the time they did, it was too late, and they were on their way out of town en route to York.

He asked his brother what they should do next, that he and Cathryn had talked about a couple of different options. Kent and London being among them. He mentioned his longing to get himself and his bride settled.

He ended the short letter with a note that he would await word from him before leaving York. Charles was surprised how easy it was to write to his twin. Even though they'd spent much of their lives apart and not knowing about the other or having vague memories of the other, Charles still felt a closeness to Arthur.

Deep in thought, he didn't hear his bride enter the room. He was busy addressing his letter when he felt a pair of arms wrap around his neck from behind as her lush lips kissed his cheek.

"Perfect timing, my love. I'm just finishing up."

"So I see. You never touched your tea."

"I forgot about it. Since I'm done, would you like to sit near the fire and enjoy some tea?"

She sat down on his lap, putting her arms around his neck. "I'd actually like you to do naughty things to me, but a cup of tea might be the perfect teaser to that."

He was caught off guard. He hadn't seen this side of her. Not that he didn't like it; he was just knocked off balance. They hadn't coupled since the first night as he was trying to be respectful of any discomfort she might be feeling. Obviously, if she truly had any discomfort now, she wasn't going to admit it to him.

"Let me call and have someone take this letter."

"I'll take your tea and plate and get you a fresh cup while you do that."

He said nothing, simply nodding as he rose and walked to the bell pull. Rejoining Cathryn, Charles noted she added sugar to her cup. When he sat down next to her, she picked up the other steaming hot tea and placed it in front of him.

"I took the liberty and added clotted cream and strawberry jam to your plate. I hope you don't mind."

"Not at all."

A quick knock on the door and a footman entered. "There's a letter on the corner of my desk which needs to go out today," Charles instructed the young man.

"Yes, milord." The young man picked up the letter and departed the room as quickly as he'd entered.

Charles turned his attention back to his wife. He picked up his tea and took a sip. "Hopefully, we'll have a response in a day or two."

"I'm sure your brother will be prompt."

"Yes, I'm sure he will be," he replied.

Cathryn picked up a small cucumber sandwich from her plate and bit into it. "Are you going to talk with someone about finding us a house?"

"I thought I'd wait and see what Arthur has to say. It's too far north here, and the house needs a lot of updating and renovations to come up to the times."

"You're right about updating. Would you still consider London?"

"Yes, but where would we go during the summer? No one stays in town during the summer. So that's a bit of a quandary right there. I thought we could find somewhere not far from London to live. That way during the summer we could either stay at my family's home in Mayfair or go home to the country."

"That's a smart move."

He reached for his scone to slather some jam on it. "You've been around much more than I have. Is there any place you'd like to look?"

"The Cotswolds is a large area and there are a good many beautiful places. It's not far from your family or London."

"Anywhere else?" he asked.

"By the sea?"

"Somewhere in particular?"

"Somerset area is quite nice. My mother's sister used to live in a house overlooking the sea. Now she's no longer with us and the house is just sitting there."

"What happened to your uncle?"

"The last time I heard my mother mention my uncle, she said he could not bear to spend time in that house and moved to Italy after accepting a position with a shipping company whose home base was somewhere in Italy."

"I've heard of that happening before. It makes for a sad situation."

She nodded. "Yes, it does."

"Who lives in the house now?"

"Their son, Monty."

He smiled broadly.

"What? Did I say something funny?"

"No. I was merely smiling because you finally shared something about your family."

"That's not true. I've shared before. I'm just not happy with them right now, particularly my parents."

"I was teasing."

She arched a brow. "Your attempt at humor? Bad, really bad, Charles." She smiled and giggled.

"Something more for you to teach me," he replied and winked at her.

"Depending on what your brother says, we're going to look in Gloucester and Somerset. What if he offers the wing at the manor house? Is that something you'd consider?"

"I'm not sure. It needs to be updated, like this house, and York is a good way off from the families."

"It's not something we have to decide today," she replied.

He nodded. The waiting was the worst part. Arthur would send a reply as soon as he read Charles's missive. He was punctual like that. Out of the corner of his eye, Charles noted Cathryn watching him intently.

"Isn't there a maze in the gardens?" she asked.

"Yes. Why? Do you want to go play in it?"

"I think we're a little old for playing, but we could make it a game."

"Or we could have a look around the greenhouse."

"Yes! I noticed it earlier today on our walk back. I'd love to see what the gardener is doing."

Charles nodded. "Come, let's go check both out."

He assisted her to her feet, and together they walked to the door. They made it to the area in the gardens where the maze began.

"Maybe we've found a place to have some privacy."

"I believe you're right. I'm used to being on my own and alone most of the time. Crowds sometimes overwhelm me, as I'm sure you've recognized."

"I have," she replied. "I can see why writing is so appealing to you. Playing piano as well. Solitary endeavors."

"I know."

It was a shame he had no real life before now. He was thought to be a bit mad, so others thought it best to leave him alone. Trying to learn how to live among people was going to be a challenge he would have to deal with for the foreseeable future. At least, though, he had Cathryn to help him.

He could see the tall hedges of the maze coming into sight. It seemed mazes were going to have a significance in their lives. Once they chose where they were going to call home, he would have to have a maze installed if there wasn't one already.

If they had to install one, he would design it himself. Something people would always remember. Challenging, that's what he wanted.

Greenhouses weren't uncommon. The estate gardeners, he understood, had at least one where they would raise plants from seedlings, graft roses, and such. He missed being able to work in a greenhouse. Again, another solitary place and occupation.

"What about the coal mine? Are we still going to go look at it?" he heard Cathryn say.

"Yes, perhaps we can do that tomorrow. I'd like to see the operation," Charles said.

"From what I've heard and read, it's a horribly dirty and dangerous job."

He nodded. "Yes, that goes without saying for any type of mining."

"True," she replied. "I would hate to be married to a miner. Not knowing if they'd come home every evening."

CHAPTER ELEVEN

THREE DAYS LATER, at the urging of Arthur, Charles and Cathryn found themselves on a train headed south. The time in between the letter being sent and Arthur's reply allowed them precious time alone. They got to know each other in ways some couples never did. Riding the estate, finding private places to make love were just a portion of what they engaged in. The mine was utterly fascinating even though they couldn't get too close since it was dangerous, and Charles deemed it not a place Cathryn should go.

Frazier took care of all the details of the journey. From the tickets to baggage handling, and when they arrived in London, they were met by the duke's coach. Not wanting to stay in London, the pair chose to push on to Kent.

It was dark when they arrived and were met by the butler. Arthur and Daphne were finishing up their dinner and met them in the drawing room.

"Have you eaten?" Daphne asked them.

"No, last time we ate was on the train. My valet had seen to having a hamper prepared for our journey."

"I'll have Cook send something up to your rooms when you're ready," she replied.

"So Cathryn's parents never caught up with you?" Arthur asked with an amused smile on his face. "They certainly let us know what they thought when they arrived home."

"No, we never saw them," Cathryn said.

"To clarify something—you two can stay in that wing as long as you want. This is a family home, and family is always welcome."

"We appreciate that," Charles said.

"Yes, we do. We just didn't want to be in the way," Cathryn echoed.

"Neither of you would be a burden. It might help Charles continue to transition to normal living," Arthur said.

"You're too kind, Arthur," Charles replied.

"If you decide this isn't for you, I do know of an estate for sale in Gloucestershire. The house is magnificent. It was built in the last century and is Georgian in design. The gardens are something to behold but since the current owner died, they need some work."

Charles and Cathryn locked eyes for a moment. "We would be remiss to not at least go look at it. If the owner died, who is looking after it?" Cathryn asked.

"The estate sits in trust until a new owner is found," Arthur replied.

"We'd like to see it if you can arrange it. It doesn't have to be right away. Just check with the trustee for us."

"I will do that in the morning," Arthur said. "How did you like York? I haven't been there in over a year. I need to make a trip and go over things with the estate manager."

"Your man does a good job keeping it up, but I must admit the house needs some redecorating and renovation," Charles said.

"I need to make a visit. If it wasn't entailed, I might think of splitting the land up, selling the house and keeping the mine."

"But you can't do that, can you?" Charles asked.

"No, I can't."

"If I may change the subject, but were my parents rude when they came here?" Cathryn asked.

"Under the circumstances, I think they were fairly well behaved. By the time they arrived, they realized there was nothing they could do and if they did try something, it would play out badly for them," Daphne said with a faint smile.

"Good."

"By the way, Charles, I almost forgot. A letter came yesterday for you from Oxford," Arthur said.

"Oxford? I wonder what they might want?" Charles mused.

"Let me go get it and you can find out." Arthur left the room to retrieve the letter.

Charles began to pace the room. Getting a letter from the prestigious university was nothing new. Since his first book was published, he'd been invited to speak at various universities. He'd accepted one or two, but Oxford, that was indeed the most famous.

He heard the two women talking amongst themselves as he walked. It sounded like buzzing to him, nothing more. His mind was elsewhere. He kept turning his head and glancing at the door. Arthur should surely be on his way back.

A moment later, his twin came through the door, waving an envelope above his head. "Here it is."

Charles accepted it and took a deep breath before proceeding. Taking the correspondence from its envelope, he began reading. "It seems they want me to come talk to them about perhaps doing lectures on a more regular basis."

"What have you lectured on in the past?" Cathryn asked.

"Overcoming a mental ailment to become an author, among other things."

Arthur arched an eyebrow. "Do they say what they want you to speak about this time?"

"They don't say. Only that they wish to discuss the matter of my lecturing more."

"You're going to accept, aren't you?" Cathryn asked.

"Yes, of course. I need to reply and accept their invitation for Friday."

His wife smiled gently. "I'd love to go, but we know what

they think of women on campus, let alone a meeting."

"I'll only be gone that day," he replied.

"And you're going to impress them," Cathryn said.

"We'll see."

"Is there anything you need?" Arthur asked. "If you do, just tell Daphne or me and we'll get it done."

"I took the liberty of having your suite aired out and having it thoroughly cleaned," Daphne said.

"Could the piano be tuned?" Cathryn asked. "I'm afraid sitting there all this time, it's quite out of tune."

"Of course. I'll have it taken care of when the man comes next week," Daphne replied.

"If you'll excuse us, I need to go write a reply to this invitation."

It wasn't that he didn't like idly talking, but there were things he needed to tend to, and he was sure his bride needed a break.

Their wing had certainly been through a good cleaning. They headed for the drawing room where Charles took off his coat and placed it over the back of a chair. He walked directly to the desk sitting at a window overlooking the gardens and beyond, placing the letter from Oxford on the mahogany desk.

He turned to Cathryn who was watching him. "If you want to get started on your reply, I'll go see if dinner awaits us," she said.

"Please. I'm famished."

Watching her leave, he sat down and studied the letter before beginning his reply. He no sooner began writing when Cathryn returned.

"Why don't we go eat before you get started on that? It'll be cold if we wait."

"It'll only take a moment to write my reply. Why don't you go on ahead and begin? I promise I'll be right behind you."

He could tell she wasn't really happy as she flounced out of the room. Still, he knew himself well enough that if he procrastinated, he might put writing his response off until early morning.

It wouldn't take but five minutes to write his reply.

As he placed the paper in the addressed envelope, Charles was intrigued with the university's request and hoped he would do a good job with whatever they wanted. He rose and placed the letter to his left. After dinner, he would call Frazier and ask him to make sure it got out.

Cathryn was sitting next to the end of the table when he walked in. He tried to muster a smile for he could see she was still unhappy with him.

"See, the reply took no time."

"So I see. I hope you like asparagus soup. It's really quite good," she said.

"I don't believe I've had it before."

"Seriously?"

"Yes, it's true. My meals were never anything too fancy."

"Oh, Charles, we need to sit down and see what you have never had and have Cook prepare them for dinner. Just one or two items at a time. That's enough, but it would be better to try them now than at a dinner party," she said.

"I would have never thought of that."

"It's important, especially in London. You wouldn't want to offend a hostess, now would you?"

He snorted as he picked up his spoon. "No, I would never want to do that."

Taking a sip, he nodded and proceeded to take a couple more spoonfuls. It was rather good and before he knew it, he'd finished the bowl. He looked over at his bride, who sat there with a wide grin on her face. She couldn't stay mad at him long.

"I take it you enjoyed it?"

"Yes, yes, I did. What's next?"

"A pork roast, I'm told. You have had it, haven't you, because I think you'll like it."

"I've had it numerous times. It's especially good with apple and cinnamon cooked in it."

"Then you're going to like this," she replied with a grin.

Moments later, footmen with the main course appeared, carrying plates for each of them. A plate was set down in front of each of them. The pork was recognizable and had a sauce over the top. Charles was intrigued and dug in and got a taste. It was moist and the sauce had notes of apple and cinnamon. There was another ingredient, he could tell by the taste, but couldn't place the flavor.

"This has an interesting taste to it. Cinnamon and apple for sure, but there is a third flavor I can't place my finger on. Ginger? A very light amount of ginger," Charles said.

"Yes! Were you told that, or did you guess it on your own?"

He snorted and took another small bite. "It was an easy guess because ginger has a very strong taste and smell. No matter how little you use," Charles replied.

"You would be correct," she said.

Their dinner turned out to be a most enjoyable evening. A couple of the things talked about were not appropriate for the dinner table because they were so personal. Charles was thankful that his bride would speak of them with him.

"I'm tired from our journey. Why don't we go sit in front of the fire in my private sitting room and enjoy a brandy?"

"That sounds very nice indeed," she replied.

Walking hand in hand, they made their way to the personal chamber. Entering his room, he watched as Cathryn made her way to the couch and sat down. He smiled as she took her shoes off.

"Feel better?" he asked.

"Yes."

"Let me pour us a brandy."

As he unstopped the crystal decanter, he slowly began to pour the deep amber liquid. He handed her one and sat next to her. They both savored their brandy in silence. It had been a long day, and he was grateful it had been pleasant.

He stretched his legs out in front of him and took another taste of brandy. Closing his eyes, he listened to the fire crackling away in front of them.

"I need to write my parents and let them know we've re-turned."

He grunted. "They're going to want to see you."

"Us. They're going to want to see us."

"Right. I think it would be best to invite them here. If they come here, we control the narrative," he said, opening his eyes and turning to look at her. "I wonder what they'll think about all of it."

"I wouldn't even want to guess," she said. She swirled the brandy before taking a small swallow, which led to her to finishing it off. She began to set the empty snifter on a table when Charles popped up and got the decanter. He poured her another drink, adding some to his own.

"Hopefully they've accepted our marriage now that they've had time to think about it," he said. Swirling the liquid, he watched it intently before taking a hearty swallow.

Glancing at Cathryn, he smiled as he realized she'd fallen asleep. She snored lightly. He reached out and took the glass away. He finished his drink before whispering in her ear. She was slow to respond, so Charles leaned in and kissed her on the lips, which did the trick. In a moment, eyes blinking, she became more aware of her surroundings.

"I think we need to go to bed," she said sleepily.

"Agreed." He stood and helped her to her feet. They clung to each other across the room and into the bed chamber. He helped her out of her dress and undergarments before picking her up and placing her on the bed and pulling a sheet over her.

His cock was rock hard and throbbing for her. Quickly he removed his clothes and climbed in next to her. Mounting her, he began kissing her skin. He suckled her breasts, nipping at her tits. Moving farther down, he kissed her all the way down to her thighs. His tongue began to lap up her wetness at the apex of her legs. She opened to him when he inserted fingers into her dripping wet cunny. Her hands held his head as she rocked back and forth to his rhythm and cried out, begging him to make love to her. He guided his cock into her slick passage. Establishing a rhythm, it became more and more frantic. When he began to come, his hands went to her arse and held her at an angle as he lost control. He could feel his body shiver before slamming into her cunny one last time. He lay over her, on his elbows. She was flush with pleasure.

"That was nice," she said, wrapping her hands around his neck. "It was unexpected."

"I like spur of the moment, don't you?"

"Hmmm, yes I do."

He certainly did enjoy being with her so intimately. So much so, he had dreams of them together. He never had that happen before. The depth of his feelings and being in charge woke up his cock one more time.

This time he turned her over and pulled her to the foot of the bed. He lifted her abdomen and spread her legs. She remained quiet as she picked up what he wanted from her. Drilling into her with precision speed, he reached around and rubbed her until she was lost in her orgasm. He followed after her. They climbed up on the bed, where he pulled her close. They remained that way, breathing slowing down, eyes heavy. They both fell asleep and didn't wake until morning.

Charles woke before she did and went to the bathing chamber where he found his valet two steps ahead of him. Water was running from the taps; Frazier was gathering what he knew Charles would need and placing it next to the tub on a stool. He climbed in the warm water and submerged himself, laying his head against the back of the tub.

HE WAS SO deep in thought, Charles never heard his sister-in-law's light knock on the door to his study.

"Charles?"

He jerked his head around in the direction of her voice. "I'm sorry, I didn't hear you enter."

"That's fine. Do you know where Cathryn is?"

"At breakfast she mentioned going to the music room to play so she could see how out of tune the piano is. Why?"

"Her sister and brother are downstairs waiting in the drawing room. I need to find her and tell her. They refuse to leave without talking to her."

"I'll get Cathryn and meet you all downstairs. Does Arthur know?"

"Yes."

"Good."

Daphne left the room as Charles went in search of his bride, which wasn't too hard to do. She was exactly where she said she would be. At the piano. He strode across to the black instrument and let her finish what she was playing.

"Your brother and sister are here. They're in Arthur's drawing room."

"They're a little early to be calling," she said.

"Daphne said they refuse to leave until they've seen you and spoken with you."

"That doesn't surprise me. They both think they're far more important than they really are," she replied.

They walked for what seemed like the longest time. The house was huge and getting from one point to another was sometimes tricky.

Cathryn just wanted this over. So much so, she refused to change for something she'd wear for morning guests. They'd come unannounced and that was a blatant no-no.

They stood outside the drawing room door for a moment. "Ready?" Charles whispered.

She nodded and the footmen opened one of the large oak doors. Inside sat her sister and brother. Arthur and Daphne sat across from them. Sam, the parrot, could be heard in the background.

Her brother studied Arthur and Daphne for a moment. "Thank you. If you don't mind, we'd like to speak with our sister—alone," he said, his eyes locked on Charles.

"Charles is my husband now. Whatever you need to say, you can say in front of him as well."

Her siblings both glanced at one another. They'd thought they could come in and take over. Cathryn wasn't having it. Once Arthur and Daphne left, she and Charles sat down across from her brother and sister.

"I expected Papa and Mother would have been here."

"They are still quite unhappy with you. You could have had your pick for a husband. Instead, you forget everything you've been taught and elope."

"It wouldn't have mattered. They weren't going to allow Charles and me to marry. Scandal or not."

"No, they wouldn't have."

"So tell me, why did you come? To gloat and report back?"

"We're here because there's the matter of your dowry. Father has no intention of seeing either of you. He's given me the papers your husband will have to sign and a bank draft for the dowry."

"All of it?" Cathryn blurted out.

"Yes."

He held up the stack of papers and glared at Charles. "Let's get this over with. We need to be on our way."

Charles pointed to a small writing desk against one of the walls. "Will that do?"

"Yes."

Charles turned to his wife. "Arthur needs to be here. Would you mind getting him?"

"Not at all," she replied, and left the room.

A couple of minutes passed before Cathryn and Arthur stepped into the drawing room. Arthur went straight to the desk and sat down to review the dowry agreement.

"This appears to be in order," he said. "Since we don't have time for an attorney to look at it, I'm going to quickly read through it."

"Thank you, Arthur."

"No problem."

Ten minutes later, Arthur nodded in approval and glanced at Charles. "It appears to be in order. Go ahead and sign it. I will make a note under my signature that the document had not been read by your attorney and date it."

"There's no need for that," the young man sneered.

"I'm looking out for my brother and his wife. You should care as much for your sister."

Saying nothing, he grabbed his copy of the papers once they were signed and both of Cathryn's siblings left the room as fast as they could without a word.

After the door shut behind them, Arthur turned to Cathryn and Charles. "Would you like me to place these in my safe?"

Charles nodded. "Please."

"Plan on going to London with me in the morning. You need to cash or deposit that check as quickly as possible," Charles said.

"Good idea. Should we plan on spending the night?"

Nodding, Arthur spoke up, "Yes."

"And the ladies?" Charles asked.

"If they'd like to accompany us, they are more than welcome. I'll see what Daphne has to say."

Suddenly, Cathryn began for the door. "If you gentlemen will excuse me, I'm going back to what I was doing."

As the door shut, Charles turned to his brother. "She's upset, isn't she?"

"Yes. Give her a little time alone and then go seek her out."

"I'm still not good at reading people's emotions," Charles replied.

"It'll come with time."

He nodded. He knew Arthur was right in that he had no real memories to go upon. All he had was the here and now. Every now and then a glimpse from his early childhood captured his mind. What Cathryn was going through was something no one should have to experience. She was bound to be hurting. It hurt him because he was partially to blame. Given some time, she would be fine.

"Charles? Where are you?" Arthur asked.

He glanced up at his brother, who was standing next to him. "I am here. Just wondering why people act the way they do."

"If you're talking about Cathryn's family, don't try and find a solution. I doubt there is one. Fortunately, she has you and together you have a future."

"I guess I need to keep her focused on us."

Arthur arched a brow. "Yes. You'll be fine—both of you will be."

Nodding, he knew his brother was right. He and Cathryn had had much going on since their marriage. Maybe now that the matter of the dowry had been taken care of, things would start falling into place.

He'd been invited to Oxford for a meeting among his peers. That was indeed special. Since he and Arthur needed to meet with their man of business, it would be a good time to let the women shop.

"A brief trip to London is in order," Charles said to his brother.

"I'll get it arranged. We can leave tomorrow."

"That's fine. Just let me know and I'll make sure Cathryn is packed and ready to go."

CHAPTER TWELVE

WHEN THEY ARRIVED in London, gray, dark clouds greeted them. The rain had not started, and it was taking real effort not to spill open.

The two women were chattering among themselves. Charles had hoped they would become friends, and it appeared to be exactly what they were doing.

The house had been cleaned and aired out for their arrival. The suite of rooms they'd be staying in had two large vases filled with flowers. Charles had accompanied Cathryn in case she got turned around. The main room had been done in a soft shade of sage green and one wall had a silk wall covering. It was cozy and not overly feminine.

"This is elegantly done, don't you think?" she asked.

He arched a brow pensively. "Yes, I'm particularly fond of the colors chosen."

"They are soothing."

"Would you like to have a cuppa tea?"

"Sounds good. I'll have it sent here."

The tea was exactly what was needed. It also gave them some time to talk about anything they felt comfortable with. They would all be busy while here. He and Arthur were going to have a meeting about her dowry and the funds. Charles was due to meet with the Oxford representatives and had been looking forward to the encounter. He would also try to meet with his editor about his novels, and there were also some things Cathryn had mentioned wanting them to do together. He'd make sure to see them done so he didn't disappoint her. One thing he'd learned about the female sex was that they got their feelings hurt easily, and they would either wear it on their sleeve or would act as though nothing had happened. Either way, he found both reactions unfamiliar. As time went by, he hoped to understand her better than he did now.

He was getting to know what she liked and what she didn't. The piano made her quite happy but unfortunately, women were limited in their options for performing. She was daring and bold and fiercely protective of those she loved and cared about.

Suddenly, Charles cursed himself. How could he have been so forgetful? When they married in Gretna Green, he hadn't a ring for her. There hadn't been time for him to get one for her. Not once did she complain. She hadn't mentioned it. He had no idea if her feelings were hurt or what she thought of his forgetfulness.

While they were in London, he'd go out to a jeweler and see if he found something. Or perhaps bring her along and let her choose what she liked.

For now, he and Arthur were off to speak with the family man of business to find out about the validity of the dowry papers he signed and the money that came with it. The other questionable item was Cathryn's brother signing off as though he were her legal guardian.

They were led into the inner office, where they sat down and waited. When their man entered the room, they exchanged pleasantries before moving on to the task at hand.

"So far, the dowry is straightforward. I'll keep reading the dowry agreement. I'll be in touch if an issue arises," Arthur said.

"What about the money?" Charles asked.

"I thought to put it into your account for now," their man of business stated.

He watched his brother nod. "That's probably the safest place for it, don't you agree, Charles?"

"Absolutely," he replied.

For a moment, Charles wondered why he'd even come along. It seemed like Arthur had everything under control, and he was merely an afterthought. True, he hadn't been exposed to business much, but this had the markings of impatience.

He and Arthur left almost as quickly as they had arrived for their appointment. As they began their departure, his brother stepped back to have a quick word. Charles continued to the door leading to the outside. Stepping out into the fresh air made him realize how confining some circumstances could be. That was why he walked as much as he did.

"That was easier than I anticipated," Arthur said from behind him.

Charles pivoted on his heel to face his brother. "I was surprised we didn't actually have more of a conversation than we did. But I understand we were added in at the last minute, but I would have liked to have asked some questions I've been pondering."

"I can see if we can see him again before we return to Kent."

"No, it's nothing important."

"Come. Let's go to my club and have lunch."

Charles shook his head. "I'd rather go and get fish and chips. It's been ages since I had that."

Arthur stared at him for a second. "You fancy fish and chips over a steak?"

"Today I do."

"Fish and chips it is," Arthur replied. "Next time, it's my choice."

"Very well. Now, do you know of a good chip shop?"

"As a matter of fact, I do. It's within walking distance from here. If we leave now, we'll arrive before the crowds."

"That's a sign of a good place to eat."

"What's that?" Arthur asked.

"The crowds."

They continued to walk through the crowds of hustling and bustling masses of humankind. Arthur led them to a street just off the main one they'd been on. It appeared there were small stalls offering things like pasties. The place Arthur had in mind was at a corner with tables outside for customers to enjoy their meal. Though it was still early, a crowd was beginning to form. Luckily, they were able to get a good spot and placed their order quickly.

Two mugs of ale and two orders wrapped in newspapers came, and once again Arthur led the way. This time to a table outside.

"This okay with you?"

Charles nodded and pulled out a chair. "It will do just fine."

"Good," Arthur replied.

"How did you find out about this place?"

"It's quite popular with local businessmen. MPs even come here to eat."

"Have they been here long?"

Arthur handed him a wrapped newspaper as he contemplated his answer. "As long as I can remember. Papa would bring me here when I accompanied him to Parliament." He shut his eyes for a brief moment as though it occurred to him that mentioning their father and what they did together hurt Charles's feelings. He might not show it, but his brother did have feelings.

Charles bit down on the hot, crispy fish. He grabbed his ale to wash down the fish and the chips. "This is some of the best."

"Told you so," Arthur replied with a grin. "Anything you'd like to do this afternoon?"

Shaking his head, Charles looked about at all the people surrounding them. "I'm not sure."

"I need to go to my tailor to pick up some shirts I ordered."

"Then let's do that."

"You're sure?" Arthur knew his brother had problems when it came to crowds or unfamiliar situations.

"Positive."

"Why don't you see about getting a couple of suits made?"

Charles nodded but didn't make an attempt at replying. He knew he had to learn to tolerate things that otherwise would have made him uneasy. "That sounds like an excellent idea since I'm speaking at Oxford soon."

"Of course. Any other stops you'd like to make?"

"Do you know a good jeweler? I need a ring for Cathryn."

"I can do you one better. I have most of Mother's jewelry. You're welcome to go through it."

"That's a thought."

Arthur grinned at his brother. "You'd still like to go to a jeweler to look?"

"Yes," Charles replied. "You don't mind, do you?"

"Not at all. The gentlemen I use are near where my tailor is."

"Thank you."

"You don't need to thank me. I'm more than happy to introduce you to the merchants I use."

Charles nodded and finished his last chip before tidying up the newspaper. "I am ready any time you are."

They both rose from the table and threw the newspapers away and placed the empty mugs on a nearby table. The crowd waiting to get inside to the counter had grown considerably since they arrived.

Arthur's carriage was parked at the end of the side street. Charles took his brother's cue and ascended into the vehicle after Arthur had told the coachman where his next destination was. Slowly, the coach started to pull away.

"It'll just be a few minutes," Arthur said.

Nodding his head in acknowledgement, Charles said nothing.

"I know somewhere you could take Cathryn some nice afternoon," Arthur said.

"Where is that?"

Nodding, Arthur continued. "Take her to Hyde Park and afterwards to Gunter's for ices or sorbet. She'll love it."

"She's mentioned it in passing before. I'll surprise her and take her there before we leave London."

The carriage pulled to the side once again. Looking outside, Charles saw several tailor shops and wondered which one his brother preferred.

"Mr. Sims has a shirtmaker on staff. It makes it easier to have them all together rather than go from shop to shop."

"That makes sense to me. I would think one would like to be able to see what a shirt might look like next to a particular fabric or suit."

The pair entered the shop and were quickly greeted by Mr. Sims himself. Arthur made a point of mentioning what Charles needed. For the next three hours he spent being measured, going through bolts of fabric for not just one suit but three. Shirt fabric was shown, and Charles was in luck that Mr. Sims had a couple of shirts already made that fit him perfectly. Given an appointment for both of them, they said their farewells and returned to the inside of the carriage.

"That was an invigorating experience," Charles announced.

"Yes, it was, and now you're set up with him, so any time you need something, he'll have your measurements and likes and dislikes."

"True."

"The jeweler is just up ahead," Arthur said.

"He's good?"

"Yes, and if he doesn't have it, he can scour the competition or have something custom designed for you."

"Interesting," Charles replied, his mind a thousand miles off as he looked out the coach window with fascination. It was a thriving city, and people from all over the world came to see it for themselves.

Since going to Scotland, he had the urge to see more of the world, and perhaps they would when he and Cathryn went on their wedding trip which they were planning on doing the next spring.

When they pulled up in front of the jeweler, they found a

large sign on the window. Arthur had the coachman get down and read the sign. The man quickly returned, telling Arthur the shop was closed due to a death in the family. They would reopen in a week's time.

"Anywhere else you'd like to go?" his brother asked him.

"No, not unless you can recommend another jeweler."

"There are one or two I have used in the past, but for something as important and meaningful as a wedding ring, I'd seek out only the best."

"I agree," Charles replied. "I'll go through Mother's jewelry and see if there's anything appropriate, if that's still fine with you."

"Of course it is."

"Very well. Anything else you fancy doing?"

"No, nothing that can't wait," Arthur replied. "Let's go home."

They rode in silence for what seemed forever. The traffic in this part of London was horrid. It always seemed to be non-ending, and there was never a good time. Early mornings the delivery men were out, then businessmen, and in the evenings, it was the ton out for everyone to see them in their finery as they made their way to balls, soirees, or the theater.

"I believe we'll have the house to ourselves when we arrive. Daphne and Cathryn were supposed to go to tea at the dowager duchess of Blackpool's house," Arthur said.

Charles nodded but said nothing. He was staring out the window at all the commotion the traffic caused.

Arthur knew Charles well enough now to know that even if he didn't respond, it didn't mean he hadn't heard the conversation.

"Charles?"

"Yes, the women have gone to have tea," Charles said.

"And..."

"You can show me Mother's jewelry without either of them walking in on us.

"Yes, would you like to do that?" Arthur asked.

"I would," Charles replied with a nod of his head.

Before they knew it, the carriage pulled up in front of the family home. Charles was out of the carriage before any of the footmen could ready the carriage. He didn't wait for his brother but rather moved quickly into the house. Removing his hat and gloves, he placed them on a nearby table. Arthur walked in and the process repeated itself.

"Join me in my study when you're ready," Arthur said.

"I'll be there shortly."

Charles needed to have a moment to catch his breath. There was only so much riding in a carriage in town he could tolerate. He found them claustrophobic. He needed to regroup and put this out of his mind. Arthur always made him feel at ease and never forced him into anything. His brother always let him take whatever time he might need.

The one thing he missed about Kent was being able to simply go out and walk whenever and wherever he wanted. It helped him in more ways than one. It not only refreshed him but renewed him as well. It had the same effect on him as taking a nap during the day did for others.

When Charles did enter Arthur's study, he found his brother setting out a box on his desk. He watched Arthur open the box and then shut it again. He glanced up upon seeing Charles.

"Have a seat. Would you like a whiskey?"

"Yes," Charles replied.

"The box is open. Go ahead and look through it. These were Mother's rings. Perhaps there might be something suitable."

Sitting in front of the closed red leather box, Charles waited a moment to open it. He wondered if he might recognize any pieces. If he did, would he remember where he saw them? So much of his early life, his early childhood, was deja vu.

Arthur handed him a glass half full of whiskey. He took a good swallow, set it to his right, and placing both hands on the box, he opened it. Inside were at least two dozen rings of various shapes, stones, and metal. Why would anyone need this many rings? He corrected himself silently. Women liked to collect, especially jewelry. Their mother was no different.

He began to pick up various rings and look closely at them, not needing any help with the pieces. Arthur tried to supply what he knew about a piece; if it was a favorite of their mother's or she rarely wore it.

Picking up a striking emerald ring, he began to look it over closely. The emerald was a good size emerald cut with three diamonds on each side of it. He put it aside and continued to look. It seemed rubies were their mother's favorite stone apart from diamonds.

"Are any of these part of a set?" he asked his brother.

"No."

He ran across two more emerald rings. Taking them out of the box, he studied them closer. Neither was as nice as the first one, so he returned them to the red leather box. He found two sapphire rings. They were nice but they were still not as nice as the emerald. Emerald was most definitely Cathryn's stone.

"You like this one?" Arthur asked, pointing to the emerald sitting to the side.

Charles arched a brow and nodded. "Emerald is the color that looks best on her."

"It's a beautiful choice."

"Do you think she'll like it?" Charles asked.

"Yes. I can't imagine any woman not liking it."

"Good, then I made the right choice."

Shutting the box, he moved it forward toward Arthur who was sitting behind the desk. Then he picked up his glass and finished the whiskey in the glass beside him.

"Are you going to take Cathryn with you to Oxford when you go to speak?"

"I haven't decided but probably not. She'd have to spend most of the time on her own."

"I hadn't thought about that," Arthur said.

"Yes, I had. In great detail."

"If you decide you want company, let me know. I'll see if I can't rearrange my day if needed."

"You're too kind, but trust me, I've been on my own for years even though I was confined to Wight. I know how to adapt to my surroundings."

"I don't want you thinking you have to be alone when you don't have to be. That part of your life is in the past," Arthur said.

It might be in the past, but it would always be a part of him. Because of the solitude, he found it hard to make friends or even be around a lot of people. Back then, and even today, people thought he was mad to one degree or another. And maybe they were right. Maybe he was a little mad.

Chapter Thirteen

B Y THE TIME they entered the theater, Charles thought the majority of London was in this one building. Inside, it was a sea of people like he'd never seen in one place all at once. He'd been to the theater a couple of times on Wight, but the patrons were a lot less than here. He felt it hard to breathe and reminded himself to relax.

The family box wasn't what he'd been expecting. It was well located in relation to the stage and was easy to see all that was going on beneath them. The evening was his and Cathryn's first public appearance as husband and wife. They sat to Arthur and Daphne's right, the two women sitting beside each other.

Immediately, he felt a thousand eyes staring up at the box, all vying for even the slightest glimpse of the newlyweds, though Charles knew better. Some wanted to see the duke's brother who'd been hidden away all these years. The mad spare.

They would be disappointed that he didn't fit the image they had in their mind's eye. As he peered down at the stage, he felt Cathryn's reassuring hand on his. It was odd to him that something as simple as her touch soothed the beast within him.

Lights began to go down and people scurried to their seats. The peerage, though, took their time. Scurrying would be like mice, and they were anything but. For them, an evening at the theater was to be seen and to add to one's list of growing acquaintances. To be seen in the company of only the best the ton had to offer.

Even in the box with the lowered lights, he felt their stares. He pretended not to notice but rather to take a great interest on what was happening on the stage in front of them. Everyone else was mesmerized about what was transpiring. He knew he couldn't leave right now. That would be rude, or they would think something was wrong. That the madman was barely civilized to be part of society. His poor wife would be pitied as they talked amongst themselves about how she could have been duped into marrying such an oddity.

Feeling her hand squeeze his gently, he gazed at her momentarily. "Are you enjoying yourself?" he heard her ask.

"Yes, I find it quite unique," he replied. "And I'm not talking about the play."

She returned her attention back to the stage and he continued with his vigilance of seeing who was who by where they were when they sat. The royal box sat empty this evening. He decided they didn't attend every performance. They saved their appearances for performers they thought well of.

Charles heard polite clapping as the first half concluded. It wasn't the enthusiastic applauding one would expect, but then the ton was never known for being over enthusiastic.

He and Arthur stood and waited as Daphne and Cathryn left the box. Joining his brother for a whiskey, he wondered how long it would take before someone knocked on the door wanting a word with Arthur. His brother was, after all, an MP now, having taken over their late father's position, and there was always someone who wanted Arthur's ear. Coming to visit him at the box was a good excuse to meet Arthur's mad brother.

The entire thing was absurd. Perhaps true to some degree, but absurd nonetheless. It would make the perfect novel. The entire idea was one he'd been contemplating for a while but he had the one project he had to finish. For now, he'd make notes, figure it out, and write it soon.

"What do you think of the play?" Arthur finally asked.

"Truthfully? I found the audience far more entertaining than what was transpiring on stage."

Arthur chuckled. "I'm afraid I have to agree with you on this one."

"Poor acting and execution," Charles continued.

A knock on the box door had both brothers tense up. "Save that thought," Arthur said as a well-dressed man entered. Overweight, hair slicked back, his face flushed from drink. He headed straight for Charles.

"You must be the mad twin," the man said without introducing himself.

"Charles, this is Percival Williams, Marquess Sutherby."

"My pleasure," Charles said. "I am afraid you've gotten your stories up. I am not mad. A twin, yes, but mad? Never."

"I apologize. How are you enjoying London?"

Before Arthur could put a stop to this, he saw his brother was going to answer the man. "It's been quite interesting. There is so much to see and do, but I long for the tranquility of the country."

"True. I do enjoy my summers at my summer country home." The marquess turned to Arthur, a slight not lost on either Charles or Arthur. "I do hope you and the duchess will join us for our famous country party."

"I'll check with her and see what's on her schedule. I've heard your parties are quite original and are talked about months after they've ended."

"You've heard correctly."

Charles heard the chimes indicating the second half of the play was about to begin. Hopefully now no one would come calling.

Just then the door swung open and in walked both women. They each accepted a flute of champagne a footman offered before returning to their seats. Quietly, Charles and Arthur took seats next to them and waited for the play to begin.

Again, the theater went dark and the first of the men moved

about back to find their wives. This time he did catch a glimpse of a small group of women sitting in a box and glancing in their direction. Word traveled fast during intermission about his attendance. Those who continued to look at the box were hoping for a sighting of him. This time, at least for now, he wouldn't give them what they wanted. He sat back in his chair and when that didn't work, he guided Cathryn to one of the chairs in the row behind them. Now they wouldn't be in the spotlight.

By the time the foursome climbed into the carriage after the performance, it was late. It had been harder than normal to get to the carriage as they seemed to be the center of attention. And that made it impossible for them to go to a restaurant for dinner. Luckily Daphne had the foresight to realize this might happen and asked the cook to make something simple for when they did arrive later in the evening.

When they finally sat down in the breakfast room, footmen served them Cornish pasties, which were still hot. Cook knew they were well liked and made for an easy dinner. With it there was a selection of cheese and seasonal fruit. Perfect for such a late evening out.

"This beats any fancy restaurant meal," Daphne muttered.

"No noise, no having to shout to have a conversation either," Cathryn agreed.

Charles, who had eaten two pasties along with fruit and cheese, pushed himself away from the table. "If you all will excuse me, there are some things I need to take care of before I retire for the night."

"It can't wait until morning?" Cathryn asked.

"No, I'm afraid not." With that, he walked out of the room, leaving the remaining three staring at each other with confusion.

Arthur spoke up first. "I believe he has a new idea for a book and just wants to write down notes, so they don't escape him."

"Oxford is coming up as well, and I'm sure he has to prepare for that," Cathryn said.

"You don't sound too happy about it," Daphne said.

"I'm proud of him, of course, and don't get me wrong, I'm fine with him going by himself. He just doesn't open up like most people."

"You knew that going in," Daphne reminded her.

"Yes, it's just he can be so eccentric and doesn't realize he's being odd."

"Give him time. He's adjusting better than I thought he would," Arthur said.

"I know, and I will," Cathryn replied. "If you two will excuse me. I'm sure you'd like part of what's left of the evening to yourselves. I'll see you both tomorrow."

Cathryn headed upstairs to their wing. Rather than bother her husband, she went to her dressing room and readied herself for bed. She picked up a book she'd started reading and headed to the sitting room. She startled when she saw Charles sitting in front of a writing desk furiously writing something down. He hadn't heard her come in, so she inched closer and gently placed her hand on his shoulder. He didn't appear to notice she was there.

"I'm going to go read in bed," she said, knowing saying anything regarding not staying up too late was wasted on Charles when he was in the middle of something.

Charles himself never recalled his wife having come to say good night. When his attention was focused on something such as his writing, he was completely immersed in his own little world. He knew he needed to try and fix that. How he wasn't sure, but one thing he was sure of was that it was late, and he was tired. The evening in particular had been exhausting. It was time to get some rest. Everything he'd just done would be there in the morning.

He hadn't realized how tired he was until his head hit his pillow. Cathryn lay beside him, facing toward the far wall, gently snoring. He snuggled in behind her, wrapping his arm around her. Immediately, he felt his body begin to respond to having her so close. He lay like that until he couldn't stand it any longer.

Turning her onto her back, he spread her legs and in moments, he was inside her. She was ready for him. How, he didn't understand, but he began a steady rhythm, and as he felt himself nearing his own orgasm, he gently placed his hand in between them, stroking her nub until she awoke. Startled by the sensation, she cried out as her body exploded in ecstasy. He found himself unable to control his own response and plunged in one final time, feeling his seed drain into her.

Rolling off her, Charles leaned over and kissed her, and she responded lazily. He pulled her close to him.

"That was an unexpected and nice surprise," she said softly, rubbing her hand across his chest.

He grunted.

Cathryn giggled at his response. "What does that mean?"

"I was agreeing with you. Did I do it wrong?"

"Heavens, no. It was wonderful."

"Good. It was for me too."

He felt her kiss the skin on his shoulder. "We should really try and get a few hours' sleep. The house will wake shortly."

"I find myself falling asleep."

The last thing he thought he remembered was Cathryn whispering the words "I love you."

Sleep overtook him before he had time to respond. Instead, he had dreams. Dreams of them somewhere tropical. He couldn't recall where as places which were hot year round didn't interest him. A year was supposed to have four seasons.

His parents appeared in his dream. It was hot and humid. Everyone was miserable. His parents were ignoring him almost like they didn't know who he was. What was this and where was he?

Not waking up, his mind found another dream, only in this one, he and Cathryn were riding horses on a beach. He liked to sneak out and do that on Wight. There was something about a horse cantering through the sand, the breeze running through your hair or standing knee high in the water that appealed to him.

In the dream, he watched as Cathryn rode her horse to him. She had a huge smile on her face and then everything turned dark. Was he dreaming this or was it real? Why was it dark?

WALKING INTO THE breakfast room, found his brother scouring the newspapers. Usually, Arthur didn't do this until he'd finished eating. This morning, he was doing both at the same time.

The two men exchanged pleasantries and Charles sat down while a footman set a plate filled with his favorites.

"Is something important going on? Are we at war?" Charles asked, picking up a piece of toast and slathering some marmalade on it.

"No, but you certainly were the talk of last evening. All the society pages are talking about you."

He shook his head and took a bite. "I don't know why. I certainly didn't do anything."

"People gossip, Charles."

"Yes, I know, but doesn't one have to do something odd to be gossiped about?"

Charles lowered his toast to his plate and stared at Arthur as reality set in. "I'm the oddity, aren't I? So now let's tell all of London since seeing me at the theater wasn't enough entertainment."

"I'm sorry."

"Don't be. I should be used to it by now. People are fascinated by me. I don't know why I can't just accept that fact and go about my life."

Arthur held up one of the newspapers. "Care to read one for yourself, or I could read it to you?"

He grabbed the paper and began reading the article. Nothing unusual. It was the author's opinion that he did not know why his brother, the duke, couldn't keep his twin out of sight and out of mind. Then they made mention of Cathryn, wondering how and why she married the eccentric gentleman.

Charles felt his teeth gnash as he continued to read the article. This was exactly why he didn't want to go out into society. He was perfectly happy with his life otherwise. Now people would stop and stare if they ran into him. Or they'd look at him in horror and back away from him. It was what had happened a few times on Wight. When it happened, he would simply disappear to his cottage and keep a low profile. He found people forgot quicker than they remembered.

"After my talk at Oxford, I think it's time to return to the country until all this blows over. Cathryn and Daphne don't need to be part of this."

"They won't be. If they are, Daphne will set the record straight, and I believe your wife is just as capable. Do not underestimate either of them."

"I'm sure you're right. Do I need to address this or ignore it as I usually do?" Charles asked his brother. He'd lost his appetite. It was easy for him to go through this. He never acknowledged any articles. The same needed to be done here. Still, he was sure it would affect Cathryn one way or another. It wasn't fair for her to get pulled into this situation. He would have to keep an eye on her and how she acted.

"Ignore it," Arthur replied.

"Ignore what?" Cathryn asked as she glided into the room. She looked breathtaking in a stunning lavender dress.

"It seems you and your husband made the society pages of some of the newspapers," Arthur said.

Cathryn sat down and, smiling, looked between both men. "That doesn't surprise me. I hope they were not too horrid."

"No, I've seen worse," Charles replied.

"The ton is so fickle. Something new will interest them and we'll be yesterday's news," Cathryn said.

"We'll return to Kent after my speech at Oxford."

"That's probably for the best," she agreed.

"You don't mind?"

She shook her head. "No, not at all. While I love London, there is only so much one can endure."

"Now you sound like Daphne," Arthur said with a laugh as he folded the newspapers neatly and moved them near his brother. He rose to his full height. "If you will excuse me, I need to tend to some correspondence."

Once Arthur left, Cathryn got up and took two of the newspapers from the small stack. Sitting back down, she placed them to one side as a footman set a plate in front of her. She wasn't a huge eater this time of day but appreciated toast along with tea.

"What are you doing?" Charles inquired.

"I want to see what they had to say."

Charles firmly shook his head. "You don't need to read such trash, and you don't need to get yourself upset."

"I'm not going to get upset, Charles."

He said nothing for a moment, mulling over how to word what he needed to say next. "You say that now. I've made a decision."

"What's that?"

"You're returning to Kent when I go to Oxford. Once I've finished my speech and business with them, I'll join you. I really see no point in staying here any longer than necessary."

"It's probably for the best, though I would rather go to Oxford with you. We could spend the night and leave for Kent the following morning."

"I suppose that would work. I just don't wish for you to be bored."

"I won't be. I'm sure they have shops and places to eat. I'll be fine, and once I've had my fill, I can go back to the room and wait for you."

Charles was once again intrigued by his bride. Obviously, she'd taken her time and thought this all out. He hadn't even thought about her being able to visit shops or bakeries. Just that she couldn't or shouldn't go with him when he went to Oxford.

He'd much rather them travel together than for her to go to Kent without him.

"Go ahead and look into it," he said.

"I have and I will. Thank you, Charles."

"No need to thank me. I simply don't want my wife traveling alone."

He stirred his tea before taking a sip. It was a delightful blend, one they served in Kent as well. He needed to find out what it was called or if it was blended in the kitchen.

"Would you like to take a walk, or have you things to do?"

"I need to finish preparing my notes. A word of advice, wife; it might be best to stay here for a day or two."

"I see. So you're hiding and expect me to do so as well? That is not going to happen."

Charles sighed. It was next to impossible for Cathryn to let things go. The better he got to know her, the more he noticed. "I was simply trying to spare you from the gossips, but if you aren't going to be bothered by their whispers and stares, go, have your walk. I have to finish preparing my presentation."

Rather than reply, Cathryn huffed, lifted her skirts, turned, and quickly walked out of the room.

CHAPTER FOURTEEN

THE NIGHT BEFORE they left for Oxford it had stormed, and Charles was worried that because of the magnitude of the storm, the roads would be left impassable. Luckily that hadn't happened, and they were able to leave with the sun shining.

That yellow sphere in the sky changed everyone's moods, including Cathryn's. She was humming and looking out the carriage window with great interest. Charles's mood was lightened because his wife was in a better mood than she had been.

Once he finished his business at Oxford, they would head toward Kent.

"Oh, Charles, this carriage is magnificent. I can't believe you purchased a carriage for us."

He had gone and spent the money to have a carriage built for them. It wasn't that Arthur wouldn't have let him use one of his, but he felt odd riding around without his brother in a coach that had a ducal seal. It was money well spent.

"I felt it was time to stop using Arthur's, even though he doesn't mind, and purchase my own. I'm pleased you like it so much. I will purchase another once we're settled in our own home."

"I thought we were going to stay at the manor?"

"We are for the time being," he replied. Charles wasn't ready to divulge to his wife that he had a man looking at some properties that he'd been told about or heard of in conversation. There was the one in Somerset and one in Gloucestershire. The latter was the one he was most interested in. The man he hired was going to see if he could find others. It wasn't that he didn't appreciate his brother's hospitality, but he truly wanted his own home. Living in the manor did give Cathryn and him an entire wing of the castle, but it wasn't the same.

Roxanne had suggested they could live in the dowager house, located on the far side of their estate. It also hadn't been occupied since Graham's grandmother's death but had been kept up as though she still lived there. She'd taken Cathryn to see it and she had adored it to use her phrasing. It was another possibility. But still, he wanted something that was their own. Not that he wasn't proud of his family and its history, but he hadn't been part of it the majority of his life and it felt more appropriate and right to have his own home. Not one that Arthur or the rest of his family gave him.

Cathryn drew him out of his thoughts with her enthusiasm. She could find joy in pretty much everything. He envied her for that.

"Charles! We're here! We've arrived in Oxford."

He nodded. "Very well. We'll go to the hotel first, so you can settle in, and I can go on to the university."

"Are you nervous?"

"No," he replied without a hint of emotion in his voice.

"I would be."

The coach pulled up in front of a hotel Charles had chosen for its proximity to shops and other merchants. It would keep his wife occupied for hours while he went to his appointment. He stepped out of the carriage and put his hand out to help Cathryn. She was taken in by all the uniqueness of a university town, looking everywhere except at the task at hand. Exiting the carriage, she was about to lose her footing, and he firmly took hold of her arm and saved her from what would have been an embarrassing situation.

He accompanied her to their room and freshened up before leaving her to her adventure. "I'll be back as soon as I can. Enjoy your afternoon. Thomas will be close by to take packages and help you if you should need it."

"Thank you and good luck," she said, lifting herself on her tiptoes to kiss him on the cheek.

He nodded and flashed a smile. One thing he never had gotten used to. Conversation that was nothing but a filler for awkward moments like this. Turning, he left the room and went down the stairs to his waiting carriage.

⟫⟪

HE FOUND DR. Richard White waiting for him outside one of the large rooms used for lectures. He appeared to be older than Charles knew him to be due to the shock of white hair he had. Otherwise, the professor wasn't much older than him.

The story of what had happened to him and what it all meant to his life fascinated Dr. White since he'd heard Charles speak to a small group of intellectuals on Wight. He had been among those who'd come to hear him. They'd stayed in contact ever since then.

"Good to see you, Charles," he boomed.

"A pleasure, Dr. White."

"Richard, please."

"We're in public. I meant to show respect to a colleague."

"Very well. I heard you married. Congratulations are in order."

"Yes, and thank you."

"Did you bring her with you?"

"Yes, we're heading back to Kent in the morning so she's going to shop and whatever else women do while I am here."

"Smart man. If you're ready, we can get started. I think you'll like this particular group. Very curious, aren't afraid to ask questions."

"Yes, I am ready."

They entered the lecture hall, Charles standing to the side while Dr. White spoke. He gave a brief outline about Charles and how they'd met, and the work Charles did in addition to how hard it had been. The smiles and smirks while he forged ahead with various projects and how he overcame them.

When his time came, Charles took to the podium, notes in hand as he began to speak. Starting from the beginning, he recounted the day when he was told of his sponsor's death and what transpired next.

Finding out he had two siblings, he was grateful for that but wondered how much, if anything, they knew about him. Social situations were complicated for him and what he found out was that he had memories of his early childhood before being sent to Wight. He had vague recollections of him and his brother playing together and how their sister tried to tag along.

Questions followed, and he was delighted at the thought put into them. They wanted to know what his thoughts were when he found out he had a brother and then finding out his brother was indeed his twin. How isolated he'd really been until he found his brother. Did he have those feelings now?

Professor White interrupted to reveal the books Charles had written and the one he'd just finished. It was a cue for Charles to introduce all of them to his books.

The books, he told them, had come as a way to learn about himself, his reactions to new situations.

Someone asked him if he ever felt as though he were very different from others and how did he cope with others' reactions.

Finally, the class ended. It had to. Other students were waiting as Dr. White's class had run over his allotted time. No one seemed to mind.

His head was swirling from all the interest and questions. As he walked out into the corridor, lingering students approached him, asking questions they needed the answer for. Dr. White stood to one side and watched. Charles found himself ready to return and find his wife. He'd been working there for some time.

"Thank you all for the interest. However, if you'll excuse me, I have other obligations needing my attention."

Dr. White took him through the hallways to his own office. "I do hope you'll consider coming again."

"I would be honored."

"Perhaps we could see about getting you on staff."

Shaking his head, Charles replied, "I don't think that would work. I have little to no background."

"If you want, I could make some inquiries," White persisted.

"In the future, perhaps. Right now, I have a lot going on with my latest book and a few other things my brother asked me to look into."

"I understand. I'll be in touch about the students' reactions."

"I would love to hear what they have to say."

The two men parted ways and Charles walked to his carriage. Satisfied by the success of his talk with Professor White's students, Charles felt he'd overcome a major obstacle. It hadn't been the first time speaking to a group, but these students took their studies seriously. For a moment, he wished he'd had the opportunity to go to university. Instead, life had dealt him an entirely different set of cards, and he would make the most of that fact.

Arriving at his waiting carriage, Charles made the decision to continue walking for a time. They could follow behind him and when he was tired of walking, he could climb in and ride the rest of the way.

Glancing at a huge clock on the side of a large tower, he noted there was plenty of time for him to meet Cathryn and have tea together.

The afternoon was magnificent. Blue skies prevailed and white puffy clouds dotted the horizon. He finally climbed into the carriage and rode the rest of the way. It was the best way to save time. He would make it back with plenty of time for him and Cathryn to have a nice, leisurely tea.

She must have seen the carriage pull up and stop as she came rushing out of the hotel. "Did you have a nice afternoon?"

"Yes, I did," she replied. "From the look on your face, I would say you did as well."

He nodded. "Yes, it was a remarkable group of students."

"Good."

"Did you enjoy yourself?"

She nodded. "There are a lot of shops unique to the university."

He patted her hand, which was tucked in the crook of his arm. "This is one of the oldest universities, so I imagine a lot of places have been here for eons. Handed down from generation to generation."

"You're right. I visited a couple like that. It made it a lot more interesting, knowing the patrons of some of the shops were part of a unique group."

He stopped in the middle of the lobby, knowing the hotel did serve tea in their restaurant in the afternoon and they also would bring it to your room. "Where would you like to have tea? In the restaurant or in our room?" He really hoped she would choose their room. He'd been around enough crowds of people for one day, but he would do whatever she chose. He couldn't force her to live life completely around his idiosyncrasies.

"Would you mind terribly if we had it in the privacy of our room? I'd like to relax, take off my shoes, and enjoy some quiet. I'm sure you would as well after being around all those young men."

He gave her a lop-sided grin. "Wait here. I'll go arrange to have tea sent to our room."

"I'll be right here," she replied.

Walking over to the desk, Charles informed the gentleman behind the desk what he wanted. Today was a good day.

Chapter Fifteen

TWO DAYS LATER, on a sun-filled cloudless summer day, Charles and Cathryn made their way to Gloucestershire to meet up with an agent over the possibility of purchasing an estate south of Tetbury.

Endless discussions with both himself, Cathryn, and even his valet always led to the same conclusion. In order to have a new life and successes, a new home not attached to his family was the best way to accomplish that.

The estate wasn't as stunning as the one in Somerset. It wasn't sitting on the edge of a cliff, which had made him nervous that the entire house could slide into the water below if the right storm came around.

The estate in Gloucestershire had been built in the eighteenth century in a Georgian neo-classical style. From the drawings and even the photograph he'd seen, Charles was positive this was where he wanted to spend the rest of his life with his wife.

There were acres and acres of gardens which had become neglected in the last year or two. The widow of the property had spent little time at the estate and wanted it sold as quickly as possible as she had no intention of ever returning. According to the agent, her thinking was if she wasn't going to live there, there was no reason to keep it up as it had been. The interior had been kept as though she was away on a trip to some exotic land. A skeleton staff had been kept on for this purpose.

As they turned onto the drive, he noticed Cathryn make a face upon seeing the grounds. He said nothing as they continued to the house.

The house was exactly as he'd seen and looked even more magnificent than he could've imagined. He glanced over at his bride and noted she was now smiling.

As the carriage came to a stop in front of the house, a dark-headed man met them. Mr. Stanley, the agent charged with finding a new owner for this estate, greeted them as they stepped out of the carriage.

"Please overlook the grounds. They've been neglected since the owner died nearly two years ago," he said. "They were once magnificent, and I know with the right gardeners they will be again."

"I have no doubt," Charles replied.

Walking into the house, Mr. Stanley gave them a brief history of the house. Cathryn didn't stay; instead, she began walking around the entry hallway with its black and white marble floor. A large round mahogany table sat in the center of the room. A vase full of flowers completed the stunning room's possibility. Just beyond the table were two joined staircases which led to the family rooms.

Stanley showed them to one of the drawing rooms which was done in shades of blue, down to the silk wall covering and matching upholstery on the furniture.

"This is beautiful, isn't it, Charles?"

"Yes, it is." He turned to the agent who was standing to one side of the room to let them take in the tastefully-done room. "Does the furniture come with the house?"

"If you want it, arrangements can be made. I have specific instructions to try and sell it as you see it. She wants nothing from the house."

Glancing at Cathryn, Charles knew she'd made up her mind. "Draw up the papers."

He noted his bride had a huge smile on her face but turned to check out a rug in the center of the room. She was happy, and he knew this was going to settle a lot of issues. Most importantly, they would have a home of their own.

"You're interested in the entire estate?"

"Yes, house furnishings, all outbuildings and land," he replied.

The agent nodded, overwhelmed, Charles was sure, that it was such an easy sale. "How will you be paying?"

"Cash. Have the papers drawn up, sent to my solicitor for him to read. If everything is as it should be, we can set up a meeting to handle the transaction. Shouldn't take more than a few days."

"As you wish, milord."

Charles turned to Cathryn, who was now looking at a vase placed on a table. "Anything you want to add?"

"Keep the staff already here. We'll figure out how many more people we need once we move in. I'd also like the house to be given a thorough cleaning before we arrive."

"That is easily arranged, milady."

"Before we leave, I'd like to walk to the stables," Charles said.

"This way, milord."

"While you're doing that, I think I'll walk through the house again," Cathryn said.

He nodded and turned to walk outside with the agent. Charles wanted to get a better look at fencing and the stables in order for him to have an idea how much work was going to have to be done. The fencing was in relatively good condition, as were the stables when they arrived. He was introduced to the stablemaster first thing. The man, James, was knowledgeable about his entire domain.

"Make a list of what needs to be done. Fencing, horses, what-ever needs repair or upkeep. We'll go over it once my wife and I move in," Charles told the man.

"I shall, milord."

"My man of business will be in touch once he's read the papers. I can't imagine there being anything wrong with them."

"They'll be just as you wish them, milord. It's a pity, but the widow has not taken an interest in any of this. I hope you realize what a sweet deal you're getting."

"Yes, I'm aware."

They walked back to the house in relative silence. Charles knew while Arthur and Roxanne would be happy for him, they might also be cautious at the simplicity of the deal. Months ago, he wouldn't have been able to do this. He'd be too uncomfortable with the strangers and would want to flee. That was before Cathryn did what she did best. Guiding him through the societal challenges.

He and Cathryn bid the agent good-bye and climbed into their waiting carriage. The man would see to getting this transaction ready. Once signed and money exchanged hands, Charles would be a landowner, an estate owner. Best yet, his wife was very, very happy.

"I'm so glad we decided to come and look at this place," she said.

Nodding, Charles agreed. "As am I. It's perfect for us and is not far from anything, like London or Arthur's estate."

"It is perfect."

"I'm glad to hear you say that. Once it is ours, please feel free to make your rooms your own. If you don't like something, replace it or redo it in the case of wallpaper and paint."

She giggled. "I didn't know we were going to sleep in separate suites."

"We're not, but it's right next to mine, and I'm sure you'd like somewhere feminine to change and bathe."

"Maybe we can make your suite more neutral."

That wasn't happening. Not unless he had no final say on everything. "We'll see. I want to move in and get a feel for it before I go redoing it."

"That's a smart idea," she replied.

"I want to wait on the rest of the house. I think we need to live there before deciding to redo anything. Besides, it was redone by the woman we're purchasing from."

"Agreed."

"I can see lots of rides to explore the estate," he said.

"Do you know if there's an estate manager still on the property?"

He shook his head. "I believe the manager is there still. I'll have to make some inquiries."

"That's a very vital position, I remember my father saying," Cathryn said.

"It is."

That was the last Charles remembered saying until his wife woke him as the carriage pulled on to the drive of the family estate. It had been some very busy days. The best being finding their perfect place to call home.

It was late afternoon when they arrived. They quickly learned that Arthur and Daphne had gone to Roxanne and Graham's for a visit. That meant he and Cathryn could go to their rooms without having to socialize with them. Not that he minded, but there were times like now when after a long ride, you simply wanted some privacy and quiet.

Cathryn went to order tea, and he made his way to their suite so he could relax. There was a lot to be done, and as soon as he had possession of the estate, there would be even more to be done. He wouldn't have Frazier begin packing until he had a date on the purchase being finalized. He'd of course tell him what was coming.

He lay down on the bed and picked up a notebook he kept and began writing. There was so much that would be coming up. The move wasn't simply just that easy. There were lots of details that would go along with it. He knew he could handle them; it was just something new. He had a wife, and her happiness and well-being were important to him.

He'd done some research on the house and property before they went to see it. The estate had been self-sustaining with cattle, horses, and numerous other types of livestock. Cheese was made, as well as preserves and smoked meats such as hams. Everything one would expect to find on a large, fully functional estate.

Making some notes to ask the estate manager, he finished up just as Cathryn walked into the sitting room with a footman following her with a large tray which he knew to be tea, sandwiches, and other sweet goodness.

"What are you doing?" she asked, popping her head in.

"Making notes."

"Tea is here."

"Let me finish this sentence and I'll join you," he said.

"Would you like me to fix you a plate?"

"I can do it."

He wasn't used to someone waiting on him the way Cathryn did. He'd turned out learning how to do for himself, because apart from his early memories with Arthur and Roxanne, he'd had to learn how to take care of himself. Relinquishing that was indeed hard for him, and he realized how much Cathryn wanted to do some of that herself.

Setting the notebook back on the bedside table, he walked out to join his wife. She was pouring two cups of tea. Beyond that were some small sandwiches and cake. He hadn't realized how hungry he was until he laid eyes on the food.

"Is that seed cake I see?" he asked.

"Yes, and there's marmalade cake as well. Would you like some?"

"Most certainly, along with a couple of those egg sandwiches."

"Go find yourself a spot to eat and I'll bring them."

He found himself going to a cream-colored upholstered chair with a large table to his right. The chair was comfortable, more than most in the room. Most were not upholstered, instead with simple cushions on the seats. They were upright and finished in dark stain. Cathryn unfortunately was going to get to occupy one of the leftovers from the Elizabethan period.

She brought him a steaming cup of tea and set it on the table near him. When she returned moments later, she carried a plate of sandwiches and cakes. He thanked her and waited for her to bring her own tea and cake.

"I'm glad you thought of this. I don't know about you, but I am tired from lack of sleep and traveling."

"I am." She glanced at the window. "Looks like a storm might be coming in."

"It does. Won't have a chance to go out for a walk before it hits. I for one am satisfied with staying indoors."

She smiled demurely in his direction. "As am I. I'm sure we can find something to occupy our time for a couple of hours."

He pretended not to have heard her or what she was insinuating. For being a shy, inexperienced lover, she now looked for ways for them to be together. He enjoyed this hidden side of her and waited to see what she would do next.

In a bold move, Cathryn stood in front of him and unfastened his trousers and coaxed his throbbing cock out of its hiding place. She lifted her skirts and impaled herself with his cock. She rode him with bold confidence Charles hadn't seen before. He knew he couldn't last, not with the way she was testing him. Taking one hand, he began to finger her, which made her jump and beg for more. As she began to unravel, he picked her up off his cock and stood her up as he did the same. Bending her over the chair, he thrust himself as far as he could go and exploded deep inside her.

Withdrawing, he fastened his trousers and ran a hand through his tousled hair. Still breathless, Cathryn came and kissed him before walking away toward her own suite of rooms.

"I warned you I had something naughty in mind," she said as she opened the door.

"Yes, you did, and I certainly wasn't expecting that."

Her laughter was the last thing he heard as she slipped through the doorway and closed the door.

THE FOLLOWING TWO weeks were filled with preparations for their move to their new home. Charles and Arthur made the trip to London together for the papers to be signed. Arthur had meetings for Parliament, but he made sure his schedule was clear when it came to the attorney and estate. Charles knew his brother wished he would stay but understood his reason for being on his own.

He had finished his latest book and was now in the process of preparing it for his publisher. His manuscripts were always pristine when he turned them over to them.

Oxford had invited him to speak yet again, only this time they wanted him to come on a more regular basis. His reputation was growing. So, while in London, he and Arthur made the journey to the university. Charles was ecstatic when it was mentioned he would be back to give the students more of what they seemed to be interested in—Charles himself.

While he was away in London, Cathryn, with help from Daphne and even Sam the parrot, got everything packed and ready for the journey. Books filled a lot of boxes, along with Charles's papers. She hadn't asked him about packing them for him, but took the utmost care in making sure everything was kept in the order he had them in.

The only people missing were Roxanne and Graham. They had departed for the Continent so Graham could conclude some business deals he had going. Vienna and Antwerp were their immediate destinations.

Arthur promised to come over to see the house and help Charles with what he needed to make it a working estate once again. Part of that would be a knowledgeable estate manager.

All the way to their new home, Cathryn was talking non-stop she was so excited. Like a magpie or Sam, Daphne's parrot. At first, Charles thought she was talking directly to him but soon realized she wasn't.

They had a perfect day for moving into their new home. It was a beautiful summer day, a blue sky with hardly a cloud in the sky. When a cloud did appear, it was a large puffy one lazily floating by.

Finally, Charles thought he best put Cathryn's non-stop chattering to a slowed down version by trying to hold a conversation with her.

"You wouldn't be excited, would you?" he asked.

"I'm beyond excited!" she exclaimed. "This is our home. I'm mistress of my own house now."

"Yes, you are."

She turned to face him more directly. "Does the estate have a name? If not, we should choose one."

"Yes, I believe it does. I found the name quite odd. Xanadu, I believe was what the widow and her husband renamed it."

"That is odd. I don't care for it at all, do you?"

"Not particularly."

"Then we must come up with a proper new name," she said.

"Yes, I suppose we should. The perfect name will come to us; you'll see."

"You're right. Once we've settled in, something will come to us."

He cleared his throat. "Have you written your sister or brother?"

"No, I thought I'd wait."

"Why?"

"I wanted my first letter to them to be from our home, and I'm thinking of asking them to dine with us."

"Perhaps ask them to stay a few days?"

"We'll see. Just letting them know where we've settled is enough for now," she said.

"Fair enough."

The carriage was nearing the estate. Charles could tell by the landscape. It had been neglected for a couple of years. Slowing, the carriage made a left turn onto a gravel drive. Majestic oak trees lined each side of the drive, just as Charles remembered.

Beyond the oaks, on either side of the drive were two cleared grass lawns. Charles wondered what, if anything, they were used for. His thoughts were interrupted by his bride.

"The house, the house! Doesn't it look majestic, Charles?"

"Yes, it does. Once we get things taken care of, it'll look even more regal."

"It's perfect."

He grunted as he continued to look out the window. As they neared the house, the tidier the grounds appeared. The remaining gardener had been hard at work and Charles was sure he'd had help, because upon the completion of the estate transfer, he'd sent word to clean it up and begin restoring the gardens and estate in general.

Knowing he didn't like change of any kind, purchasing this estate was a major change. All had been since he had left Wight. Charles thought he'd come a long way in accepting people as they were, and as long as they didn't get into his space, he was content.

Sometimes he would even go as far as to force himself into socializing. At first, it had been extremely difficult. Now it was still hard, but he was learning what triggered his anxiety.

"We're here! We're home, Charles!" Cathryn grabbed his hand, the one closest to her, and squeezed it so hard he thought it might break off.

"We are indeed. You may let go of my hand, my love." He rubbed his aching extremity as she continued looking out the window of the carriage. Love, my love. Where had that come from? It was odd. Endearments were foreign to him. He rarely used them because he found them out of character for himself. Was this the beginning of a change?

The carriage came to a stop in front of the house. He thought Cathryn was going to burst through the carriage door rather than wait for a footman to open it and escort her out. She was that excited. Instead, he opened the door and disembarked, putting his hand out to assist his bride.

The front door had opened in the meantime and the butler walked out. He neared them before bowing to them both.

"Milord, milady. I trust you had an uneventful journey?"

"Yes," Charles said. "Did our things arrive?"

"They did, milord. Everything was taken care of. If you want anything moved, feel free to tell me and I'll have it taken care of."

"Thank you. I'll keep that in mind."

"I'm sure you'd like to freshen up after your journey." He extended a hand and followed behind them to the main hall.

Picking up a letter that had been sitting on a center table, the butler passed it to Cathryn. "This came for you this morning, milady."

"Thank you," she replied. She took the envelope and looked it over carefully. It was a fancy script but she had no idea who could have sent it. She'd open it in the privacy of their chambers.

"Would you care for something to eat?"

"A light lunch would suffice," Charles said. "A pot of tea, some cheese, bread, and fruit should do."

"Where would you like to dine, milord?"

"In our chambers. The sitting room."

He and Cathryn made their way to the chambers. When he closed the door behind them, she took off her shoes and set them to one side. With her letter in hand, she sat in a chair nearest the windows.

She broke the seal and removed the letter. After reading and rereading it, she burst into a smile. "Charles! I've been invited to play for the Prince of Wales and his wife, Princess Alexandra, in two weeks' time."

"That's wonderful! Where will you perform?"

"It doesn't say. Only that the prince's secretary will be in touch with details."

"That's quite an honor."

"It is. I'll write a reply once we've finished our meal."

"That would be smart, letting them know you accept and add any questions you may have," he said. "I'm proud of you."

"I wonder if there's some specific occasion or if it's simply another one of their parties."

"I'm sure you'll find out soon," he replied.

"The prince is known for enjoying a good party," she said, placing the letter and envelope on a nearby table.

"We'll go to the music room after we eat and see if the piano needs tuning. If it does, I'll get someone out here immediately."

"I can still play it as is. It would just be nice if it were in tune," she replied.

She walked over to a small round table near the windows. It had obviously been used as a place to take meals if the occupant didn't care to go downstairs to eat.

At that moment, someone knocked on the door. Charles went over and opened the door to let the footmen in with their meal. He instructed them where to leave the food and waited until they left before joining Cathryn.

He sat down and watched as she poured them each a cup of tea. She passed one to him and placed the other where she was going to sit.

"This is nice," she said, surveying the various plates. She passed an empty one to him and sat down. He watched as she chose a piece of each cheese, some apple slices, a piece of warm bread, some cold roasted chicken.

He slathered butter on the chunk of bread in his hand. "I agree. This is nice."

"It is. Not too much. Just enough choices," she replied.

"What would you like to do when we finish eating?"

"First, I would like to see what condition the piano is in. After that, see if my things are being put away. Perhaps take a bath and change clothes."

"Yes, I suppose I should check on Frazier and what he's up to."

He watched as she picked up a piece of cheddar and popped it in her mouth. It was sensual how easy it came to her.

"While you're doing that, I should find the housekeeper and set up a time for us to meet in the next few days."

"What for?" Charles asked.

"The housekeeper is the one who makes sure the household is running smoothly. We meet regularly, and she comes to me if something urgent occurs."

"Makes sense. Like an estate manager, only inside."

"Yes. I'm going to meet her in the music room. If the piano needs tuning, I can instruct her to get someone out immediately."

"I thought…" Charles stopped himself. She was so excited right now with everything going on, she probably didn't recall something she said an hour ago. He'd let it go. It was nice to see her in this state.

"What?"

"Never mind. I answered my own question."

"I'm going to reply to the Prince of Wales's letter first and I'll ask what he would like me to play," she said.

"Very well. I'm off to find Frazier."

His wife was so engrossed in writing to the prince that Charles doubted she heard a word he said. He left the room in search of his valet. After that, he decided to take a walk to the stables and make sure their horses had settled in and to introduce himself.

CHAPTER SIXTEEN

N O ONE WAS in the music room when Cathryn walked into the room. It was a large room, perfect for what she needed. In the center of the room was a black grand piano. The black shone in the sunlight. To one side was a harp and in another corner there was a harpsichord. The entire room had recently been re-done in a musical theme. Chairs and a settee were all done in a pattern of musical notes while others were simply a dark cream. With a smile, she noted the wall covering matched the upholstery. Someone had put a lot of thought into the room.

Sitting down at the piano, Cathryn began to play something simple to hear the notes and see if it was out of tune or not.

"The piano and harpsichord were tuned two months ago, milady," a voice from the doorway said.

Turning to look, Cathryn noted a woman dressed in dark gray, clutching a book of some sort. Probably her diary where she kept notes on the household. She thought the woman's statement was odd.

"That's good to hear as I play every day," Cathryn replied.

"It'll be nice to have music back in the house."

"You must be Mrs. Thompson," Cathryn said. "I'm Lady Cathryn."

"Yes, milady. Would you like to go over details of the house-hold?"

"Yes, I think that will suffice for today." Cathryn stood from the piano bench and walked over to the woman. "Please sit."

Mrs. Thompson sat in a cream-colored brocade chair across from the chair Cathryn had chosen.

"I thought we should at least meet. You've answered my big question about the piano. I must have it in perfect pitch so I may rehearse. You see, the Prince of Wales has invited me to play for him and the princess. Once I hear when it is and what he'd like me to play, I'll be able to practice with some direction."

"That's quite an honor, milady."

"Yes, it is. Unexpected, I must say. I'm not sure where he heard me play."

"I'm sure you'll do splendidly," she said. "Where should we start?"

"How many on staff and do we need more? I know my husband will want more staff for the gardens."

"Of course. For now, I think we have enough staff."

"That's good to hear," Cathryn replied.

"If you like, I can arrange for Cook to join us. She can best tell you what she might need."

"The kitchen is her domain, I assume."

"Yes, it is."

Cathryn smiled. "I can respect that."

The housekeeper had opened her book and quickly read whatever it said. "What time do you like to dine in the evening?"

"If we're alone, probably seven-thirty. Later, of course, should we have guests."

Mrs. Thompson began writing in her book while Cathryn discreetly watched. The woman had been here quite a while so Cathryn decided the housekeeper knew a lot more about the estate.

"How long ago did the previous lady need to purchase things like sheets and bath towels for the house?"

"Everything is pristine and new. Since she knew the estate was up for sale, and would probably be sold as is, furnished, she instructed that everything be replaced with new."

"Which you did?"

"Of course," the housekeeper replied.

"That's awfully thoughtful for a woman who is selling her home."

"I suppose since she moved in here when it was in a neglected state, she would make sure the next resident wouldn't have to deal with that."

Cathryn took a moment to digest what she'd just been told. It was highly unusual for a mistress of the house to do something so generous, but the gesture wasn't lost on Cathryn. "Is there anything I should be aware of?"

"No, but if you'd like to meet, I can take you through the house tomorrow morning."

"I think that's a splendid idea. The only thing I ask is that the temperature in this room be kept consistent. It's better on the instruments and I'll be using this room quite a lot."

"Yes, milady. Is there anything else?"

"Not now. I'll meet you here in the morning."

Mrs. Thompson nodded her head, turned, and walked out of the room. Cathryn decided she and the housekeeper were going to get along quite well. Mrs. Thompson wasn't condescending because her new mistress was young and seemed to listen to everything Cathryn had to say. Having someone who knew what she was doing and didn't need to be watched over gave Cathryn peace. The last thing she wanted to do was spend most of her days taking care of household matters.

Returning to the piano and sitting down, Cathryn began to play a piece by Beethoven she liked to play for practice. As her fingers flew across the keys, she kept going. She would practice something extra for the prince in case there was time during her upcoming performance.

Noticing a stack of music on a nearby chair, Cathryn left the piano bench and stood over the sheets. There were many pieces of various composers; the two who seemed to stand out were

Mozart and Handel. Mozart's music could be quite dark.

She decided to separate the music sheets by composer. It would give her a good idea of what she had to work with. One by one she made piles on the floor, and if a sheet came up by an unknown composer, she placed it in a pile of its own. Unfortunately, there were none like this, so she stuck with her task until it was finished.

One by one she picked up each pile and stacked it neatly in its own file on a small table. She ended up with five different composers, all of whom she had played at least one piece of theirs. Everything was now neat and tidy, making all easier to go through the piles.

Wondering what Charles was doing, she left the music room in search of him. She knew he wouldn't have been able to stay in one place for long, so she backtracked to where Frazier was working.

"How long ago did he leave?"

"It's been a while now, milady," came Frazier's reply. "He did mention he was heading to the stables."

"Makes sense."

"Is there anything I can help you with?"

She shook her head. "No, I just thought I'd see what he might be doing," she replied.

"He doesn't seem as overwhelmed with everything that was entailed with this move. When we moved from Wight, he was quite anxious."

"That was different. It wasn't his choice. This time it is his decision."

Frazier arched a brow. "You're right. I hadn't thought of it that way."

"He's going to be okay, Frazier."

"I've always known that. He's simply never been given a chance."

She agreed with the valet and turned to leave. "I'm off to explore the house. Thank you for all you do for Charles."

He truly wasn't expecting a compliment and Cathryn could see his face redden ever so slightly. He mumbled something, but she didn't stay around to find out what it was. She didn't want to embarrass him more than she already had. He deserved to be complimented. Charles wasn't easy at times. She knew that, even in the relatively short time she'd known her husband. He wasn't a man to share his feelings. Even being excited for her chance to play in front of royalty was hard for him. He didn't understand what all the fuss was about. Instead, now, he said little, leaving himself the ability to absorb what he'd just learned and respond appropriately.

She was confident having moved to their own estate would be a great help to his self-esteem. He was smart, but because of some idiosyncrasies, he'd been deemed mad. There were more epithets, but mad was the easiest one people used. Charles was anything but mad.

CATHRYN PROMPTLY RECEIVED the music the Prince of Wales and his wife wanted to hear the night of her performance. She had four pieces of their choosing, and two could be of her own. The pieces weren't complicated or overly long, but they weren't ones she played on a regular basis, nor did she believe they were compositions the public heard at concerts often. They were what their majesties wanted, and who was she to challenge them? She would choose one popular piece for one of her two. The other she wasn't sure of yet.

Practice became all-consuming for her. She would begin right after breakfast and play non-stop until she was satisfied with how each piece sounded and how well she played them. There was little time for anything else. Everything had to be perfect. If she impressed their majesties, it could lead to her playing for others privately like this soiree or publicly.

She hadn't given thought that her non-stop practicing might get on others' nerves, but her parents had raised her that if you were good at something, you perfected it even if that meant disrupting the daily harmonic balance of the house.

In the evenings during dinner, she would listen attentively to her husband tell her about his day and accomplishments about the estate. Cathryn listened, but her mind was never far from her music.

"Cathryn, I'm afraid I have a conflict," he said, a serious tone to his voice.

"What sort of conflict?"

"I am supposed to do a talk at Oxford the day of your performance for their majesties."

"We can meet at the house and go from there. I don't see the conflict," she said.

"I'm expected to attend a dinner afterwards."

She mulled over what he just told her. "How long have you known about this?"

"Since yesterday."

"I see."

Charles cleared his throat. "I apologize for the inconvenience."

She slammed her hand down on the table. "This is the most important night of my life and all you can do is offer an apology for being unable to attend. I demand you cancel or change the date."

"I can't," he replied.

"Can't or won't," she barked. "For God's sake, Charles, I'm playing for royalty. I think that trumps anything you might have going on that evening."

"You're being selfish, Cathryn."

She shook her head. "I'm not. If I were in your shoes, I'd cancel."

"I'll meet you at the house," he said.

"Don't bother. I'm going to go on alone. This way you don't

have to rush."

"I appreciate your gesture, but I simply can't cancel."

"Can't or won't?"

He sighed and repeated, "Won't."

"That's rich," she replied. "You know what? Accompany me if you want, or go do whatever it is you think is more important. I'll be just fine without you."

Without another word, Cathryn bolted from the room. Her anger was growing, and she didn't dare stay and continue the conversation for fear of making the situation worse. She kept walking until she found herself at the door of her bedchamber. Hesitating for a moment, but still angry and frustrated, she opened the door and walked in. She locked the door behind her before crossing the sitting room to the door that adjoined their two suites. She locked that door as well.

Before she spoke to Charles again, they both needed to cool off. They were both angry and wanted things their own way. Normally, she would work things out with him, but she was playing for the prince and princess and there was no negotiating that. He'd either accompany her, or he wouldn't. It was his choice.

She walked around the room several times before continuing to the bed chamber itself. Slipping out of her slippers, Cathryn shut the heavy drapes and climbed onto the bed. As soon as she was comfortable, she felt her eyes grow heavy. She thought of taking a hot bath to loosen up her tense shoulder muscles but decided against it. She was too tired to get everything ready. It felt good to lie down somewhere comfortable after spending the day once again bent over the keyboard. After playing as much as she had been, it was near impossible to keep good posture.

That was the last thing she remembered. When she opened her eyes a crack, she realized she'd slept through the night. If she hurried, she could change and have breakfast. Should Charles be there, she would not bring up their heated conversation of the night before.

She needed to choose a gown to wear to the soiree. There wasn't time to have one made; besides, she had three gowns she'd not worn before. She'd had them commissioned when they'd been in town. After she had breakfast, she'd look over the gowns and make her decision.

Entering the dining room, she quickly noted there was no sign of Charles. His place was untouched, newspapers to his left where they always were kept. Perhaps he'd gone for a ride. His horse needed the exercise, and it was a good way for him to get to know the estate.

She sat down and waited for a footman to bring her a plate with eggs and bacon. A second plate with a good chunk of toasted bread was all she needed. Pouring a cup of tea, she waited for it to cool and instead spread blackberry jam over the toast.

Halfway through her meal and with no sign of Charles, she decided she would go in search of Frazier and see if he knew where he was. The valet had much more understanding of Charles's routines.

She heard a faint knock on the door and looked up and saw Mrs. Thompson and the cook enter.

"Cook has the menus for the next few weeks. I thought you'd like to go over them, make changes or additions."

"Yes, by all means. Now's a perfect time."

She motioned for the two women to sit. They hesitated for a minute but did sit down across from her.

"Perhaps you'd like to tell me some of your favorites," Cook said. She was a woman in her fifties, her gray hair pulled back. From what Cathryn understood, Cook had never worked for anyone else and apprenticed her skills right here in this house.

"My husband is the odd bird. He will try most anything and if he doesn't like it, then it will never grace our table again. As far as meat, the only one he will not eat is lamb or mutton. No game except for the occasional venison. There isn't a piece of fruit he doesn't like, and the same can be said of vegetables."

"What about fish or crustaceans?" Cook inquired.

"He eats both, but both must be extremely fresh."

She noted desserts hadn't been mentioned, which she decided she should address. "He likes most any sweet but is perfectly content with fruit and cheese as a dessert."

"He's not all that difficult. I've had worse," Cook said. "As far as guests, just let me know in advance so we can make adjustments or changes."

"No problem. I expect some time soon, my husband's brother, the duke and his wife, will come for a visit as will his sister."

"Just let us know," Mrs. Thompson said. Turning to Cook, Cathryn noticed the housekeeper make a gesture to the older woman. "We've taken enough of your time, milady."

Cathryn looked at Cook. "Let's just go through the menus and we'll see what works. I think that'll work best."

Cook nodded before both women left the room. This was something she was going to have to get used to, and it was going to take her a while to learn.

Finished with her breakfast, she left the dining room in search of Frazier, who wasn't hard to find. He was in Charles's dressing room putting things in their proper place.

"I haven't found him. Any suggestions?"

"None. He must have left in the middle of the night. From what I can tell, he took a change of clothes, which is not unusual for him. He's meticulous in that way. I'm sure he took some things from the kitchen. Outside of that, I haven't a clue. He was upset and when he gets that way, he goes and spends a day or two by himself."

"He never mentioned he did such," she said.

"He does it less and less, but it is good for him to do. Never goes too far, so I figure he's somewhere here on the estate."

"But he doesn't know the lay of the land."

Frazier smiled. "He's smart like that. Just give him a day or two. He'll be back just like new."

"Very well. You know him best."

"For now."

"If you'll excuse me, I've got a concert to prepare for," she said.

Frazier nodded. She left the room and found her way back to the music room. Charles certainly had impeccable timing for doing something a young boy might do. Still, she understood why, but that didn't mean she had to like it.

Sitting down at the elegant glossy black piano, Cathryn took a deep breath and began to play as though she were in front of the Prince of Wales and his wife. Putting everything she had into each piece, she didn't stop until all six pieces were played.

Then, sitting quietly with hands in her lap, she critiqued her work. How well had she played? What needed to be worked on and improved? Overall, she knew she'd done an excellent job. Three of the pieces, two picked out by the royal couple, were complex and harder than the others, but that's where she thrived.

Reminding herself she was her biggest critic, Cathryn readied herself to play it all again. When she finished, she would walk away for the day, no matter how she did.

Then there was the matter of Charles and where he'd disappeared to. While he was known to disappear when he had something on his mind or just needed to get away from people, Cathryn worried. He didn't know the estate yet as well as he knew the one on Wight, and she was afraid of where he might be. Except for the forests, the large pieces of natural land left untouched, Cathryn didn't know where he could be. She worried he might encounter a wild animal and couldn't defend himself. As far as she knew, he hadn't taken a gun with him for protection.

She would have a horse saddled and take a groom with her and go in search of her husband. If they couldn't find him, she would pray he was fine and simply needed time to himself.

Thinking back to the words they had exchanged made her tense. How could he not understand how important the evening meant to her? She was sure his colleagues would understand. After all, it wasn't every day a gentleman's wife was invited to play for royalty.

First, she had to find him in order to try and make him understand. She needed to be less demanding and more herself.

She went to her dressing room and changed into something appropriate for riding. As she was on her way upstairs, she asked a young boy in the kitchen to go on ahead to the stables and have her horse readied, along with a groom the stablemaster could spare to go with her. The young boy jumped up and went through the open door and down the path.

If it was any consolation, Charles knew how to survive. Survive. It was as though he was off in some exotic foreign land when he was on his own estate. Frazier wasn't too concerned, even with Charles being in new surroundings. If he wasn't concerned, maybe she was overreacting. Still, the idea that he spent the night outside rather than in the comfort of his own home was nerve-wracking to her.

She would look for as long as she could, alone. Not comfortable in anyone besides Charles's valet knowing, she didn't want the rest of the household discerning the real reason she would be riding today.

CHAPTER SEVENTEEN

CHARLES HAD BEEN up since the new day began to break. His first thoughts weren't about Cathryn or about the disagreement they'd had the day before. Having spent the night next to a fallen tree, he was ready to explore some more. The tree was near a large creek. He decided to follow the creek and see where it went. If he went right, he would end up near the house, and he was not ready to have to grovel. He was also going to stick to his plans and attend Oxford, even if it meant missing Cathryn's small concert in front of royalty. He was proud of her, but she needed to understand they were in this marriage for the long term, and that meant she didn't always get her way.

Following the creek to the left led him deeper into the vast wooded land. He could tell some of the trees were old growth, probably having been there for decades, if not longer. As he walked farther, Charles came across an old, deserted cottage. By the looks of the structure with weeds and vines growing on the walls, it was safe to say no one had lived here for many years.

Glancing at the roof, he was certain it was in decent shape. He walked to the front door and stepped in. There was nothing but an old table and chairs. Whatever else had been here was long gone. The likely scenario was the cottage had been lived in by a tenant. He couldn't think of anyone else. In fact, it was rather far from the others. Maybe it had once been used as a hunting cottage. That made more sense to him.

The structure wasn't easily seen. A person would have to know of its existence. For now, it would be a perfect place to go when he needed to be away from society. He looked around and spotted a much-used broom and took it and began sweeping the floor.

Hours passed when Charles stopped to admire his handiwork. He had a lot of work needing his attention, but he was satisfied it would make a perfect place when he needed solitude. He could slowly begin to furnish the cottage with what he might need. Mostly for the kitchen. He knew where the cheese was kept to age and where the smokehouse sat. He would pay both a visit and bring back what he would need. Water was easy since the creek was close by. This would be perfect indeed.

Charles was certain there was no search party looking for him. Frazier and Cathryn were probably the only ones who would do so, and they would do that discreetly so as not to alert the rest of the staff.

Recalling his "disappearances" while living on Wight, the more he went off by himself, the less anyone worried about him. He knew his way around, and people began to realize it was his way to recover. Frazier was the only one who knew exactly where he went, and even if he didn't go to his usual place, his valet always had a good idea of where he was.

One time, he managed to slip off Wight and ended up in London. He stayed there for over a week, using money he'd put aside for adventures. He never stayed where his family or their friends might run into him. He explored some of the villages on the outskirts of London. Some of the neighborhoods were less than pristine but he found them to be almost another world.

He would need to find some straw and blankets to make a place to lie down. The straw would scratch but, in a few days, it would pack down and he would have a bed of sorts. He didn't need much when he was off like this. Being ready to go back was the only way he'd return. He saw a side of Cathryn he'd never seen before. At least not directed at him. Just because she was playing for royalty, at their invitation, didn't mean that what she did was more important. This was something they were going to have to figure out together. Neither one was more important than the other, but she didn't see it. Yesterday was all about her. He needed for her to see they both were important in different ways.

Feeling his stomach protesting from the lack of food, Charles pulled out a crude fishing line and an apple. He would be having fish and knew exactly where to find it just by reading the water. He began to hike down to the water's edge when something made him freeze. Standing perfectly still, he listened closely.

Branches breaking, horse hooves. Slowly, he moved and slid in behind a rather large boulder to wait and see who was coming.

A moment later, he could see the outline of Cathryn. She was by herself, riding along the creek. She was looking for him. Though glad to see her, he wasn't ready to interrupt his time. His biggest hope right now was that she didn't veer away from the creek and find the old cottage. It couldn't be seen from the water's edge, which was good for him. She was looking around at her surroundings, looking and hoping she would find him.

He watched her until she was out of sight. Then stealthily, he followed behind her to see exactly where she was headed. She wasn't quiet about what she was doing. If she were hunting, she would chase all the animals away with her noise.

She would be in a meadow in a few minutes. That's where the creek ran, and hopefully she'd get tired of riding around without finding him. He would go to the creek's edge and drop a fishing line. Hopefully the fish would be biting.

For not knowing his wife for long, he certainly could figure out her movements. He just had to learn how to hold a conversation with her without making her angry. This time he had done it. Made her mad.

He hunted for wood of any kind to use in the hearth to cook. It would stand to reason a fire in there might go unnoticed during the day. There were lots of branches from nearby trees. He picked those up first and took them back to the cottage and dropped them in front of the door.

The sun was beginning to lower in the sky. He walked back out to the creek to check his lines. Both were empty. Determined to outsmart the fish, he dropped the lines back into the creek. He'd seen fish in there, but they weren't having anything to do with being someone's meal.

Back at the cabin, Charles picked up all the branches and put them either in the hearth or in a neat pile next to it before going in search of more.

Sometime during the night, a storm rolled in. Lightning was ferocious and the rain pelted down hard. He lit a candle and tilted his head toward the roof. It seemed to be holding well. He could find no cracks or water on the floor.

Lying back down on his makeshift bed, Charles closed his eyes. It was impossible not to notice what was going on around him. He hadn't caught even one fish, so rather than dinner, he went hungry. His stomach growled in protest. He had a chunk of cheese he brought with him. He dug it out and pulled off a piece. He had to force himself to slow down and not to take any more. These were his rations, and he needed to stretch them out as long as possible.

When he woke up again, the storm still raged. Rain had not let up at all, and rumbles of thunder in the background told him there wouldn't be a break anytime soon. He would need to go down to the creek to check his lines and to get some fresh water. He'd get wet, soaking wet, but he had to try. He'd start a fire when he returned and try to dry out his clothes.

He walked into the rain and quickly walked to creek side where he checked his lines and filled a bucket with water. This time, the lines held one fish, a good size one. He took it off the line and carried the fish to the bank of the creek. Now to find a way to cook it. Grabbing the fish and the bucket, he almost ran to the cottage. He was indeed soaked through, so he removed his clothing and lit a fire in the hearth. Hopefully, it wouldn't take too long because he needed to clean the fish and prepare it for a meal.

Charles hated being cooped up inside; he always had. He much preferred to spend his time outside. There was so much more to do. But for now, he was stuck indoors. At least until this storm moved on. It seemed to him this was an unusual storm. It was intense and certainly hadn't weakened or strengthened since it started.

He hadn't expected to be stuck in this cottage, but with the intensity of this storm, he had no choice. Once it stopped or weakened, he would head back to the house. He was ill-prepared to stay much longer. Now that he'd found the cottage, he would begin to bring supplies for the next time, because there would be a next time. It was simply the nature of his personality.

Before he did return, he needed to decide about Cathryn's performance. Should he give in and cancel his plans? He shouldn't have to, but something told him his wife wasn't going to be happy unless she got her way. Getting her way meant he would cancel or postpone his scheduled talk at Oxford, and he wasn't ready to do that.

So what was the solution?

He paced the floor of the cottage to come up with a solution that would be beneficial to them both. It was going to be no easy task. What he could do might be to give his scheduled talk and afterwards leave and stop by the family home and change. He'd then meet Cathryn either at the house or at the Prince of Wales's residence. That meant giving up his dinner at Oxford, but at least his wife would be happy. Charles was certain no one would be offended by his cancellation to the dinner. Once they understood his wife was playing for royalty, anything else would be forgotten.

The rain continued for most of the day, but that did not deter him. He grabbed his things and left the cottage. He was heading home, and hopefully Cathryn would not be too upset or angry with him for disappearing like that. It was simply something he had to do, the only way he could cope with life when it overwhelmed him.

Now wasn't the time to be overwhelmed. There were too many things to be done that needed his attention. He needed to get things on the estate organized. Find out what had been done and what needed to be done.

Once this performance was finished, he and Cathryn needed to have a talk, so that they better understood what they each expected. He didn't want to become like so many other husbands who simply ignored their wives; the only time they spent together was for social events or making love in order to produce children.

He wanted to do everything with her, but they had to understand what was more important. This performance was particularly important for her, but she needed to know she couldn't have her way every time something came up.

How he was able to enter the house without being seen by the staff concerned him. Even though the house wasn't at full staff, one almost always ran into a footman or maid. Deciding it wasn't for him to question such luck, he quietly found his way back to his own chambers.

When he entered, it was as quiet as the rest of the house. He walked over and checked the door between his and Cathryn's rooms. Unlocked. Interesting.

Turning around, he saw Frazier, arms folded, watching him with great intent. "You're back earlier than I expected," his valet said.

"I would have returned earlier, but the rain kept me."

"Lady Cathryn will be happy to see you."

Charles arched a brow. "She's not still angry?"

"Concerned would be the word I'd use. And no, she isn't angry. I think the storm made her reconsider how she felt."

"Hmmm."

"What's that supposed to mean?"

"Nothing."

"I trust you'll want a bath before changing your clothes."

"Yes. Where is she?"

"I imagine you can find her in the music room," Frazier replied.

"Of course." He sat down and removed his boots and socks and headed into his bathing chamber. Luckily the previous owner had updated all the plumbing. Footmen weren't needed to carry buckets of hot water from the kitchen.

As his valet prepared the bath, Charles undressed and laid the filthy set of clothes on the floor. He was positive he would probably not see them again. If Frazier couldn't get them clean, they'd end up going to someone less fortunate.

"I take it you found somewhere out of the weather last night?"

"I did. It will be perfect," he replied, not daring to look his valet in the eyes.

"Come on, you're not planning to run off every time you and your missus have a spat, are you?"

"No. I simply like the fact I have somewhere."

"There's always the attics," Frazier said with a grin.

He shook his head. "She'd find me too easily."

"Your bath is ready. I'll go lay out clothes for you."

"Thank you," Charles replied.

Frazier said nothing. He'd been with Charles for far too long. The man didn't need to thank him continuously. He'd do whatever the man wanted. Before leaving, he picked up the pile of filthy clothes and headed into the dressing room.

Charles leaned against the back of the tub. The hot water felt good on his skin. He still had a chill from the night before. If he sat here for a while, that feeling would leave. He had nothing to do. If Cathryn was practicing, he wasn't about to disturb her. She needed complete concentration. Besides, sitting here kept him from the inevitable. Groveling and asking her forgiveness because he was sure his wife would demand it. Everything would be his fault. If she hadn't slept last night, it would be his doing.

On the other hand, that was better than the way she was when he left her. Angry. Once he dressed and was presentable, he'd go search her out.

CATHRYN WAS IN the music room going through more sheet music she'd found sitting on a bookcase. Whichever of the former owners had been musically inclined wasn't much on organization. She'd found music in the oddest places and placed in no particular order. No sooner had she thought she had organized it all, than she found another pile. Her goal was to organize all of it by composer, but that was a job for another day.

Right now, she needed to keep her composure. She had to focus on the upcoming performance for the Prince of Wales. Charles having disappeared had to be secondary. His valet assured her this was not uncommon, and he would return any day. It was a reaction for him. Having been isolated for so long, fleeing was his way of coping with a situation that made him uncomfortable. The way she'd left that day was something he was unsure how to handle. So he fled to have time to digest it. Being they'd just moved into the estate, his valet hadn't had time to find places Charles might go to.

Hearing a faint click of the door shutting, she turned and found Charles standing there. He'd recently bathed. His hair was slightly damp. He stood with his hands clasped behind his back.

They stood staring at the other for what seemed to be the longest time.

Charles broke the silence first. "I need to apologize if I put you through any undue stress. I take full responsibility for my actions and hope you'll forgive me."

She hadn't expected that, him apologizing. "Apology accepted. Frazier explained things to me and assured me you'd return quickly."

"I've had quite a bit of time to think, and I've decided not to go to the dinner after my talk."

"I see. What made you decide this?"

"My wife has been invited to play for royalty, the Prince of Wales, no less. That's more important than a dinner with stuffy academics."

She turned so he wouldn't see her smile. "Thank you for that, Charles."

"You're welcome. I look forward to hearing you play."

As hard as she tried to be a little bit angry with him, she couldn't do it. She understood this was difficult for him and that apologizing was enormous for him. She would take whatever she could.

"Would you mind if we stayed an extra night in London?" she asked.

"Of course. I take it you'd like to visit your modiste?"

Why hadn't she thought of that before? This was a perfect excuse. "Yes. I need to have a fitting on a couple of gowns she's making."

"While you're doing that, I can make a few calls of my own."

Hearing him cough caused her to walk closer to him. "You weren't out in that storm, were you?"

"No, I managed to avoid that," he replied.

"You don't sound like you did."

"I'm sure the dampness didn't help."

"No, I'm sure it didn't. Come sit by the fire and I'll order us some tea."

She watched him nod and walk to a settee in front of the fireplace. The upholstery was perfect for this room. Black and white musical theme with notes floating on a sea of white. He stood before the fire for a moment before sitting down.

Tea was served a few minutes later and she passed him a cup. He sipped before setting the cup on a table beside him.

"That's what I needed," he said.

"Good," she replied.

"Are you ready for your performance?"

"Yes. I am very confident about it. I'd like to play it for you later. If you don't mind."

"Not at all. I love to hear you play."

He was right about that. He was an accomplished musician himself, but he'd never pursued it. Since they'd first met, he had always been available to listen to anything she played. Especially new pieces. It was always good to have someone to critique.

"I'm trying to make some sort of order with all this music," she said, picking up her cup.

"Composer?"

"Yes. Composer first. Then perhaps years written?"

He nodded. "That would work if you knew when or could find out when it was composed. Otherwise, I'd place it alphabetically, I think."

She smiled. She couldn't stop smiling. One of the things she loved about him were his ideas. Even the far-fetched ones always showed the depth in which he thought things through. He was meticulous.

"What's so humorous?" he asked.

"Thinking about you meeting the prince. It ought to be interesting."

He shook his head. "I met him on Wight. He was on holiday."

Her eyes widened at his statement. "Wait. You've already met the Prince of Wales?"

"Yes, that's what I said."

"Were his wife and children with him?"

"Not that day, but I assume they were wherever they were staying."

"Tell me the circumstances. How did you meet him?" she asked.

Shaking his head, he sat back. "We were both riding that day. His horse spooked at something, and he was having difficulty regaining control of the beast. His men weren't able to get hold of the horse's bridle. The animal looked as though it were going to bolt, prince or not."

"What did you do?"

"I was able to grab the bridle to the chagrin of his soldiers and calmed the horse. He thanked me and we went our separate ways. Not a big thing."

She patted his hand. "Yes, it was. You kept the prince from falling off his horse and onto the ground. That would have been quite an indignity for him."

"Embarrassing."

"It doesn't sound like he's much of a horseman."

"He's not. Nothing extraordinary. He didn't appear to be one who did for himself. He had people for that. He's the Prince of Wales, after all," he replied.

"So he's going to remember you as the man who kept him from falling off his horse and onto his ass."

She giggled as Charles appeared horrified by her statement and choice of words. "Don't tell me you hadn't thought that."

"Yes, of course I have," he said. "Do you know how many people are going to your concert?"

"No, but from what his people have told me, the more the merrier with the prince. Why?"

"Just curious."

Cathryn watched his face for changes. She didn't want to let him know the count she'd been given. It might set Charles into a meltdown. "I imagine it'll be an intimate group of friends of the prince and princess."

"Good. That's more doable."

"You'll do fine, Charles."

"Yes, I will."

Smiling, she patted his hand and picked up her tea. "Maybe when we return, we can go to the village and look around. Have dinner?"

"I'd like that. We should probably get to know people who

work and live in and around the village."

"I'm surprised we haven't heard from people who live here. Not even the vicar has come to pay a visit."

He arched a brow. "That's highly unusual. They're usually the first ones."

"I know. I thought perhaps he had something else going on."

Grinning, Charles offered his idea on the lack of a visit from the vicar. "Perhaps word's gotten to him that a mad man purchased the estate. He hasn't visited us yet because he's afraid. I hadn't thought of that. Afraid of what? Me?"

"Yes. You know how fickle people can be."

They were. It didn't matter if it were family or friends. The less they had to deal with an uncomfortable situation, the better. Somehow, she had to keep his thoughts off that. Everything would be fine, and Charles would overcome his hesitation.

"Have you seen the greenhouse?" she asked.

"No, but I gather you have."

"I have. The gardener does graft various plants, starts seeds. He keeps the young plants in there until they're ready to be moved."

"Interesting. Are you interested in showing me?"

"We certainly can. Did you know we have a pineapple stove? We'll be able to enjoy the fruit anytime we want."

"Do you want to show me or leave it for another day?"

"Let's see it now," she said with great excitement in her voice.

She was sure this was something that would interest Charles. It was also a place she could talk to him without worrying someone was close by listening. Word of their disagreement the other night had made for gossip among the staff. This should put a nip in it.

They both left the music room and made their way through the house and exited by the drawing room. The greenhouse was in an unusual place, at the far back of the house. Trees and bushes kept it obscured, out of sight of prying eyes. Good enough for them to do naughty things. The windows needed to be washed because no one could see inside and there was a lock on the door, making it the perfect place for an afternoon rendezvous. The old gardener was smart; he wouldn't bother them.

CHAPTER EIGHTEEN

THE CARRIAGE RIDE to London had been uneventful until they got closer to town. By the time they hit the outskirts of London, the weather was changing. Not for the better, either. What had started as a partially cloudy day with a variety of clouds quickly changed. The clouds and sky had turned to an almost dark-gray in color. The wind had whipped up, and there was the smell of a storm brewing nearby.

Cathryn had been peering out the window for quite a while watching not only the landscape but the worsening weather rolling in. "Do you think it'll blow over?"

"Yes, the wind has picked up. It won't stay long."

"I hope you're right," she replied.

Charles smiled and looked out the carriage window at the darkening sky. "Of course, I am. I believe it'll stay for the afternoon and evening, but everything will be back to normal tomorrow morning."

"Where did you learn to be such an expert on weather?"

"Wight. The weather was always changing, and changing at the spur of the moment. I began to see a pattern."

"Of course, you did. I imagine Wight is no different than any other coastal area."

He nodded. "You're right. The coast is where the storms come in and start out with a vengeance."

"You see," she said, looking at him, "living on Wight taught you a lot of things most men would overlook."

"It did, but you must remember the season is beginning to slowly change. Autumn is coming, and that's why we see more bad weather than usual."

She settled into her corner of the carriage, pulling a blanket around her. "I think I'm going to rest my eyes. The carriage ride isn't agreeing with me today, and I don't know why."

"Of course," he said. This was quite unusual for Cathryn. Usually, she was the rock when it came to things that made some women swoon. The roads were in good order. No unusual holes to cause the carriage to sway unnecessarily.

The swaying of the carriage was lulling his eyes heavy. With the inside now quiet from conversation, he couldn't help but give into sleep. Besides, he figured he was probably still tired from his adventure a few days ago and the lovemaking he and Cathryn shared last night. He always figured her for a passionate woman, but last night brought it out two-fold. She was becoming quite the seductress.

Charles shut his eyes and tried to void his mind of everything. If he didn't, he would find himself wide awake, unable to sleep. His mind would grab on to something he hadn't solved earlier and wouldn't let go. It didn't matter what it was. Today was no different. He focused on a curtain in the carriage. Its movement and how much the movement of the carriage made it sway.

That didn't last. His mind had moved on. Moved on to the Prince of Wales. Would he remember him? Maybe he wouldn't. That would be just fine with Charles. To put it mildly, the prince was loud and boisterous. A narcissist. Everything revolved around the prince, as he had to be the center of attention. The man disliked being around people who wanted to discuss something meaningful. He would turn the conversation around to him in a matter of minutes, and those involved would find themselves listening to the prince once again manipulate what he thought was important.

Subject matter could also go to matters best suited to an audience of only men. Bedroom talk was one of the prince's favorites, and he didn't mind the ladies being near. He had a very unusual sexual appetite and was quick to point out he liked to watch or try new things. Things that he could do with his large girth. After all, after sex, food was the Prince of Wales's favorite topic. He liked only the best. It didn't matter what it was: caviar, steak tartar. As long as the prince wanted something, he kept his staff hopping to find what he wanted. Charles tried to keep this sort of thing tucked away in the back of his mind.

He would be going to the prince and princess's musicale where his wife would be the top billing. All he could hope was that they would be enthralled with Cathryn's playing and that would be that. But the prince being who he was wouldn't be so tolerant. He'd want to show her off to anyone who would give him time. He would probably brag to his wife about what a superior piano player he was but that he hadn't pursued it because of being who he was. He had so many other duties, practice eluded him, but he was known to have house parties that went on for days and at which he sometimes played. Another way to keep himself as the center of attention.

This was what happened when Charles had too much time on his hands. His mind wrapped around something and wouldn't let go. His thoughts never truly left him. Something always was waiting to grab on to his attention.

He glanced over at Cathryn who was sound asleep and envied her for being able to peacefully sleep through anything. She looked like an angel lying there. His life certainly had taken a sharp turn when he met her. She was the only person in a long time who understood him and his oddness. Not to say she didn't have her limits. Despite differences, they complemented each other, and he was thankful for that. Before Cathryn, he never considered that he would ever find a woman who would become his wife. A solitary life is what he imagined was in store for him. Being alone never bothered him, but as soon as he met her, that all changed.

Closing his eyes for a matter of minutes, he tried to guess where the carriage was as they neared London. He could tell when they were getting near because the carriage would slow and then the horses would liven up again before slowing because of the traffic. People like them headed into London. Some on business, some for pleasure, and others both.

The change of pace woke Cathryn. He heard her move around next to him. Her hand gently touched his shoulder.

"Charles, are you awake? I think we're getting close to town. The traffic has everyone slowed down."

"I'm awake," he replied. "I was wondering when the slowing down and speeding up was going to wake you."

"You're beginning to know my habits, Charles."

"Your likes and dislikes too."

She giggled and edged closer to him. "Really? Do tell."

He danced around her question. "Your nap must have agreed with you."

"How's that?"

"You weren't feeling well and appear to be much better now."

She nodded. "I feel much better. I'm not sure what brought that on."

"You've had a lot going on lately. Some days you go from the moment you wake up until you get into bed. It would wear the best man or woman down."

Leaning her head on to his shoulder, Cathryn sighed. "I don't like to make excuses for my actions, but I do like this."

Charles had to agree. The more they were together, the more he liked even the simplest of gestures like this. "As do I."

He turned his head to peer out the window on his side. The carriage had slowed down to a walk and from what he could tell, there was a very long line in front of them. There would be no relief until they were farther into London and carriages began to veer off to their destinations.

Ordinarily, he would exit the carriage and walk to his destination. The carriage would come, but a bit later, and by then he would be sitting back in front of a cozy fire. There would be none of that today. She'd just gotten over him disappearing on the estate and he didn't need to pull another one. So he'd just stay put.

"Who knows? Maybe some of these people have been invited to hear you play."

"If you're trying to make me even more nervous than I already am, it's working," she said.

"You're nervous? I find that hard to believe."

"What has me on edge is the idea that I have no real experience playing private parties. Except for my parents' soirees, of course."

"Can you not pretend no one is in the room with you?" he asked.

"That's what I try to do, but if there are even a few who insist on whispering during my performance, it takes all I have not to stop and reprimand them for being rude."

Charles burst into a fit of laughter. He could imagine her doing that. Stopping midway through a piece, getting up from the piano, and confronting the offending party.

"I'm glad you think that's funny," she said. She was trying not to smile.

"I apologize, but I can see you doing this."

"That's because I have."

"What? Do tell."

Cathryn smiled and turned to face him better. "It happened at one of my mother's teas. I was in the middle of a piece by Mozart. An entire table, sitting off to my right, had sat there the entire time I'd been playing, whispering and just being rude. I stopped playing and stood in front of them and told them off. One of the women was a dowager duchess, who I shan't name. She looked at me like 'how dare you.'"

"Did you continue? Or did you quit?"

"I went back, sat down, and started the piece from the beginning. And before you ask, no, the duchess and her friends continued on as though nothing had happened."

"They didn't!"

"Oh, yes. The duchess even told my mother I was rude and had no manners and that my mother needed to fix my bad behavior before it was too late."

He snorted. "Sounds like the duchess had the bad manners."

"Yes. I've never seen her since that day. My mother said she'd bought a home in Paris and had moved there."

"I'd say she'll get along just fine with the French."

She nodded, saying nothing for a few moments. Charles could tell she wasn't feeling well again. He kissed her on the forehead.

"Why don't you lie down for a while? You look as though you're not feeling right again."

"I hate to because we're so close, and the jerking of the carriage doesn't help."

"I can imagine. Unfortunately, we're going to have to endure it for a while longer."

"Hmmm."

She had removed her hat hours ago and laid her head in his lap, kicking her feet up on the seat. Situations like this still made him uneasy. He wasn't sure how he was supposed to act. Running his hand up and down her arm seemed to comfort her.

Finally, as the carriage drove up on to the cobblestones, he felt at ease. They were at least in town and his driver would know alternative streets to use to help speed up the last of their ride.

"Where are we?" Cathryn asked without sitting up.

"In London. Not sure where. I instructed the driver to try and find alternative routes to get us home quicker."

"Good. I'm ready to get out and walk about."

"Perhaps you should consider taking a hot bath. Maybe that'll help you feel better."

"You know you're right, and I believe we're only a couple of blocks away."

He peered out the carriage window. She was right. They were about three blocks away from the house, and things were looking familiar. At least he was more comfortable. He could put the old fears away. At least, he thought he could. He wasn't avoiding situations like he had.

Finally, the carriage turned onto the small drive of the house before coming to a complete stop. Cathryn sat up and smoothed back her hair before putting the hat back on. Curious, he watched her as she made sure everything was in place and she was ready to step out of the coach.

Charles followed her as she walked up to the front door where they were greeted by the butler and others. Cathryn requested tea be served in their suite and that dinner be served at the usual time in the breakfast room.

He entered the room behind her, where he deposited his hat and gloves in the arms of a waiting footman. Catching up with her, Charles climbed the stairs and followed her down the hall to their suite. While she immediately removed her slippers and laid her hat and shawl on a chair, he went in search of Frazier.

His valet was in the bathing chamber, arranging things on a stool beside the tub. Steam was coming up as the tub filled. "If you don't mind, Cathryn is going to bathe first. She wasn't feeling well on the way back, so I suggested a bath."

"Not a problem. Let me take these back and I'll go fetch a maid to assist her."

"Thank you."

Charles walked back out and found his bride looking out the window. Hearing him, she turned back around and smiled when she saw him.

"Frazier's gone to find a maid to assist you with your bath."

"Aren't you sweet?" she said. Walking up to him, she placed a kiss firmly on his lips and put her arms around him. "Hopefully, this will help me feel better."

"I'm sure it will."

Moments later, Charles's valet returned with a young maid to assist Cathryn in getting out of her outfit and whatever else it was women did to get themselves ready.

He spied a small pile of letters on the far side of the room. Who could possibly know they would be here? There was one addressed to Cathryn. He recognized the writing as being that of Cathryn's mother. Now he was intrigued. He assumed they still weren't speaking, and how she had found out they were here in London was puzzling. He hoped it wasn't something that might upset her. Had her parents received an invitation to the Prince of Wales's party? Nothing would surprise him.

He hated the idea of having to give her the letter, but he couldn't keep it from her. Or could he? If she read the letter now, she'd be upset from today until after her performance. If he didn't tell her, he could feign ignorance when it came to the letter. However, if she found out he'd kept it from her, it would cause friction between them, and he didn't wish to go through her wrath again any time soon.

That quickly solved his dilemma in a hurry. He'd go ahead and give it to her once she finished her bath. Cathryn would not let her manipulative mother get too close.

When Cathryn returned, he was sitting in a dark-blue wing-back chair reading a newspaper he had requested Frazier to find.

"You look refreshed," he said, noting her dark-gray dress trimmed in black. It was nothing fancy, but he knew she preferred to wear it when at home because it was comfortable.

"Yes, I feel much better. That was just what I needed."

He nodded in agreement, his newspaper still folded to the story he wanted to read. "There's a letter for you on the table over there." He pointed in the direction of a square mahogany table used for such things.

"Who's it from?"

"Not sure. Saw it was addressed to you and put it on the table."

He watched as she picked it up and looked closely at it and

sighed. "It's from my mother. Now how would she know we'd be here in London at this particular time?"

"Perhaps she heard about you playing for the prince and his wife."

"Perhaps." She studied the letter for a few more seconds before opening it.

He watched as she read it, and from the facial expressions, he gathered she read it more than once. Then he saw her smile and shake her head.

"Problems?" he asked.

"It seems my parents have heard about my playing for the Prince of Wales."

"What do they want? For you to get them invited?"

She shook her head. "Oh no. She simply is letting me know that they've secured an invitation because they are my parents and are looking forward to seeing me and hearing me play."

"Don't let her get under your skin."

"I'm not. I do find it amusing at how she has to tell me how important she and my father are. They wouldn't have secured an invitation if I wasn't playing for the prince. They're not the sort of people the prince keeps as friends."

"I'll look after you, my love. Just concentrate on what you are there for."

"I plan to. I just fully expect her and my father to want to hover because who knows, Father might find a business deal while he is there."

She walked toward him and handed the letter to him. "Read it for yourself."

He did, and more than once. Her mother was a miserable woman. Cathryn had neglected to tell him that his mother didn't think it would be a good idea to bring him along. He might embarrass them all with his lack of social skills.

He barked out a laugh. "I don't know what to say that hasn't already been said."

"You're right, and you're going to accompany me. You're my

husband, and she'd just better get used to that."

"I never intended not to go with you," he replied.

"I know."

"Now it's just gotten a little more interesting."

"It certainly has. We'll have to make sure to make her un-comfortable when she's around us," she said.

"How's that?" he asked with a smirk.

"You know, kissing, holding my hand, just be attentive to each other. It'll drive her crazy because she can't control the narrative."

Charles chuckled. "You, my dear, are an excellent judge of character."

"Thank you," she replied with a smile.

She had to be, with parents who were like chameleons, changing their personalities to suit the scenario around them.

⇶⟫⟪⇷

THE FOLLOWING MORNING had a delightful pink and gray to the sky, Charles thought as he paused to look outside a window on his way to the breakfast room. He hesitated as a footman opened the door for him.

He had no sooner gotten a plate filled with eggs, sausage, and fried potatoes than the door opened once more, and his wife walked in. She sat across from Charles. As she stirred her tea, he noticed she was quieter than usual.

"Good morning," he said.

"Good morning," she replied, pulling a folded paper out of the pocket of her brown and rust dress. "This just came."

"What is it?"

"I've been invited to check out the piano I'll be playing and to rehearse if I like."

"That's good, isn't it?"

She nodded and chose a piece of toast and began to slather it with strawberry jam. "Yes, it is. There aren't many hosts who would think to do such a thing. The prince and his wife are different."

"I know you're going to go, but may I suggest I go along with you? Afterwards, we could grab a light lunch."

"How did you know what I was considering? I was going to ask you to accompany me. I'd prefer not to go alone."

She didn't have to give him an explanation for what she was asking. Charles knew what she was uncomfortable about: the Prince of Wales showing up unannounced, and she would feel ill at ease about being alone in the same room with him. The prince did have a reputation.

"Good, it's settled. I'll accompany you so you can practice and afterwards we'll have lunch."

"Thank you, Charles."

"No need to thank me. I'm your husband. While a lot of husbands would simply send a footman to accompany their wife, I'm not like that."

Nodding, Cathryn placed the letter back in her pocket and took a sip of tea. He knew she felt better just knowing he'd be with her.

He watched as she pushed her toast and remaining dollop of strawberry jam on the plate. "Is there something wrong with the toast?"

"No. I'm not as hungry as I thought I was."

"How can you not be hungry? You haven't eaten since last night."

"I'm just not hungry. I'll eat this toast, and by lunch I'll be more than ready to eat. It just takes me a while sometimes for my appetite to wake up."

"Understood. Think about where you'd like to go."

"I will."

He continued to watch her as discreetly as possible. Though she did eat the toast, it took an effort on her part. She finished her tea and began to rise from the table.

"When would you like to leave? Did they give you a specific time to go and practice there?"

"All it says is any time after ten and before three."

"We have plenty of time."

"Why don't we plan on leaving at ten?" she asked.

"Very well. That'll give us plenty of time."

She walked out of the room. Charles went back to reading his newspapers quickly before deciding he needed to make sure he was appropriately dressed for their stop at the prince's. He took a last bite of egg, set his newspaper down, and rose to leave the room. This was going to be a busy day.

He ordered the carriage readied before going upstairs. He knew it took a while to harness the horses and have them ready.

They left precisely on time. It didn't take long to get to the prince's residence. Charles looked up at the structure in amazement. This was where the prince also entertained. The palace was huge, with plenty of room for various sizes of functions. The prince and his wife loved to entertain.

Arriving at the entrance, the couple disembarked the carriage and were led to a small room where they waited and waited for someone to direct them. Finally, a young man wearing spectacles entered the room. From the looks of his dress and mannerisms, Charles concluded he must work for the prince himself.

"I apologize for my tardiness. I'm Mr. Temple, one of the prince's secretaries. I understand you're here to practice on the piano you'll be using?"

"Yes, I am. The prince invited me."

"If you'll just follow me, I'll show you to the ballroom."

She was outside the room. As soon as Charles tried to go with her, he was stopped. "I'm sorry, sir, only your wife can come. You'll have to wait here."

He was about to protest when Cathryn spoke up. "Either my husband accompanies me, or I'll leave now without practicing."

"I'm just following orders, milady," Mr. Temple said.

"Understood. Now what are we going to do to resolve this?"

"Your husband still can't go with you."

"We're at an impasse then. I'm leaving in that case."

Charles had remained close-mouthed the entire time as he'd been treated badly. Cathryn seemed to have everything under control. He extended his arm and pulled her closer. Together they walked through the palace to the main door to take their leave. Mr. Temple followed close behind, trying to get them to change their mind.

No matter how much he groveled, Cathryn stuck to her belief. Ladies shouldn't be alone. Especially in a situation like this where any man would love to take advantage of a woman like her. She was a married woman, and if she wanted her husband to accompany her, he would. If men like Mr. Temple wanted to play the prince's game, she would simply remove herself from the situation.

"Very well," Mr. Temple finally said. "Your husband may accompany you."

"Thank you. I want the room cleared unless the people are working on readying the room for the party."

Temple sighed, knowing he'd met his match. "Very well. Most everything has been done and anything else can wait until you're finished."

She and Charles followed Temple to the ballroom. The shiny black piano sat on a large riser. Stairs were just behind the piano stool. "Very nice," Cathryn said.

"Did I tell you the piano has just been tuned? You should find it a delight to play."

"No, you hadn't told me that. I appreciate that being done."

Charles found a chair to sit in and set it off to one side. He watched his wife climb the three stairs to the large piano and sit down on the bench.

She ran her fingers across the keyboard and began doing some exercises to loosen not only her fingers but also to test the piano. Each one was unique, and it was up to the player to know what it was.

First, she broke into one of the pieces requested by the prince. She'd decided to play the pieces at rehearsal in order to hear how it would be played later. Charles closed his eyes and listened to the sound. While he played and played well, his talent did not come close to matching his wife's. Her playing seemed to soothe him and help him relax.

By the time she was through with the requests of the prince and his wife, Charles was almost asleep.

"What did you think?" she asked.

"Superb."

"You don't think I need to play them one more time?"

"No, not unless you're unhappy with something. I think you've done what you set out to do."

"I'm satisfied. I think I can leave feeling good about everything," she replied.

He got up from the chair and walked toward her, meeting her at the bottom of the steps. "Shall we go to lunch like we planned?"

"Absolutely."

"I think you'll enjoy the place I picked out."

"You've got me curious, but first I'd like to find Mr. Temple and thank him for obliging me."

"Good idea."

They followed the hallway in the direction Mr. Temple had brought them. Nearing the door they'd entered through, they found it was not as busy as when they arrived. Charles spotted Mr. Temple outside, speaking with none other than Cathryn's mother. He glanced over at his wife and saw she'd seen her mother as well.

"What is she trying to do?"

"Why don't we thank Mr. Temple and leave? I have a feeling she's trying to get in to listen to you rehearse."

"Yes, let's. I'm counting on you to get us away from her."

They walked over to the prince's man and thanked him, before acknowledging Cathryn's mother.

"I was trying to get in to hear you rehearse. You can always use a good critique."

"No need for you to come here, Mother. I'm quite satisfied with how things went."

"You may think so, but your father and I think you need someone to represent you, speak for you if you're going to continue playing for the public."

"And I suppose that someone would be you and Father?"

"Of course! Who better?"

Charles decided to use this as a perfect place to extract his wife. "If you'll excuse us, we have a couple of appointments and we can't be late."

"Mother, we've got to go, but understand this: I'm not playing professionally. This was a special request which I accepted. Now if you'll excuse us."

Charles led her out to their carriage, leaving his mother-in-law stunned by being snubbed by her own daughter. Or, in her eyes, she was being snubbed.

He sat down next to Cathryn, and as he did, the carriage slowly began to move. "You were brilliant, my dear."

"I've learned through trial and error it's the only way to keep my mother's bizarre actions under control."

He smiled. "You do it so well."

"Enough of my mother. We'll have to deal with her antics again tonight. I'm hungry, and you promised lunch."

"I did, didn't I? We could either go to the Brown Hotel and eat at their brand-new restaurant or we could go to a chip shop. Arthur introduced me to one."

"Let's go to the new restaurant. Although I adore fish and chips, I'm afraid all that grease would be a bit heavy to eat today," she said.

"The Brown Hotel it is," he replied. He then knocked twice on the roof, telling the driver where they were to go.

"I'm intrigued at what this new place serves, aren't you?"

"Yes. I understand it's become popular in a short period of

time," he said.

"Hmmm. May I ask a question?"

"Of course you can."

"Are we still leaving the day after tomorrow?"

He nodded. "Yes. Unless you'd like to stay on."

"No. I just have a couple appointments and will need the carriage."

"Very well. We can talk about it later. I only have one or two appointments myself. Should be no problem."

"Thank you."

He peered out the window at all the people walking in a hurry around him, having always done this at earlier stages of his life. He got through some of his discomfort of riding in a carriage by ignoring everything around him and solely concentrating on the people, strangers all off to an appointment or to visit with a friend.

Charles always wondered why he was odd, different than his two siblings. No matter how he tried to come up with a logical answer, it was something that wasn't talked about. Looking at all the people outside, he couldn't be the only one.

"I know that look, Charles. Get out of your head."

He turned to her, nodding. "I was watching the people, wondering how many more people like me are out there."

"Well, stop. I've told you before you're unique and no one is like you. You're one of a kind."

He patted her hand which had been on his thigh since they'd entered the carriage. "Thank you for reminding me."

They passed the Brown Hotel. Charles tapped on the roof of the carriage and finally, they came to a halt. He'd been very specific in where they were going. He opened the door and stepped out. "I thought I told you this was where we were going for a meal."

"You did, it's just there's no room in front of the establishment to do that," the driver said.

Charles looked back towards the Brown. What he saw was a

swarm of people lined up waiting to gain entrance. "Send a footman and see how long a wait there is."

He opened the door to the carriage and found Cathryn in the spot he'd been occupying moments before. "I've sent a footman to see how long a wait we'd have."

"It's certainly a popular place if all those people are waiting for a table."

He nodded and closed the door. Walking back to the coachman, he could see the young footman and Coachie discussing something. Charles imagined the wait was probably longer than anticipated.

"How long?" he asked, approaching the pair.

"More than an hour. Starting tomorrow, you must have a reservation to dine here. They weren't expecting this reaction."

"I can imagine," Charles replied. "In that case, let's return home. I'm sure Cook can come up with something."

He climbed back into the carriage. "We're going home. The wait is well over an hour."

"Oh my. They must be good if the line to get in is that long."

"Evidently so."

"The day is lovely. We could go home and eat on the terrace if you'd like."

He nodded. "That sounds nice. Just you and me, none of the crowds."

"Not that I don't like to eat out, it's simply the fact you can rarely hold a conversation because of all the noise. People just don't know when to be quiet or enjoy the ambiance."

"You're right," he said.

They kept riding along. It didn't take long before the commercial shops began to turn into residences. Traffic reduced as well. When they pulled up in front of the house, Charles led his wife inside. Immediately, she went to the kitchen to get things started with the cook. It would be an easy meal, and probably better than anything she could find at a restaurant.

A short time later, she met Charles on the terrace. The day

was sunny, which needed to be enjoyed. Cooler weather would soon be on its way. He was standing against a baluster looking out at the gardens.

"We could have gotten a hamper and gone to one of the parks," she said, approaching him.

"This is nicer. We have the place all to ourselves, and we don't have to deal with the bugs and sit on the ground."

"I concur on all."

CHAPTER NINETEEN

CATHRYN STARED AT the person standing in front of the full-length mirror. Finally, she chose a new periwinkle silk gown she recently had made. She chose it in part because of its color. Having considered emerald-green or red, she decided she didn't want to draw unnecessary attention to herself. Tonight was about the music.

Grabbing a shawl, she left her dressing room in search of Charles. He wasn't far, sitting in front of a fire in the drawing room. He rose upon seeing her enter the room. She effortlessly glided across the floor to his side.

"What do you think?" she asked.

"You look beautiful."

"You always say that," she said.

"Because it's true."

"Flattery will get you everywhere, husband."

"Good to know. Would you care for a drink before we depart?"

"No," she said. "I'm fine, but we should be leaving," she said.

They walked out of the house to the waiting carriage. He handed her up and then followed as a footman shut the door behind them. The evening was quite comfortable, the night sky clear. Stars were beginning to come out. Soon they would be twinkling against a black backdrop.

"Are you nervous?" Charles asked as the carriage came to a halt in front of the same entrance they had used the last time they'd been at the prince's home.

"Perhaps a little. Once I begin playing, I forget all about it or anyone around me. Don't you feel the same when you play in front of people?"

He chuckled. "I have only played a handful of times in front of anyone, unlike you."

"The only reason I'm playing here is because the Prince of Wales invited me, and one doesn't say no to the prince."

They were shown down a hallway to outside the ballroom where she would be playing shortly. All around them staff were busily preparing for this evening's event.

"Would you and your husband like to sit here, or do you prefer to come through the main entrance when the prince announces you?"

She glanced at Charles. "I really prefer sitting at the chairs you showed us earlier. All I'll need to do is stand, walk across to the piano, and play."

"As you wish, milady," the man replied.

"Would you be so kind as to tell me if the prince has arrived?"

"He hasn't. You'll know when he does."

"Would you like me to place the music at the piano?" Charles suggested.

"If you wouldn't mind," she said with a smile. "I've arranged them in order so it would be simpler."

She watched Charles walk to the center of the room where he placed the sheet music. Cathryn then glanced in the direction of where guests were settling in for the performance and waiting for the prince to be announced so the evening's festivities could begin. There were more guests than she'd imagined. If this was an intimate soiree, she wondered what an actual ball might look like. The prince's ideas and hers were something entirely different.

She hadn't seen her parents. That was probably because they

were telling anyone who would listen that this evening's guest was their daughter. If they didn't act quickly, they weren't going to get a front seat, and she knew how her mother hated being in the back of a room. The only reason her parents were even here this evening was because of her mother non-stop insisting they be included.

The sound of a gong pealed across the room, telling everyone to find their seats. The prince and princess had arrived. Moments later they were announced and walked to their chairs. Once the prince was certain everyone was settled in, he rose from his seat and introduced Cathryn. Later on, the words the prince spoke would come to her.

Cathryn stood and smiled not only at her hosts but the audience as well. She then walked to the magnificent grand piano and sat down at the keyboard. Making sure the music was before her, she closed her eyes and began to play. Her fingers flew across the keyboard effortlessly. She lost track of time and anything else as the melody flowed through her veins.

Ending the last piece, Cathryn sat for a moment, listening to the prince's guests' vigorous applause. Finally, she stood and faced everyone. To their surprise, Cathryn turned toward the royal couple and melted into a deep curtsy. She glanced around the room looking for Charles, who was where she'd left him. He had an odd smile on his face, obviously proud of her.

She began walking toward him, the sound of people complimenting her as she smiled back at them, keeping pace. As much as she'd like to, Cathryn knew stopping to chat with anyone would delay their departure. As she reached Charles, she was redirected back. The prince and princess wished to speak with her.

With Charles in tow, they stood in front of the royal couple in no time. Again, she dropped into a curtsy.

"You play most elegantly," Princess Alexandra said.

"Thank you."

The prince reached out and took one of her hands in his beefy one. "We must have more, my dear. Say once a month?"

"I am honored you think that highly of my musical abilities. I will take some time to think about your offer."

"If it's a matter of money, I'm quite sure we can come to a figure that will benefit both of us," the Prince of Wales said.

"Money is not the issue, though it's generous. I'm not a professional pianist. Should you like for me to play for you again, I'd be happy to, but I need to think about it before doing it on a regular basis."

"Of course you do. We just wanted you to be properly thanked for a magnificent evening and look forward to hearing you again," Princess Alexandra replied.

"Thank you, your highness," Cathryn said.

Curtsying one last time, she and Charles walked to where they'd been sitting. She knew they should leave, for Charles's sake, but it appeared her mother was waiting in prey for her to return.

"Good evening, Mother."

Her mother stood there with her mouth agape, a look of mock horror on her face. "Good evening? That's all you can say? You completely ignore and embarrass your father and me and all you can say is 'good evening'?"

"How did I embarrass or ignore you? I didn't even know you and Father were here. Now if you'll excuse us, we were just leaving."

"You can't leave yet. There are so many people you need to meet."

Cathryn shook her head and linked her hand through Charles's arm. "No, we don't. My only purpose for being here was to play for the prince and princess. We've done that. We're leaving."

"You ungrateful cow," her mother hissed.

Charles moved his body in such a way he blocked the two women, standing in between them. He was about to say something when Cathryn tugged at his arm, trying to lead him away.

"She's not worth it, Charles."

He nodded. "You're right."

She let him lead her out the same door they had come in through, leaving her mother alone, her mouth once more open in disbelief.

Neither spoke while walking down the hall to their waiting carriage. What could be said? Her mother wasn't worth the words it would take to describe her actions.

A footman opened the door to the carriage and stood aside as Charles helped her up the steps leading into the carriage. He immediately followed her and sat down next to her. The footman closed the door, and the carriage began to roll forward.

"You were extraordinary this evening, love," Charles said.

"I was quite satisfied with my performance, but I'm glad it's over with."

"Your mother?"

"No. I've gotten to the point where when she gets like that, the best thing to do is ignore her. It's almost as though she wants you to get into an argument with her," Cathryn replied.

"I was very proud of how you handled her."

Cathryn smiled at his compliment. It wasn't something he did a lot so when he did, it was something to be cherished because it came from his heart. "Thank you."

The carriage was moving at a slower than normal pace due to the congestion in the streets.

"When do you want to go back to the estate?" she asked, leaning her head against his shoulder.

"Would tomorrow be too soon?"

"I can be ready," she said.

"I'm afraid if we stay, your mother is going to start calling on you."

Cathryn laughed softly. "I hadn't thought of that, but you are correct."

"From all I've observed of your mother, I would say she lives vicariously through you," Charles said.

"You might be right. She's not a very good player even though she's practiced and practiced. She simply is an average player, and it makes her crazy. Not everyone can play at my level."

The carriage finally pulled up in front of Jameson House. They walked into a relatively quiet house. Cathryn had made sure no one waited up for them by giving the staff the night off. She took off her shawl and placed it in her arms.

"Come, let's go upstairs. I asked Frazier to leave a bottle of chilled champagne in the sitting room in our suite. I thought a celebration was in order," Charles said.

"How thoughtful."

They entered the room and indeed found a bottle of champagne chilling on ice. It was set on a small marble-topped table with two glasses beside the champagne. The bed was turned back waiting for them and a fire was still lit.

"Would you like to get more comfortable first or enjoy a glass now?" Charles asked.

"Let's enjoy a glass now. Afterwards we can change and enjoy the rest of our evening," she replied, kicking off her slippers. She sat down on a settee and waited for him to bring a glass to her. It hit her right then how tired she was. Having been on the go all day, she hadn't stopped at all until now.

"I like that idea," he replied. A cork popped, and she watched as he poured two glasses.

Cathryn accepted the glass. "To Charles for making this day far less stressful."

"This is for my extraordinarily talented wife who makes my life brighter with each passing day."

They consumed the glass slowly, enjoying the flavor of the wine. Cathryn placed her empty glass back on the table. "If you'll excuse me, I'm going to change. Don't go anywhere. I'll be right back."

She found an ecru night gown and robe set out for her. Quickly she began to disrobe, finally remembering she needed

Charles's help with loosening the corset. Walking back into the main room, she found it empty.

"Charles?"

His head popped around the corner. "I was getting comfortable as well. Is there something you need?"

"Help with my corset? I really can't do it alone."

He walked near her. He had no shirt on, and she couldn't help but stare at his muscled chest. The next thing she felt was him spinning her around so he could loosen the laces of the corset. His fingers worked quickly to get her waist out of the contraption.

"I don't know who came up with this. There has to be a simpler way."

"Let me know if you find it. You could probably make a fortune," Cathryn said.

"If I did, what would you ladies do with the time it takes to tighten one of these?"

"Have more time to get ready for bed," she replied. "I'll be back in a moment."

Quickly she finished getting ready for the night by brushing her hair. She decided not to braid it but let it hang loose. It felt better being free. Putting the brush down, she went to join Charles. If this evening's outing bothered him, he handled it well and never let on. Most importantly, he didn't bolt.

CHARLES AWOKE THE next morning to the sound of Cathryn throwing up. She was in the bathing chamber, but it was so forceful it could be heard anywhere in the suite. He pondered what might be wrong with her. They hadn't eaten at the party, so it wasn't that. The champagne? They'd had it before, and it'd never bothered her. Perhaps it was her nerves. Yesterday had been a stressful day for her, especially the confrontation with her mother. That was probably it.

With this going on, he wondered if they should leave today. Grabbing his robe, Charles made his way to the bathing chamber. When he opened the door, she was sitting on a chair with a basin in front of her.

"I couldn't help but hear you. Anything I can do?"

"I'll be fine. I think the worst is over. I'm going to take a bath and then dress."

"Do you think you'll be up to traveling today?" he asked.

"Yes. If you wouldn't mind, would you have some toast and tea sent up? That should help tremendously."

He nodded. "Of course. I'll get Frazier to take care of it."

"Thank you. Now go finish getting dressed and have breakfast. Then we can leave," Cathryn said.

Again he nodded, not really sure what to say. He'd rarely been sick in his life and hadn't been around others who were. He hoped he wasn't missing anything, and should he leave her by herself? Too many questions. Frazier might have the answers to a lot of them. He always did.

He needed to look for his valet. Cathryn needed tea and toast.

Charles found him readying his clothes for the day. "Would you mind having some toast and tea sent up here? Lady Cathryn is feeling poorly. Too much champagne last night and no food."

Frazier nodded and was gone. Charles decided to use the time to dress himself. His valet would want to do a shave, which he didn't mind most of the time.

The valet returned faster than Charles anticipated. "Tea and toast are on the way. So, tell me about last evening. Was she as wonderful as she sounds here?"

"More. She was extraordinary," Charles replied.

"I imagine the Prince and Princess of Wales were enthralled."

"They were. His Highness wants Lady Cathryn to play on a regular basis."

"That would be quite the honor," Frazier replied.

"She doesn't want to play that often. She said she'd think

about it."

"Well, we know what sort of reputation the prince has. I'm sure that was part of her reasoning not to."

Charles nodded. "Yes, that and the fact her mother showed up and wants Cathryn to do it, and more. She's quite odd, that one. She sees her daughter as unable to make her own decisions."

"She forgets her daughter is married and her life is none of her concern," Frazier said. He picked up the shaving razor after soaping up Charles' face. "You need to speak with Lady Cathryn and set some rules when it comes to her parents. Otherwise, her mother is going to try and take over."

Charles knew his valet to be opinionated but wouldn't have it any other way. Frazier had helped him through many difficult situations over the years. He owed the man a debt of gratitude for helping him maintain his sanity and show him the ways of the world.

"We've tried and she complies with our wishes for a while, but then she's back to interfering with us."

"You'll work it out. Lady Cathryn is a smart lady and knows her mother better than her mother thinks. Just keep an open line of communication between the two of you," Frazier said.

"Absolutely. Now, let's all go home," Charles said cheerfully. In the past, nothing seemed to make him happy. He did what he enjoyed, things that seemed to bring him joy, but not like the happiness he felt whenever Cathryn was near.

He met up with his wife, who seemed to feel much better than earlier. It must have been the champagne and nerves, like Cathryn mentioned.

The ride back to Gloucester was quiet. The sky was a mixture of dark and white clouds, like the weather was unsure what it was to do. Neither of them seemed to notice after their initial inspection. Both fell asleep to the rhythm of the carriage as it headed home.

Once they arrived at the estate, the clouds had gotten even more ominous. Darker, grayer, black. The wind had picked up since leaving London, leaving the impression rain was not far off.

"I'm going to go to my study and see if any correspondence came in," Charles said as he and Cathryn entered the drawing room.

"Would you like me to have tea sent?"

"Please, that would be nice."

"I'm going to have tea and sit near the fire to warm up. After that, I plan to check my correspondence," Cathryn said with a soft smile.

Charles leaned down and kissed her. "I know where to find you."

"Indeed, you do," she replied.

Much to Charles's chagrin, there was a large pile of unopened correspondence waiting for him on his desk. A lot was the usual monthly bills. He began to sort everything in the stack, making it easier to know how to respond to each one. The estate ledger was to the right side of the desk. His estate manager must have gone through it for the month. The man probably wanted to meet so they could discuss any work needing to be done. Cold weather would soon be upon them, and he was sure there were jobs which involved making sure things stayed dry over the course of autumn and winter.

He decided to go through the one stack and see what it was. Then when the estate manager came in the morning, bills could be paid and invitations answered. There were the usual household expenses, a few larger ones for the gardens and overall renovation of the grounds. That would be reduced or eliminated once the gardener and his crew got things done to improve the look of the estate.

A letter from Oxford that he would read tomorrow. Probably about making up dates or confirming them. Nothing out of the ordinary.

One bill caught his eye. A bill from a doctor in London. Cathryn, it seemed, had been the patient but had not said a word to him about going. She usually told him everything going on with her, but not this. If she had, he didn't recall. He would have to ask her about it later.

The tea had come but he hadn't taken the time to pour himself a cup. He put all the papers on his desk in place and walked over to the tea tray. The pot was still quite warm, so he prepared himself a cup. Noting a slice of seed cake on a plate, he picked it up and took everything to the couch to eat. The fire was a warm welcome. He took a bite of cake. It was delicious. Some of the best seed cake he'd had in quite a while. The only place he'd had it better was on Wight. There was a shop on the outskirts of town that had the best baked goods. The seed cake was one of their most popular. Whenever he was on one of his walks and had some money, Charles always stopped and purchased something from the small shop.

He was shaken out of his thoughts by the sound of hard rain hitting against the windows. The storm had arrived. Hopefully there'd only be rain and wind and no thunder and lightning. And he also wanted it to be gone by morning. Being cramped up inside wasn't one of his favorite pastimes.

Perhaps he and Cathryn could play cards, or he could introduce her to chess. He could set up a board and invite her to play and see if she was good or not. If she knew how to play, it would make it nice to have someone in the house who also knew the game.

He finished his tea and cake and headed out into the hall, sure he'd find Cathryn in the drawing room. When the footman opened the door, he found her still sitting in front of the fire, a teacup and plate of fresh scones on a table in front of her. She had a handful of embroidery threads she'd purchased in London. She was sorting them and deep in thought when he approached.

"Scones?" he asked. "Why didn't I get any?"

"They probably weren't finished baking. Take one. They're quite good."

"I think I will after I pour a cup of tea. Would you like some more?"

"Yes, please," she replied.

He reached across and poured another cup for her. "Do you need any help sorting those?"

"No, but I think I'm going to take a break and enjoy your company."

He took a bite of the scone which she had slathered with marmalade and clotted cream. The scones were melt-in-your-mouth delicious, and the added jam and cream made them even more so. He heard Cathryn trying to suppress a giggle as he licked his fingers.

"Are they good?"

"None better. I want these every day," he replied. He picked up his cup and took a swallow of tea.

"I'm sure Cook will be more than happy to oblige."

He reached for another scone and bit into it. "The woman is a master in the kitchen."

"Hmmm."

"I went through all my correspondence so I can jump into it in the morning," Charles said, his mouth half full of the scone.

"I take it there was nothing overly important if it can wait."

"End of the month bills," he said, watching her reaction. "There was one I wasn't familiar with. Doctor Foster in London? You're not ill, are you?"

"Not at all. I just went to see him about some female issues. Nothing to concern yourself with," she replied.

Charles noted she wasn't looking at him directly but something behind him. What was going on with her? "Care to elaborate?"

"This isn't the way I imagined talking to you about this, Charles."

"Are you going to tell me?" he asked. He was trying not to get frustrated with her attitude, but it might not be easy for her.

"Very well. Since you insist," she said. "I'm with child, Charles."

He was flabbergasted. That was the last thing he expected her to tell him. "How, what, are you sure? When are you due?"

Her eyes lit up and she was trying very hard not to giggle. "The doctor confirmed my suspicions. The babe is due in seven months, and how? You should be able to figure that out. I probably conceived the very first time we made love. The doctor said it was more common than you'd think."

"You're okay, aren't you? What can I do to help?"

"There's not a thing you can do. Really. I just need to rest as much as I can."

"That's easy enough," he said.

Cathryn leaned closer and kissed him on the cheek. "You're going to be a great father."

How could he be a great father? His entire childhood had been unlike what other children experienced. He'd been sent away because he was peculiar and odd. Surely their child wouldn't be like that and inherit his traits. If it was a boy, he wanted him to have the best of everything. Everything to make him into a successful man. The best schools and tutors to show him everything he needed to get ahead above everyone else. If it were a girl, she would get the same, at least as much as young girls were allowed. He wouldn't hold her back from anything.

"Charles? Charles!" Cathryn said strongly. "Where are you? I've been talking to you and you've been somewhere else the entire time."

Charles jerked his head around toward the sound of her voice. "I apologize, my love. Your news was unexpected."

"You don't like that we're having our first child?"

He shook his head fiercely. "No, no. Nothing like that. I'm ecstatic. It was just unexpected so soon."

"I felt the same way. I thought we might at least have a year, but we don't, so I've accepted it. The more the news sinks in, the happier I am. I'm sure you will be too."

"I'm sure you're right," Charles replied.

"Could we agree on one thing?"

"What's that? Not to tell your parents until after the babe is born?"

"Something like that. She's going to try and move in with us on the grounds of 'helping' me. I want to enjoy every single moment of this, and I don't need my mother trying to take over," Cathryn said. "I know that sounds horrible, but given my mother's history, I think it would be best."

"You'll get no argument from me. Besides, if I remember correctly, she and your father are supposed to travel to southern Italy in the next month or so."

She smiled. "I'd forgotten all about that. That'll keep her busy for a couple of months."

"Can we tell Roxanne and Arthur?"

"Of course we can tell them," Cathryn said.

Charles reached for another scone. This time he was met with a soft slap on the top of his hand. "It's the last one; I don't want it to go to waste."

"Very well. Go ahead. I suppose we are celebrating."

"Yes, we are," he replied. Just as he reached for the lone scone on the plate, a bright flash of lightning followed by an ultra loud clap of thunder jolted him.

"See. I told you not to take the last one. The gods have spoken and agree," she teased.

"They're just jealous they can't enjoy it. I mean, you know gods; they can't eat."

Another large bolt of lightning hit somewhere close by. By the loudness from the clap of thunder, Charles was sure the lightning hit somewhere very near, possibly on the estate.

"That was close. Very close," Charles said. He rose and walked to the windows and looked out on the terrace and gardens. The rain was coming down sideways and hard. Lightning flashed. Two strikes back-to-back. The thunder even louder. Perhaps the storm was moving on. Time would tell. He hoped it would move on soon.

"I hope it hasn't hit anything, and if it did, it only hit the ground."

"If it's hit a building on the estate, the only way we'll know with all this rain is if a hit structure catches fire."

She arched a brow. "You're right. We've certainly had our share of bad storms this summer. I wonder why that is."

"Some years are just worse than others. I'm not sure why," he replied. He returned to Cathryn's side and wrapped his arm around her shoulder and pulled her close to him. The familiar scent she wore filled his senses. "This certainly has been a day for surprises and celebrations."

"Ummm."

He peered down at Cathryn and found she had fallen asleep that quickly. She was content and felt safe with him. It was a new concept to him. One he liked immensely. One he never wanted to end. From a forgotten spare to a man with visions; he certainly had come a long way. It sounded like things which needed to be shared with the world. A new book to be written indeed.

The End

About the Author

J R Salisbury writes Victorian era English and Scottish historical romance with perfectly imperfect heroes and strong, sassy heroines.

Writing has always written. It was the continuous encouragement of a high school creative writing teacher to further her craft. Bit with the self-publishing bug in 2011 she started out her on-line eBooks as contemporary romance before switching to her preferred and loved genre, historical romance. Her books can be found at the majority of on-line bookstores.

Raised outside Seattle with three years in the South American country of Chile, traveling is in her blood. Dividing her time between Atlanta, GA in the United States and the UK gives her a unique perspective on history.

Author Links

Website: www.jamiesalisbury.com
Facebook (historical): JRSalisburyHistoricalRomance
Facebook Profile: JamieRSalisburyAuthor
X (aka Twitter): @JamieRSalisbury
Book Bub: jr-salisbury
Instagram: authorjamiesalisbury
Email: jamiesalisburyauthor@gmail.com